THE HEART LISTENS

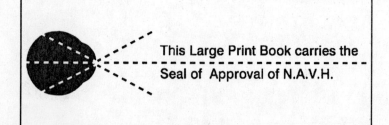

This Large Print Book carries the
Seal of Approval of N.A.V.H.

THE HEART LISTENS

CAROLYN MCSPARREN

THORNDIKE PRESS
A part of Gale, Cengage Learning

GALE
CENGAGE Learning®

Detroit • New York • San Francisco • New Haven, Conn • Waterville, Maine • London

GALE
CENGAGE Learning·

LIBRARY OF CONGRESS CATALOGING-IN-PUBLICATION DATA

McSparren, Carolyn.
　[Listen to the child]
　The heart listens / by Carolyn McSparren. — Large print ed.
　　p. cm. — (Thorndike Press large print clean reads)
　"Originally published as Listen to the child in 2002."
　ISBN 978-1-4104-4588-9 (hardcover) — ISBN 1-4104-4588-7 (hardcover)
　1. Large type books. 2. Veterinarians—Fiction. 3. Deaf—Fiction. I. Title.
PS3563.C84L57 2012
813'.54—dc23
　　　　　　　　　　　　　　　　　　　　　　　　2012000342

Published in 2012 by arrangement with Harlequin Books S.A.

Printed in the United States of America
1 2 3 4 5 6 7 16 15 14 13 12

*This book is dedicated to the fine zoos
around the world who are trying to create
a happy and challenging environment for
their charges, and to the people who are
working so diligently to preserve
endangered species.*

ACKNOWLEDGMENT

The Memphis Zoo is one of the best in the country and employs an exceptionally fine staff of veterinarians and technical assistants. They took the time to show me around and answer my questions. The zoo and staff in *The Heart Listens* came strictly out of my head and bear no resemblance to the real people I met — except that they're also superb at looking after the creatures in their care. I especially want to thank Dr. Michael Douglas, Karen Jackson and Linda England.

CHAPTER ONE

"Will he live?" Nancy Mayfield asked.

John MacIntyre Thorn tightened the final suture closing the incision along the little brown-and-white corgi's flank. "No thanks to that idiot who brought him in," Mac snapped. "Another hour and that kidney would have burst. We'd have had to deal with peritonitis. He can live a full life on one kidney. *If* we can keep him from getting infected, and if his numskull owner doesn't kill him before he gets well."

Mac gently stroked the corgi's head. The anesthetized dog could feel nothing, but that didn't matter to Mac. "You're going to be fine, little guy," he whispered.

"We're going to keep him in ICU a day or two, aren't we?" Nancy asked.

"Yeah. At least a couple days, maybe longer. The longer we keep him, the less chance there is of anyone screwing up what we've done."

"I don't think she realized —"

"It's her job to know when her dog's in pain! Hydronephritis hurts."

"But dogs don't always show they're in pain. You know that."

"A decent owner ought to recognize a sick dog the way she'd recognize a sick child — she may not know *what's* wrong, but she sure should realize *something* is." He stripped off his latex gloves and dropped them in the waste bin in the corner. "I suppose you want me to speak to her."

"Uh . . . that might not be the greatest idea right now. Why don't you have a cup of coffee? Calm down a little."

"Calm? I'm calm! Who says I'm not calm?"

"Sure you are."

He ignored her. "She in the waiting room? What's the fool woman's name, anyway?" He pushed through the swinging doors of the Creature Comfort Veterinary Clinic's operating room and marched down the hall without waiting for an answer. Nancy raced to keep up with him as he barged into the waiting room.

There were only two people in the reception area. Alva Jean Huxtable — usually the day receptionist at Creature Comfort, West Tennessee's largest state-of-the-art veterinary clinic — was working the Saturday-evening shift as a favor to the night receptionist, Mabel Halliburton. When she looked up from the magazine she'd been reading, her eyes widened, and she managed to give the impression she was ducking for cover without moving anything but her shoulders.

The other woman stood looking out over the parking lot. She wore cowboy boots with heels that added a couple of inches to her five-foot-ten or so frame. From her short haircut and broad shoulders, Mac might have taken her for a man until he saw her narrow waist.

She moved, and the fluorescent light flashed on her hair. Dark red. Not a color one saw every day.

Nancy grabbed at his sleeve, but he jerked away. "Your dog's probably going to live, no thanks to you."

The woman didn't react. She stared out the window without so much as turning her head. He was already mad as anything over the corgi — he didn't plan to put up with bad manners from this woman who should be down on her knees thanking him for sticking around after hours on a weekend to save her dog's life. Few veterinary surgeons could have done the job as neatly and with as little trauma to the animal.

11

"Hey, Miz . . . um —"

"Her name's Kit Lockhart," Alva Jean said from behind the reception desk, "but I don't think —"

"Miz Lockhart, you nearly killed your dog."

Still no reaction. Okay. No more Mr. Nice Guy.

"I said you nearly killed your dog. Don't you care?"

The instant he touched her shoulder, she jumped and swung around to face him.

She had green eyes. Not jade green or leaf green, not even gold green, but the clear green of emeralds. He'd seen maybe one or two sets of eyes that color in his entire thirty-seven years.

What was the matter with her? Nancy grabbed his arm again, and again he shook her off. "I saved your dog's life in there. What kind of blockhead ignores a distended stomach, gums that are practically white, and a dog that's almost in a coma from the pain?"

She stared at him for a moment, then raised a hand and cut him off in midsentence. "Please speak slowly and form your words more carefully."

"What?"

"I said, please speak slowly and form your

words carefully. I got 'blockhead' and 'coma' but that's about all. Since I can't imagine you think my dog is a blockhead, you must think I am."

"Well, yes, I think you're a blockhead . . ."

Again the hand in front of the chest. "Call me anything you like, but please tell me that Kevlar is going to be all right."

"I already did."

"Please, repeat that?"

"I said, he's . . . going . . . to . . . be . . . okay. Do you understand?"

She nodded. She relaxed and closed those miraculous eyes for an instant. "Thank you. I was scared to death I'd waited too long to bring him in for treatment. I've only had him a couple of weeks. He really seemed fine this morning, just a little listless. I didn't realize there was anything wrong until this evening. I came as soon as I figured it out."

"I removed the distended kidney."

"You had to remove his *kidney?*"

"He can live forever on one healthy kidney."

"I hope so, the poor dog." She'd been watching him carefully and nodding throughout his speech. "Can I see him? Please?"

"He's still unconscious."

"I just need to see he's okay. Touch him."

So she did care. "Okay, you're not callous, you're just stupid. Wouldn't have mattered to the dog. He'd have been dead either way." He turned. "Yeah. I guess you can see him now."

He felt her fingers on his arm. "Say again?"

He looked over his shoulder at her. She stared hard at him.

Then it hit him. *He* was the idiot. And he called himself a doctor. If he hadn't been so mad at her . . . "You're deaf."

"The politically correct term is hearing impaired, but I prefer deaf. It's short and ugly."

"Nobody told me." He glared at Nancy.

"I tried, Mac, so did Alva Jean."

"Yeah, yeah." He ran his hand over his hair. Nancy told him again and again that he never listened. In this particular instance, obviously she was right.

"You're good at lipreading."

"I'm nearly perfect with people I know well. With strangers, it's tougher. If you keep looking at me and . . ."

"Speak slowly and carefully."

She nodded. "Right."

"So, is this recent?"

"Not quite a year yet. I used to be a cop."

This last was said with an offhandedness that didn't conceal the underlying bitterness.

"Total loss? No residual hearing at all?"

"Nearly total. Ninety percent. I can sometimes hear thuds. Kevlar is my hearing ear dog." She swallowed convulsively. Those emerald eyes filled with tears. "Maybe he whimpered in pain, but I couldn't hear him. I'd die if I let anything happen to him. I truly didn't know he was sick. I'm so sorry."

Now he felt like a toad. "Didn't they teach you anything about dogs when you got him?"

"Teach me anything?"

He nodded.

"They taught me how to work with Kevlar, all the things he can do for me. But they didn't teach me about kidney infections. I brought him in when I first got him and let Dr. Hazard check him out and bring his shots up to date. He was fine. What could have caused this? Why didn't Dr. Hazard catch it then?"

Mac took a deep breath and spoke carefully. "He was born with a narrow ureter that finally kinked. Everything backed up, and his kidney became like a water-filled balloon. Sooner or later it would have simply burst. He also had some built-up scar tissue and some stones. Only an ultra-sound and X-rays would have caught the disease at the chronic stage. The other kidney is fine. He shouldn't have another occurrence."

She kept nodding. Her eyes flickered from his eyes to his mouth. Disconcerting.

"I got most of that. Will he need a special diet?"

"Small meals and dog food formulated to handle kidney problems. Nancy will talk to you about that before you leave with him."

Now she did look up at him. "How long will he have to stay here? I mean, I've only had him two weeks, but I already depend on him." She dropped her eyes. "And I like him."

He touched her arm. "Come on. They'll have moved him to ICU by now. You can see him."

She eyed him with suspicion. "Are you making some kind of exception for me?"

This time Nancy touched her arm. She said slowly and with a smile, "No special treatment. Dr. Mac is an equal-opportunity offender."

Back in the ICU, the little dog lay on his good side on an air mattress in the middle of the floor. Cages holding dogs and cats were stacked almost up to the ceiling, and despite the low light, several animals woke and began to bark or whine when Mac opened the door to let Kit in.

She went down to her knees on the mattress and began to stroke the dog and croon to him softly. After a moment Mac recognized the melody — an old Scottish folk song, some kind of lullaby. His Highland-born grandmother had sung him songs like that when he was a child.

"Kev's such a burly little dog," she said. "He seems like such a tough little character, and now this."

He reached down and squeezed her shoulder to reassure her.

She looked up at him. "Will there be somebody here with him tonight?"

"Dr. Liz Carlyle will be here all night. As soon as he starts to wake up, she'll move him to one of the cages."

"Doctor Something will put him in a cage? Is that what you said?"

"Close enough." He offered her his hand, but she stood up easily without assistance. She was as lithe as a dancer.

"Thank you for letting me see him. Can your receptionist call me a cab?" She walked out ahead of him, but turned her head to watch his reply.

"You need a cab?"

She stopped in the hall and faced him. "I can drive legally, but I try not to drive at night without Kevlar. During the day I keep a close eye out for ambulances or police cars bearing down on me, but after dark, I rely on Kev to alert me. My mother brought us over tonight."

"Won't she come back to get you?" He was beginning to learn the cadence of speaking to her.

"This late — it would be complicated. A cab will be fine. But unfortunately, I can't call one myself. I can give them the address, but if they ask directions, I won't be able to hear."

He'd never have thought of that. "In the rain and this far out, a cab could take a while. Where do you live?"

"I have a town house in Germantown."

He made a decision that ordinarily he wouldn't make in a hundred years. He never, ever, got involved with clients. Their animals, yes. But not the clients. "I live in Germantown, too. I'll drop you. We can go now before another emergency comes in."

She looked confused. "I got about a quarter of that. But you don't have to take me home."

"Come on."

He picked up one of the telephones on

18

the wall and told Alva Jean he was leaving. "Nancy gone yet?"

"Uh-huh. And Dr. Carlyle is on her way to check the patients. What about Mrs. Lockhart?"

His stomach lurched. In the last few minutes, he'd grown used to thinking of her as a woman alone, unmarried. It suddenly seemed important to him that there not be a husband lurking somewhere.

If there was, why wasn't *he* picking up his wife?

He'd find out somehow on the drive home.

"I am driving Mrs. Lockhart home."

"You are?" Pause. "You just *better* be sweet to her, Dr. Mac." She hung up.

He stared at the telephone in his hand. Alva Jean didn't exactly cringe when he walked by her desk, but she seldom said anything more to him than to announce his appointments. He'd have been less surprised if Kevlar had stood on his hind legs and roared like a lion. He glanced at Kit Lockhart who waited patiently. Sweet? He'd never been sweet in his life. He certainly wasn't about to start now.

At first he found the silence in the car disconcerting. Because she couldn't see him in the darkness, there was no way to speak to her. He felt frustrated because he wanted to talk. He wanted to ask her how and when she'd gone deaf, and what, if anything, could be done to correct it.

He was amazed to discover he wanted to know everything about her. There was an irony here, he realized. Most of the women he knew talked too much. They seemed uncomfortable with companionable silence. But then, he wasn't exactly the companionable type. And until now, he was the one who decided when he needed silence.

But this woman could tune *him* out simply by turning her head. That gave her control of the situation. He loathed loss of control.

His entire life was based on keeping an iron grip on himself and his environment. If things started to get out of hand, he bellowed until somebody fixed them. He tried to use his bellow sparingly so it wouldn't lose its effectiveness, but he'd found over the years that sometimes a little shouting worked wonders.

Most of his colleagues here in Memphis had learned to ignore his tirades. Nancy Mayfield had worked with him so long she knew he was a marshmallow inside. Rick Hazard, the managing partner of Creature Comfort, laughed at him. Apparently even

Alva Jean was losing her fear.

Not good. His reputation as a terror was his only protection from the world. Without his shell, the only defense a snapping turtle had was to bite. Mac didn't like biting.

He could bellow his head off at this woman. She wouldn't care any more than if he'd whispered.

"Second driveway from the corner on your right," she said.

He'd been so deep in his own thoughts that her voice startled him. "Sure," he said automatically.

The moment he stopped his Suburban, she opened the door and jumped out, then turned to him. "Thank you for helping Kev. I'll be by to see him first thing tomorrow morning."

"He'll still be groggy."

She pointed at the ceiling of the SUV. "Lean into the dome light, please. Then tell me again."

He started to growl, but realized that wouldn't impress her, either, so he did as she asked, then repeated his statement and added, "Come late morning or early afternoon."

She nodded. "Thanks again."

"I'll walk you to your door."

"I beg your pardon?"

"I said . . ."

She shook her head. "I got it. Don't bother." She grinned. "I can handle myself." She strode up her walk with an athlete's arrogant swing.

He clicked off the overhead light, but didn't start the car until she'd unlocked her door and gone inside.

Inside, Kit leaned against the front door and flung her shoulder bag across the room onto the sofa so hard that her wallet and makeup spilled onto the carpet. She picked everything up, stuffed her bag again and set it on the chest at the side of the room.

She leaned both hands on the top of the chest and took some deep breaths. Some tough cookie she was, breaking down every time she got safely home from one of her encounters with what she was coming to think of as "them." People who could hear.

At least Dr. Thorn didn't dole out great gobs of pity. She'd had her fill of that. She looked at the mirror above the chest and grinned at the streaks of mascara running down her cheeks. "First purchase tomorrow morning — waterproof mascara," she said. She wiped her cheeks with the flat of her hands. Better.

Not being able to hear her own voice

resonate inside her head was perhaps the oddest thing she'd had to adjust to. That, and the continual whistling sound.

The stairwell lights went on, and a moment later, her mother came down the steps and stopped directly in front of Kit. "Darling, how's Kev?"

Kit headed for the kitchen. She badly needed some comfort food. "He's going to be okay, but they had to remove a kidney."

She got a bag of chips and turned, realizing her mother had probably reacted to the news. Now Catherine Barclay sat at the kitchen table and held out her hand to her daughter. "Emma's been terribly worried."

"I'll tell her the minute she wakes up tomorrow."

"Tell me he's okay." Emma appeared in the doorway, blinking in the light.

Kit nodded. "He'll be home in a couple of days."

"What was wrong with him?" The ten-year-old padded into the room and leaned against her grandmother's shoulder.

"His kidney went bad. They had to remove it." Kit saw the alarm in Emma's eyes and held up her hand. "Whoa! I promise he's fine. Everybody's got two kidneys and can get along with one."

"You're sure?"

"Absolutely. Now, go back to bed. You've got soccer practice tomorrow, remember."

"Do I have to?"

Kit could almost hear Emma's patented whine in her head. There were occasional blessings about being deaf. Not having to listen to Emma's histrionics was a definite plus, but as Emma grew more used to her mother's deafness, she was becoming more and more adept at pantomiming her emotions.

"Yes, you have to. Now, back to bed, please. It's late. And take Jo-Jo with you."

Emma reached down and picked up the bobcat-size yellow tabby that was winding himself around her ankles. "I think he misses Kev."

"One less creature to terrorize."

Emma waved one hand over her shoulder as she wandered into the shadows while Jo-Jo looked back at them.

Her mother reached out to get Kit's attention. "She worries about you. I had a tough time getting her into bed tonight."

"She's taking advantage of you. Worrying about me is a great excuse to stay up late. She managed to get to bed on time when I was with the T.A.C.T. squad. If she worried then she never showed it."

"She was too young to realize how dangerous your job was. Small children trust that their parents will always be there — hale and hearty. First she lost her father when you divorced him, then your accident proved you're breakable. She's afraid she might lose you to something worse than deafness."

"She hasn't lost her father. She sees more of Jimmy now than she ever did before the divorce. At least he's on scheduled visits, when he deigns to show up."

"Not the same thing."

"And as for Emma's worrying about me, she'll have to deal with it. I used to worry about *you* all the time when you were on the job. Every time a cop got killed I'd think, 'That could be my mother.' Didn't stop you being a cop, and it hasn't stopped you being a P.I., either."

Catherine took a deep breath. This was hardly a new discussion. "Being a P.I. is not dangerous. I spend most of my time combing through financial records."

"Any situation can turn dangerous," Kit said. "That was the first thing you taught me, remember? Always keep your guard up? Anyway, Emma doesn't have to worry I'll get caught in a shoot-out or anything. Not anymore."

"That's not the point." Catherine took the half-full bag of chips out of her daughter's hand and shoved it into the garbage. "Until *you* were hurt, losing a child was something that happened to other parents. Then when your father and I got called to the hospital, I realized I could actually lose you." Her mother's voice clouded.

This wasn't the way Kit and her mother ever spoke to one another. Her mother's sudden emotion made Kit uncomfortable. She tried to laugh. "I wasn't at death's door, Mom."

Her mother raised her eyes. "You certainly looked as though you were. I'm sure you looked half-dead to Emma. Suddenly the impossible — being abandoned by her mother — became possible. You don't get over that quickly."

"So on top of everything else I'm supposed to feel *guilty* that I got blown up, because I scared my parents and my child? I know this is hard for her, Mom. At first she fell all over herself being helpful — mommy's little nurse. Treated me as though I was some sort of invalid. Brought me tea in bed. Refused to let me out of her sight. But that gets old fast when you're ten. Now I embarrass her."

"Yes, you probably do." Catherine sounded defeated. "You and I never could communicate. I don't suppose you and

Emma can actually talk all this through, can you?"

"That would just make things worse. She's adjusting at her own pace. I'm not going to rub her nose in my infirmity. Remember when I shot that guy and had to go to the shrink, Mom? Now every time I hear anybody say, 'And how did that make you feel?' I want to hit something. I'm not going to do that to Emma."

"She's your child." Catherine walked to the kitchen door. "Time for me to go home." She turned to face Kit. "I almost forgot to tell you. Vince Calandruccio called. Said to call him at the Dog Squad tomorrow morning to tell him about Kevlar."

"Vince is a good guy. A lot of the guys I worked with on the job have stopped calling to check up on me, but Vince keeps coming over and bringing Adam, of course. He never goes anywhere without his dog."

Catherine nodded. "You look wiped out. Go to bed. And if you don't make it to practice tomorrow, don't sweat it — I can take Emma. Just call me."

"Thanks for watching Emma, Mother."

"You're welcome." Catherine picked up her purse and walked through the door.

Suddenly Kit felt so exhausted she wasn't

certain she could drag herself up the stairs to her bedroom. The doctors had warned her about that. After any kind of stress and particularly after a long session of reading lips, her energy could suddenly bottom out. And sometimes she lost her balance. The doctors said that was the physical trauma of the blast and the psychological trauma of nearly winding up both deaf *and* blind.

She didn't like to remember what a close call that had been. The scar that bisected her right eyebrow and touched the corner of her eye was barely noticeable thanks to a great plastic surgeon. And her vision in that eye was almost normal, thanks to an ophthalmologist in the trauma center who'd removed splinters from her eye without damaging it.

The doctors told her she'd never remember the blast itself, but she'd heard the story of her accident so many times she almost felt as though she could.

She'd come through plenty of hostage situations and drug takedowns without a scratch. It was embarrassing to lose her hearing and her job with the police department in what amounted to a comedy of errors.

Keystone Kops, Vince Calandruccio called it.

Start with one rookie who kicked in the back door of a crack house a second too early so that Kit had to cover him to keep him from getting shot. Add another cop at the front door with a flash-bang grenade who didn't know Kit was already in the vestibule. Toss in a commander who waited a couple of seconds too long to rescind his order to lob in the flash-bang.

What do you have? Kit Lockhart standing practically on top of the grenade when it went off.

She still had to watch herself on the stairs. Her depth perception wasn't perfect, but it was improving.

Unfortunately, Emma had eyes like a hawk, ready to spot the least sign of weakness in Kit.

Life was better with Kevlar. Emma seemed willing to hand over some of the responsibility she felt to him. Kit was so grateful he was going to be all right.

She leaned against the wall at the top of the stairs for a moment, panting.

"Oh, this is not a good thing," she said as she bent to catch her breath. "It is high time we went back to working out, Kit, my girl. You've been lazy too long. You're getting soft." She walked into her bedroom, shucked off her sweater, then pulled off her boots and dropped them beside her.

Oops. She hoped the noise they made wouldn't wake Emma. She slipped down the hall and peered into her daughter's bedroom. Emma lay curled up asleep. From the crook of the little girl's knees, Jo-Jo raised his flat head and looked at Kit for a moment before subsiding into sleep again. Kit crossed to the bed and bent to kiss Emma's forehead, damp with nighttime perspiration.

On her way back to her own bathroom, she jabbed hard at the heavy punching bag in the corner of her bedroom. "Ow! Wimp. Next time wear gloves." She kicked at it. "Wonder how Dr. John MacIntyre Thorn keeps up those muscles. He certainly wouldn't risk injuring his hands on a punching bag."

In the bathroom, she began to cream her makeup off. Then she stopped and leaned both hands on the sink. *I owe everything to those hands of his for saving Kevlar. How can I thank him?*

Across the hall, Emma opened her eyes. It was much easier to feign sleep now when her mother couldn't hear her breathing.

She heard the sound of her mother's fist as she thwacked the heavy bag, then her exclamation. She couldn't understand the rest of the words.

Her mother never used to talk to herself — not out loud. Emma wasn't certain she even knew she was doing it since she couldn't hear her own voice.

Weird.

Even weirder to think that she could play her stereo all night. Her mother wouldn't know about it unless Emma woke the neighbors, and they called to complain.

At first she'd thought being able to get away with stuff behind her mother's back was cool — her friend Jessica definitely thought so. But it wasn't. She'd always relied on her mother to set boundaries. Before, when she played her music too loud, her mother told her to turn it down.

Before, her mother knew when she was playing a video game in her room when she was supposed to be doing homework just by the pinging sound the game made. All the way from the kitchen, too.

Emma hated feeling guilty when she took advantage of her mother's deafness. She hated having to find her mother and look at her to tell her something instead of just yelling from upstairs or the backyard. It made every word they said to each other too important. Why couldn't they just go back

31

the way they were before the stupid accident?

Chapter Two

Mac slept late on Sunday morning. He deserved a little extra time after having worked on that corgi until nearly ten o'clock on Saturday night.

His first thoughts on waking were of Kit Lockhart. Mrs.? He hadn't asked her last night, but he definitely wanted to know whether she had a husband.

Not that he was likely to see her again once Kevlar was fully recovered. His life was entirely too busy to complicate with women, and definitely not with women who unnerved him.

Even though it was Sunday and he wasn't officially on call, he dressed, grabbed a doughnut and an espresso from the drive-through and drove to the clinic to check on his patients.

He went straight to the small-animal ICU. Bigelow Little, the kennel man and general clinic help, was on his knees in front of the corgi's cage.

"Hey, Dr. Mac," Big said. "He come in last night?" Big stood up.

At six foot four Mac was used to being the tallest person in the room, but when Big was around, Mac knew how Chihuahuas must feel around Irish wolfhounds. Big was immense — nearly seven feet tall, and half as broad. Not an ounce of fat on him. He looked capable of breaking Mac in two, but was in fact the gentlest soul on earth.

"Removed a kidney. We had any bodily functions this morning?"

Big grinned and ran his huge hand over his cropped white-blond hair. "Yes, sir. Downright apologetic about it, though. Acted like he'd done dirtied in the churn."

"You had him out?"

"Cleaned up after him is all. Didn't know what you wanted me to do."

"If you have time, you might try walking him around in here. He's pretty sore, but he needs to use those legs. Don't want him throwing a blood clot."

"I'll do it."

And he would. Big Little had been the greatest find the clinic had made since it opened. An inmate at the local penal farm, Big had been one of the members of the first team to work the new beef-cattle herd

34

at the farm. Dr. Eleanor Grayson, now Eleanor Chadwick, had been the veterinarian in charge of that program, and had picked Big out immediately as having a special rapport with animals.

When Big was pardoned, Creature Comfort had hired him at once. Now he had a small apartment on the grounds behind Dr. Weinstock's laboratory, and acted as night watchman as well as a jack-of-all-trades in the clinic. If anyone could coax Kevlar to walk, Big could.

Mac checked his other patients, then went to look over his schedule for Monday. He wondered when Kit Lockhart would come to visit Kevlar today, and realized he hadn't told Big she was deaf. He started to go back, but Rick Hazard stuck his head out of his office door and called him.

"You keeping banker's hours?" Rick said.

"It's Sunday, Rick." Mac bristled. "And I was here late last night removing a kidney."

Rick raised his hands. "Whoa! I'm just kidding. How come you didn't let Liz Carlyle handle it? She was on call for small animals last night."

Liz Carlyle was an excellent vet. At the moment she was working on an advanced degree in veterinary ophthalmology and her surgical skills were top-notch.

"I trust her, but I trust me more." Besides, Kevlar's kidney problem was an interesting and delicate case and a welcome change from neutering dogs and spaying cats. "I didn't have anything better to do."

Rick nodded. "Like you don't have anything better to do this morning. Hey, podner, you ought to get a life."

Mac forced a smile. "I *have* a life. And I have patients in ICU. Where else would I be? You're the one who's usually on the golf course by now."

"That's where I would be if I weren't on call here. Eighteen holes, then a late brunch with Margot at Brennan's, a long post-brunch snooze in front of the television set and a late supper."

"And you think *I* should get a life?"

"Actually, I think you should get a wife."

"You sound like my mother. Don't." Mac pivoted on his heel and walked back to his office, then stopped and turned. "Look, since I'm here already, I'll handle the calls, if any, until Liz gets in. Will that give you time for your golf game?"

"Nine holes, at least. Forget what I said about getting a life. You just go right on being a lonely workaholic as long as you want."

After Rick dashed for the parking lot and his golf clubs, Mac propped his feet on his desk and picked up the copy of the Sunday paper he'd brought with him. He might take in a matinee this afternoon, maybe try a new restaurant tonight. Or he could work out at the gym. He had plenty of friends at the gym.

Except they seldom showed up on Sunday.

More annoyed by Rick's gibes than he was willing to admit, he pulled open his desk drawer and took out a dog-eared black leather address book. Maybe he'd take someone to dinner tonight.

He wasn't quite certain when he'd given up dating. It hadn't been intentional. Recently he hadn't been involved with anyone. He never had been able to master the juggling techniques of some of his bachelor colleagues. Dating should entail real emotional attachment.

He ran his eye down the names in his address book. Cindy was married — pregnant, he thought. Marilyn had moved away to Seattle or someplace. Jennifer would probably be free, but her endless prattle about social functions would give him a migraine. Claire would hang up on him.

Sarah Scott and Eleanor Chadwick, the two large-animal vets, were both happily married, and Sarah had a baby. Mac couldn't barge in on either of them on a

Sunday. Bill Chumney, the exotics vet, was out in the Dakotas somewhere building a census of black-footed ferrets, and Sol Weinstock was at the international equine clinic in Lexington, Kentucky, working on his experiments with EIA vaccine.

Mac wandered back to the kennels. The cages were cleaned and all the animals had fresh water and food.

"You about done, Big?" Mac asked.

"Uh-huh. Got the little guy out and walked him around some. He's a real happy fellow, isn't he?"

Mac nodded. "You doing anything this afternoon?"

Big turned his seraphic smile on Mac. "Me'n Alva Jean are taking her kids to the zoo." He looked hard at Mac. "Hey, why don't you come along? They got that new baby gorilla out. Ain't nothin' cuter than a baby gorilla."

Mac shook his head. "Thanks for the offer, but no. I'm here until two. Then I'll probably take in a movie."

"You ought to come with us. Alva Jean wouldn't mind."

Alva Jean had recently been through a nasty divorce. The last person Mac might have expected her to take up with was Big Little. Well, maybe not the last. She'd walked out on her husband because he had abused her and the two children. It took a great deal to rile Big Little, and he would as soon raise a hand to a woman or child or animal as he would take up brain surgery. At least with Big she'd be physically safe from her husband.

Unfortunately, if the husband tried to hurt either his ex-wife or his children again, *he* wouldn't be safe from *Big.*

Mac had no intention of spending all afternoon with this unlikely pair, and definitely not with Alva Jean's two small children in tow.

It wasn't that he disliked children, exactly, but they always acted like — well — children.

He avoided them even in his practice. Nancy usually spoke to distraught parents about Bobby's rottweiler or Betty's kitten.

You could count on animals to act like animals, so he preferred to devote himself to them and not to the owners who caused so many of their problems.

He said goodbye to Big and walked back up the hall to his office. His footsteps echoed on the tile floor. All the treatment rooms were soundproofed, so once he had closed the door on the kennel, he could no longer hear the whines and barks of the patients. The clinic felt almost eerily quiet.

As he reached the door of his office, the front-door buzzer sounded.

Good. An emergency. Maybe something to get his teeth into, to keep him from feeling as though he was the last human being on earth.

He walked into the reception room and peered through the glass doors.

His heart bounced into his throat. It was that Lockhart woman. He'd know that hair anywhere.

He opened the door for her.

"I'm here to see Kev."

"Yeah. Come in." He stood back and held the door.

She turned away from him and called, "Hey, Em, it's okay."

The passenger-side door of an elderly but well cared for red Jeep opened and a slight figure jumped out and ran up the stairs.

A child! A tall, skinny girl in jeans and a sweatshirt. Obviously Kit Lockhart's child. There couldn't be half a dozen people in the city with hair that extraordinary dark red. As she bounced up the steps, he saw that she had missed out on her mother's green eyes. Hers were hazel.

She might be a beauty someday. At the moment she was as uncoordinated as a day-old foal.

He took a step back.

"Is he okay? Can we see him?" the child asked. "We brought him some of his toys." She held out a brown paper sack.

"Whoa, girl. This is my daughter, Emma. Emma, this is Dr. John MacIntyre Thorn. He's the man who saved Kevlar's life."

"Uh-huh. Can we see him now?" She slipped past him.

"Um, yes. Please follow me. And be quiet."

Fat chance, he thought. He'd learned about the habits of prepubescent girls from growing up in the same house with his younger sister, Joanna. They invariably squealed every chance they got. No doubt this one would do the same.

As they came to the door of the ICU, he pointed to the Quiet sign. He pushed open the door and stood aside. The child shoved past him, then stood stock-still a foot inside the door. He nearly tripped over her.

"Oh," she whispered into the immediate stirring of whimpers and meows.

"Kevlar's over there on the bottom tier."

She went to the corgi and dropped to her knees in front of his cage. "He's Mom's dog, really," she said, pressing her open palm against the wire. "He works for her.

Can I get him out and pet him?"

"Carefully. Don't let him run around. Just hold him and pet him. You can give him his toys before you leave."

"Thanks," said Kit as she joined her daughter on the floor. "Hey, Kev," she crooned. He came into her lap, licked her chin and settled quietly while mother and daughter bent those extraordinary red heads over him.

Mac felt the need to talk, to tell them about the incision, the prognosis, how beautifully the dog was doing — anything to interrupt this tableau that pointedly excluded him. But he couldn't speak to Kit — she couldn't see his lips. He had no idea how to speak to the child.

Emma solved the problem for him. She stood up awkwardly, but with the fluidity of young joints, and began to wander around the room while her mother continued to pet Kev.

"What's wrong with this little dog?" Emma asked.

"What? Oh — let's see." He prided himself on knowing his patients. "That's Chou-Chou. A bichon frise. Cataract surgery on the left eye. We'll do the right one in about six months."

"He was going blind?"

"You know about cataracts?"

"My granddad had them. What about this one?"

"Her name's Rebel. She's a boxer. Had a flipped intestine. Not all that rare in large dogs. But it kills quickly if it's not surgically corrected."

She poked a finger into the next cage where a large black-and-white cat slept and shivered from time to time. "This one?"

"Her name's Folly. She got hold of some antifreeze. There's been so much liver damage we may not be able to save her."

"Oh, poor kitty! We have a cat named Jo-Jo, but he never goes outside."

"How does he get along with Kevlar?"

"When Mom brought Kev home, Jo-Jo spent four days under the towels in the linen closet. Then he decided that if Kev was going to stay, he'd better get used to him. Now they're good buddies."

Mac had fallen into step beside Emma as she checked every cage. He found himself explaining all his cases almost as though he were talking to an adult.

Exactly as though he were talking to an adult, actually. Emma seemed to understand what he said, and when she didn't, she asked for explanations.

He discovered he was enjoying himself.

"Hey, Em, let Dr. Mac off the hook," Kit said as she unfolded from the floor with the same ease her daughter showed but with much more grace. She held Kevlar against her chest. "He's got stuff to do."

"Doesn't look like he's got any other stuff at all," Emma said.

"Emma Lockhart!"

He laughed. "She's quite right. I was reading the Sunday paper and getting ready to check the large-animal patients in the back when you arrived."

"Large animals?" Emma asked suspiciously. "What kind?"

He shrugged. "Cows, sheep, horses —"

"Horses? You got *horses?*"

Kit groaned. "You just hit the hottest button you could. This child has never even been on a horse, but she is horse crazy."

He glanced at Emma's shining face. "I don't work on the large animals so I don't know if we have a horse in the clinic at the moment," he said. "I haven't checked the charts."

"Could we see? Could we, please?"

If she'd whined, he probably would have said no, but she sounded enthusiastic and excited.

"I don't see why not."

"Listen," Kit said, "you don't have to . . ."

He didn't attempt to answer her, but took Kevlar gently from her arms, put him back in his kennel and gave him his toys. "Here, boy, play with these."

"Bye, Kev," Emma said. It was obvious she was eager to get going.

"See you tomorrow, sweetie," Kit said. She touched Mac's arm so that he faced her. "When can he come home?"

"Tomorrow, if he doesn't develop an infection. But he won't be up to par for a couple of weeks."

"Can he work for me?"

"So long as it doesn't entail running up and down stairs too often, I doubt that you could *keep* him from working."

"Come *on!*" Emma's exasperation was aimed at her mother.

Mother and daughter followed Mac down the hall toward the heavy door that separated the large-animal area from the small. The room beyond was cavernous, with a broad central hall. On the left were offices, operating rooms and storage areas. On the right was a large open pen for cows, and past that were raised padded cells for animals coming out of anesthesia. Past the padded stalls were a number of smaller stalls that could be used for recuperating animals.

Mac picked up a clipboard from a hook beside the first office door and ran his eye down the list of patients. "You're in luck."

"You have a horse?" Emma practically danced a jig.

"Not just a horse. Follow me."

They followed him past the enclosed stalls. As the space opened out, both Emma and Kit said "ooh," as he knew they would. If he'd expected Emma to run to the stall, he was mistaken. She froze as though afraid to approach.

The big gray Percheron mare didn't raise her head from the bale of hay she munched. The black foal, however, scrambled awkwardly to its spindly legs and leaned against its mother's broad side.

"What's wrong with her?" Emma whispered.

Mac started to tell her, then looked at Kit and raised his eyebrows. He wasn't quite certain how much this child would or should know about the processes of delivering babies. Kit, however, nodded at him and kept her eyes on his mouth.

"The filly's fine. It's the mother we worked on. See those sharp little hooves the baby has?"

Emma nodded.

"Well, when the baby was coming out, one

46

of those hooves tore the inside of the mare. She was bleeding so badly we had to bring them both into the clinic to stitch her up."

"Wow." It was a long-drawn-out whisper. "Could I touch the baby?"

"I doubt you'll get that close to her. Stand here quietly, stretch out your hand and don't move."

Emma did as she was told. After an interminable two minutes in which Emma's hand didn't wobble, the foal reached out a velvet nose and touched her fingers. Then it bounced away and nearly fell down.

Emma broke into delighted laughter. "She has whiskers! They tickled my fingers."

"Now it really is time to go, Emma," said Kit. "I mean it. Don't forget your dad's picking you up at two."

He saw Emma's shoulders drop. "Yeah, okay. All he wants to do is watch football on TV, then he goes to sleep on the couch and snores. I get sick of video games."

Kit glanced at Mac, who looked away quickly. "Maybe he'll take you to the park. Thank Dr. Mac and let's go."

As he locked the front door behind the pair, he felt a pleasant glow. He hadn't done too badly with the child. Obviously unusually intelligent and mature. And her mother was either separated or divorced. He'd bet on divorced.

The child would be off at her daddy's tonight.

He wondered if he could think up a reason to call Kit up and maybe take her to dinner.

Call her up? Just how did he expect to do that? Even if she had a light on the phone and picked it up, she wouldn't be able to hear a word he said.

"Em," Kit called up the stairs. "Your dad's here." Then she turned to the tall, handsome man who stood just inside the door. "You're late, Jimmy. It's almost three."

He grinned sheepishly and shoved an unruly shock of sandy hair back from his forehead. Once that gesture and that grin had won him forgiveness for every lie he told, but they no longer had the power to charm her.

"Sorry, babe. Saturday night, you know how it is."

You bet she did. Cop bars, pitchers of beer, too much laughter invariably leading to some sort of confrontation. She'd dragged Jimmy away too many times not to remember.

Jimmy's shifting eyes and even broader grin told her that Emma had come down the stairs behind her. That was one of the things she most hated about her deafness — Godzilla could walk up behind her and she'd never know until he bit her head off.

Emma grabbed her mother's arm and turned her around so that she stared directly into Emma's eyes. "Mom, will you be all right by yourself?"

"I think I can just about handle it, thank you."

"You going to Granddad's for dinner?"

"I can probably manage to microwave something all by my very own self." But she smiled to show she was kidding.

"Oh, Mother," Emma said. "Come on, Daddy. Can we go to the park?"

"Yeah, well, about that . . ." He pointedly turned away so that Kit couldn't read his lips. She could, however, see Emma's face and the look of resignation that came over it.

"Jimmy, playing video games while you sleep on the sofa is not much fun for a child. Couldn't you do something Emma wants to do for a change?"

He turned back to face her. This time he didn't smile. "Hey, she's my kid too, okay? You don't run my life any longer."

Kit bit down a reply. Not in front of Emma. "When will you be back? Emma has school tomorrow."

"Yeah, I do remember about school. Eight, maybe nine."

"Try seven, maybe eight. She has to be in bed by nine."

He didn't say anything else as he herded Emma out the door and into the front seat of his yellow Mustang.

Kit leaned on the door. The psychologists said that divorced parents weren't supposed to let the child hear them snap at one another or say nasty things about each other. They were especially not to fight over the child. Kit tried hard.

Emma was too smart. When Kit and Jimmy had finally put an end to a marriage that both had known — almost from the start — was a mistake, Emma had been devastated. She'd been Daddy's girl. Jimmy could do no wrong. The breakup was all Kit's fault.

Kit knew that the divorce rate for cops was higher than for the rest of the population, but when she and Jimmy met at the police academy and married soon after they graduated, she'd never expected to become a part of that statistic. Now she wasn't even a cop any longer — just a pensioned-off ex-cop. Jimmy would probably ride a squad car until he retired. That had been part of the problem — she'd had too much ambition to suit Jimmy, while he hadn't had nearly enough to suit her.

Now Emma had endured two years of Jimmy's canceled visits and his endless succession of empty-headed girlfriends. They either treated Emma like an interloper or fawned all over her to get close to her father. Just when she'd get used to one girlfriend, the girl would disappear to be replaced by a clone. There were so many that Kit had stopped asking their names, merely calling all of them "New Girl."

Kit was having a harder and harder time convincing Em to spend Sunday afternoons and alternate Friday nights and Saturdays with her father. Jimmy kept promising that they'd go to see the latest movies, then reneging when New Girl preferred to see something R-rated that was unsuitable for Emma.

Occasionally, he simply got in a babysitter and left. At first Emma had refused to admit she'd been left with the sitter. Finally, however, she'd confessed in a welter of tears.

It was far worse, though, when Jimmy dumped Emma at his mother's Germantown condo for the day. Kit carefully avoided saying anything negative about Mrs. Lockhart to Emma, even if there were times she had to bite her tongue. Jimmy's mother didn't keep to the same rules.

Mrs. Lockhart had never liked Kit. Not that she would have liked any woman who married her son. She'd been civil to Kit until the divorce. After Kit threw Jimmy out, Mrs. Lockhart switched from kid gloves to brass knuckles. And used Emma as her punching bag.

Kit remembered the Saturday afternoon when Emma came home from her grandmother's with her eyes red from crying, slammed the door on her father and announced, "I won't go to Meemomma's ever, ever again."

Since the scene took place shortly before Kit's accident, she could hear the frustration and fury in her daughter's voice. It had taken an hour of cajoling for Kit to get the whole story about the afternoon. By that time she was even angrier than Emma.

"All she does is bad-mouth you, Mom." Emma switched to a Mississippi Delta twang that was such a good imitation of Mrs. Lockhart that Kit was startled. "If your momma took care of her family like a decent woman, your daddy would still be living at home instead of that puny little apartment. I told Jimmy when he said he was gonna marry her, I said, 'She's a mean 'un, you mark my words. Never cook you a decent meal or iron your shirts or keep a halfway decent house.' "

Kit had to laugh in spite of her anger. "Don't you ever let her hear you do her that way, Emma Lockhart. Don't let your daddy hear you, either." She wrapped her arms around her daughter and pulled the child into her lap. She could hear Emma's sniffles against her shoulder. "*I* don't care what she says about me, Emma, but you shouldn't have to listen to that stuff." She smoothed her daughter's hair. "She loves you, sweetheart, and she loves your daddy. She's unhappy, is all." What Kit actually wanted to say was that the woman was a harpy. "I'll tell your dad she upset you."

"No, Mom, you can't! He'll just get mad at me for telling. She goes on and on about how Daddy's perfect, and you're some kind of monster who goes around shooting people. She says you spent all his money and now he's poor because he has to pay child support when you already make more than he does. She says I'd be better off living with her. I don't want to live with her, Mom! I'd die. Where she lives smells like old people, and she hates cats."

"Don't you worry about that, baby. I wouldn't let you live anywhere but with me." *Besides, Jimmy never wanted custody of you.* She could never tell Emma that.

Emma touched her mother's cheek in that way that melted Kit's heart. It generally got her everything from a new doll to an ice-cream cone before dinner. "You can tell Daddy I don't have to go back there ever again, right, Mom?"

Kit wished that were possible, but Jimmy would never agree, and once Emma was out of her sight and under his care, he could drop her anywhere he wanted. All she could do was talk to him and tell him that Mrs. Lockhart was making Emma unhappy. If he held true to form, he'd talk to his mother, but it wouldn't change her behavior for more than one visit. Kit cuddled Emma and rocked her as she had when she was a baby. She ought to feel some sympathy for Mrs. Lockhart. She'd had a hard life. She'd had Jimmy when she was well into her forties in some unpronounceable Delta town in Mississippi.

Apparently, Jimmy's father had spent his days over coffee at the local diner and his nights playing poker and drinking illegal booze with his farmer buddies. His wife had not only worked the farm pretty much by herself, she'd canned, sewed and baked biscuits from scratch three times a day.

Her experience should have made her applaud Kit's desire to become a police officer and not be dependent on her husband. Instead, she resented anything Kit did that didn't involve pampering Jimmy. Kit cursed the day Mrs. Lockhart had rented out the Mississippi farm and moved to a retirement condo in Germantown.

"Daddy keeps saying he's going to take Meemomma and me down to the farm in Mississippi so I can ride a horse. He says he wants me to see where he grew up." She sighed. " 'Course, he never does."

Until Kit's accident, Emma had used the sudden and unexplained onslaught of stomachaches or even extra homework to keep from going with her father. Since Kit's accident, she'd tried to use "looking after Mom" as an excuse.

Of course, Jimmy blamed Kit when Emma didn't want to stay with him. He would never admit that after so many broken promises, a child like Emma would simply stop asking to be disappointed.

Kit knew Jimmy loved Emma, but she didn't fit into his lifestyle.

He didn't seem to realize that all too soon she'd be a teenager and then an adult, and he would no longer fit into *her* life.

Kit hadn't wanted to ask him about his support check this afternoon. It was two weeks late. Before, when Kit had been making good money with the police department, the money hadn't mattered so much. Now, even with her disability pension, she had to watch every penny. Jimmy's check could at least buy Emma a new pair of Nikes from time to time.

Pushing herself away from the front door, she went to the kitchen. She opened the cupboard and reached for a box of cookies, then stopped and snatched an apple off the counter instead. Her mother was right. She didn't have a problem with food now, but boredom could very well lead to a major one if she didn't watch herself.

Apple in hand, she walked from the kitchen to the den, where she turned on the television and stretched out in the recliner. She had closed captions on a number of channels, but there never seemed to be anything she wanted to watch. She tried to practice lipreading, but the faces were too often turned away or backlit.

So how to spend the afternoon? Running? Didn't appeal to her. Besides, it was probably going to rain again any minute.

Riding her bicycle? Without Kev in the basket to warn her about traffic, she was asking for trouble.

The flower beds in the backyard badly

needed to be cleaned up and weeded for spring, but she couldn't get up any enthusiasm for that, either.

She needed a job. A job that she went to and worked at and then came home and rested from. A job that paid actual money and gave her actual satisfaction. She'd never been a stay-at-home housewife and mother.

What was she going to do with the rest of her life? Live on her pension? Sure, if she wanted to sweat every bill. She'd never wanted to be anything but a policewoman from the time she was five years old.

But when the single thing that defines you as a person is taken from you, who are you?

CHAPTER THREE

Monday morning Mac met Mark Scott walking down the hall of the clinic with his little black-and-white mutt at his heels.

"Morning." Mac bent down and scratched Nasdaq's ears while the little dog wagged its whole body. "I need to talk to you. Ten o'clock."

"Okay," Mark said, looking at Mac suspiciously. "Please don't tell me you've discovered the newest piece of equipment to make you the perfect surgeon and it only costs two million bucks. I get enough of that from my beloved wife."

"Sarah simply believes in buying the best for our clients," Mac said with a perfectly straight face.

Mark rolled his eyes. "She'd been after me to buy the best from the first day she walked into this place. She made my life a nightmare until I gave her what she wanted." He grinned. "I got payback, though. She's not only made me the perfect wife, she's given me the perfect daughter. Not a bad trade-off for an ultrasound and a laser. So what do *you* want?"

As business manager of Creature Comfort as well as vice president of Buchanan Industries, Mark split his time between his cubbyhole in what had once been a storage room at Creature Comfort and a palatial office on the top floor of Buchanan Towers. Since Coy Buchanan — Rick Hazard's father-in-law — had bankrolled Creature Comfort in the beginning, it was only right that Mark keep an eye on the clinic's bottom line. However, clinic revenue had increased so much in recent months that he was around less and less these days.

"I do not want equipment." Mac looked down at Nasdaq. "And put that dog on a diet." He turned his back on Mark and walked toward his office.

He met Nancy coming out of his office with a sheaf of files in her hand.

"Oh, there you are," she said, and thrust the files at him.

"And I'm supposed to do *what* with all this?"

"That's a leading question, Doctor. Drink the coffee I just put on your desk and read them. You're spaying a couple of cats at nine."

"Great," he muttered. Spaying cats, neutering dogs, stitching up gashes and pinning broken bones of animals whose owners let them loose in traffic. Was that all his life had become? He'd wanted to make a real difference. At least Sarah and Eleanor got to work on a variety of animals. The only time Mac saw the inside of a horse was when one of them needed his help, which, given their levels of proficiency, they seldom did. He badly needed a new challenge.

Maybe he should do what Liz Carlyle was doing — go back to school for a year and pick up an additional specialty.

But he had a specialty. He was the best veterinary surgeon in the South — possibly the United States.

Yet he spent his nights watching television and his days spaying cats.

Maybe he should sign on for a tour of duty at one of the big African parks — they always needed vets. He could certainly afford six months of little or no money. Ngorongoro, maybe, or Kruger.

His partner, Rick, would have a heart attack if Mac even suggested a six-month leave of absence. He had responsibilities to the clinic.

"Your kitties are waiting for you," Nancy said from the door.

"Shaved and prepped?"

"No, Doctor, I thought I'd leave all the prep work to you," Nancy said with a sniff. "Of course they're prepped. Come on, get your rear end in gear. You've got a full schedule, as you might know if you'd bothered to read what I left you."

"Someday I'm going to fire you!" he called after her.

"One can but hope."

He grinned. Anytime he started feeling sorry for himself, Nancy brought him up short. No matter how he snapped and snarled occasionally, he was doing the thing he'd been put on this earth for, and doing it well.

Nancy, on the other hand, had been an up-and-coming professional Grand Prix show jumper on the verge of the big time — long-listed for the Olympics. Then the degeneration in her cervical vertebrae progressed so far and so fast that riding became agony for her.

Three operations had relieved most of the pain, but she could never ride again. She seldom talked about her neck, and when she did, she joked about it. But every time a horse came into the clinic, whether it was a small pony or that Percheron mare with the foal, she would go back to the stalls on her lunch hour to pet and hug it. Her eyes were always suspiciously red afterward.

Mac and Nancy worked steadily, and as usual, once he was immersed in surgery, he lost track of everything except the creature in front of him.

He didn't hear the door to the surgery swing open behind him. "Thought you said ten o'clock," Mark Scott said.

Mac looked over his shoulder. "Give me five minutes."

"Go on, Doctor," Nancy said. "I can close for you."

He nodded and stripped off his gloves and mask as he followed Mark into his office.

"Okay, what do you want money for?"

"Marriage has made you suspicious," Mac said as he slumped into the chair across from Mark. "How's the kid, by the way?"

"Since Sarah's been bringing her to work, you probably see more of her than I do." Mark's lean face split into a smile that could only be described as beatific. "Smartest child ever born, and the prettiest, which you'd know if you ever bothered to play with her."

"Can we change the subject? I have a proposition for you."

Mark rubbed his hand over his hair. "What is it?"

"I want to hire two more vet techs — one surgical and one nonsurgical."

"We have Nancy for small animals and Jack for large animals."

"They take vacations and get the flu. They are human, in case you haven't noticed."

"Sure, but I never imagined you did. We job out when we need extra help. There are plenty of people out there looking to work with animals for zilch money, which is what we pay."

"I'm aware of that," Mac said. "I want somebody I can train from the ground up to do what I want done in the way I want it. Nancy reads my mind. I need someone else who can do the same thing."

"The woman's tougher than I thought if she can stand to probe into that mind of yours."

"I want to start advertising today, put the word out among the other clinics for somebody who has some experience and wants more — somebody willing to do the scut work."

Mark sighed. "Okay, let me run the numbers. If they work out, you got it."

"Just like that?"

"Just like that. I'd appreciate your starting

with a part-timer until I'm certain the practice can bear the freight of a full-time surgical trainee. Maybe Alva Jean or Nancy knows somebody who'd be interested."

Mac stood up. "I'll ask. Now, Nancy needs me back to remove a steel pin from a Labrador's hip. It's starting to push through the skin and cause an abscess."

"Thank you for that pretty picture. Come see us sometime. I'll tell Sarah to bug you."

"Yeah, right."

He worked straight through lunch, which meant Nancy did too. At four o'clock she watched him finish off the final suture in the ear of a Border collie that had misjudged the distance between his ear and the horn of the ram he was herding. The ear had been nearly torn off and was bleeding profusely when the farmer carried him in.

Now the owner came out of the waiting room twisting his John Deere cap in his hands. "He gonna be all right?"

"Fine," Mac said. "He's groggy, but you can take him home. He's had antibiotics and I'll give you some more. The sutures should dissolve in ten days or so."

"Poor old Ben."

"He's not old — I'd say under two," Mac said.

"Little over a year. No, I meant this might

64

set him back a tad when he faces down his next ram. You have never seen a more embarrassed dog than ole Ben was when that ram tossed him down the pasture."

"Well, we saved the ear, so he won't bear the scars of his encounter."

"Thanks, Doc. Wouldn't think of running livestock without my dogs. I'm too old, too lame, and they're smarter than I am."

As Mac turned to go back to his office he came face-to-face with Kit Lockhart. The wind had tossed her hair, and the sunlight from the west-facing window turned her eyes to emeralds.

Coming this close to her had a visceral impact on him that unnerved him.

"Can I take Kev home?" she asked.

He stepped back from her and composed his face. "Haven't had a chance to check him out today, but I would have heard if there was a problem," he said, speaking slowly and letting the sun fall on his face. "Come on back."

He noticed she held a harness with a bright orange pad that said Working Dog on it. A much smaller version of the gear he'd seen used on Seeing Eye and helper dogs.

She caught his eye. "Kevlar's on duty all the time," she said. "The harness is for his protection so people don't distract him in public."

"Does it work?"

She grinned. "Almost never. Everybody still wants to pet him."

As he started back toward the kennel, Mabel Halliburton called out to him, "Dr. Mac? When you have a minute I need to ask you something."

He nodded.

Kevlar had been moved from ICU to the regular recovery kennel area in the next room. He opened Kevlar's cage and picked him up, carefully avoiding the incision along his flank. He set him down on the examining table in the center of the room, and reached for a thermometer.

Kit stood silently while he checked the dog over. Kevlar whimpered a little when Mac touched his incision, but the chart indicated that all Kevlar's kidney tests were normal.

"No fever," Mac said. He had raised his head to look at Kit when he spoke. "He needs to stay quiet for a while, and he probably won't feel like doing much running around for some time."

"When should I bring him back here?"

He wanted to tell her tomorrow — just so he could see her again. But that was stupid and juvenile. Besides, she'd never fall for it. He heard himself saying, "You're on my way home. I'll be happy to check him out in two or three days. I'll give you a call . . ." He felt his face flame.

She laughed. "Just come by. If the Jeep's in the driveway, I'm home. What symptoms should I worry about with Kev?"

"Worry about a sudden rise in temperature, inability to urinate, whimpering . . . never mind that one — Emma can tell you if he cries. If he does, get in touch with me immediately."

"Can I use a regular thermometer?"

"Right. But tie a string around the end of it before you insert it. You don't want it to get lost. Normal for a dog is about a hundred and one. You should worry about general malaise. I'll send you home with a bag of special dog food, but you can get it cheaper at your local pet store."

"One thing, Doctor. I know this is going to cost a fortune. I really hate to ask, but is there any way I can space out the payments over time? Or even do some work here at the clinic to help pay my bill? I'm strong as an ox and I'm not afraid of hard work. And I'm really good with computers."

Now her face was the one that was flaming. He could tell she hated asking him. The

Saturday surgery and the aftercare would add up to a hefty sum. She was probably on disability if her accident was work-related. Maybe she was hanging on with welfare and disability payments.

He realized he had no idea what she did or how she had been hurt.

"Don't worry about it. We'll work something out."

Nancy came toward them. "Little guy going home with you? Big's going to hate that. He's fond of him."

"Big's fond of everything that walks, flies or swims."

Nancy touched Kit's arm so that Kit looked at her. "I overheard what you two were saying."

Kit sighed. "Money's pretty tight. I'll pay my bill, I promise, but sometimes I can't pay all at once. I wish I could get a part-time job, but I really don't even know where to look. I have to pick Emma up at school unless I make arrangements. It's not easy finding a job where I don't have to hear. I can't clerk in a convenience store or anything."

"What do you do all day now?" Nancy asked.

Kit's blush intensified. She had that clear, pure redheaded skin that showed the movement of every corpuscle. "I . . . get my daughter off to school, and pick her up, do housewifely things and exercise and shop."

"You're probably getting bored."

"*Getting* bored? I've been bored out of my mind for the last three months. I can only take so much daytime television, even with closed captioning. And I never did learn to knit."

Mac realized he'd been cut out of the conversation completely. Kit could concentrate on only one person at a time. He felt annoyed that Nancy had butted in until he heard what Nancy had to say next.

"You said you could use a computer?" she asked.

"I type about a hundred words a minute, actually. You have no idea how much paperwork I had to fill out before my accident."

"Impressive speed."

"But anybody can use a computer."

"Not Dr. Mac," Nancy said. "He's a dinosaur."

Both women looked at him with pity. He made a face at them and pulled Kevlar closer.

"So how would you feel about scrubbing cages and mopping floors?" Nancy continued.

"Since when have you been the Creature

Comfort human resources manager?" Mac asked.

"You've been muttering about hiring a part-timer. And Mabel's been telling everybody for a month that if she doesn't get somebody to take the computer work off her hands she's going to quit."

"When did she say that?"

"Oh, about every day. But you veterinary types never listen to us peons." She turned to Kit again. "You could come in after you take your daughter to school, and leave in the afternoons in time to pick her up. You'll probably start by scrubbing cages or taking the animals for walks. We never know from one day to the next what we'll be doing. Are you physically all right? Except for the hearing, I mean?"

"Absolutely." Kit's face lit. "But could I bring Kev?"

"Don't see why not. He doesn't fight with other dogs, does he?"

"No, and he loves cats. He lives with one."

Nancy turned to Mac. "Well, how about it, Doctor?"

"We'll have to discuss it at the staff meeting tomorrow morning," he said, although he knew in his heart he would press to have Kit hired. It had nothing to do with the fact that she intrigued him. She was a woman who needed a hand up. Maybe it was time to be Mr. Nice Guy. It would certainly make a change.

"Well, peachy," Nancy said. "You do that." She took Kit's arm. "In the meantime, Dr. Mac's got one more cat to spay."

Kit gathered up Kevlar, put his harness on him gently and lowered him to the floor. He sat at once and looked up at her expectantly. "Home," she said.

He stood and walked off at her heel.

"Now that's the kind of dog to have," Nancy said.

"Pretty high-handed, aren't you?" Mac jabbed.

"Absolutely. You know how she went deaf?"

"No idea."

"Me, neither. But I'll sure find out."

Mac pressed his palms against his eyes. "Okay, where's this cat?"

"There isn't one. I just said that because if you don't have at least some peanut butter crackers and potato chips out of the machine, you're going to pass out facedown in somebody's intestines."

"What about you?"

"I brought myself a healthy lunch. Turkey sandwich and an apple. I just finished. You might consider packing yourself a lunch. Or don't you do that sort of thing?"

"Even I, Miss Mayfield, can make a turkey sandwich," he said and headed for the conference room.

As he munched his peanut butter crackers, he remembered that he'd promised to drop by Kit's house in a couple of days to check on Kevlar. In the meantime, he could consult with his partners about trying her out on a part-time basis. The scrubbing and cleaning part of the job required no special skills. She said she had the computer skills already. Why not give her a chance?

Mac had promised to check on Kevlar. Tonight — Wednesday — was the night. He nearly lost his nerve when he saw a dark-green van parked behind Kit's Jeep. Then he told himself that since this was a purely professional call, and since he couldn't have telephoned ahead to let Kit know he was coming, he'd simply ring the bell and assume she wasn't having a party.

The instant the bell sounded, he heard Kevlar's bark from inside the door, and a moment later, Kit opened it.

"Dr. Thorn?" She sounded surprised.

He felt tongue-tied and dry-mouthed. Ridiculous. He drew himself up to his six feet four. "I'm checking to see that you're looking after Kevlar properly."

"Oh, really. See for yourself."

"I don't want to intrude. You have company."

"Hey, Doc," a male voice called from the living room. A stocky young man with a buzz cut stuck his head around the corner of the door. "It's me, Vince Calandruccio. Adam's daddy."

A moment later the largest black German shepherd Mac knew — and he knew plenty — stuck his head around the door as well.

Mac grinned and said, "Hey, Adam, how's the arthritis?"

At a hand signal from Vince, Adam came forward, carefully sidestepping Kevlar, who stood quietly beside Kit. Mac dropped to one knee and began to ruffle the shepherd's ears.

"Adam moves a whole lot better, Doc, since you put him on that new stuff. You should have seen him do the police obstacle course last Friday. Fast as he was when he was a pup, weren't you, boy?"

Mac looked up and saw that Kit was getting only a few words of their conversation because Vince was behind her and Mac had bent his head over Adam. He stood, looked at Kit and spoke slowly. "Since Kevlar seems to be doing well, I'll be on my way."

"How would you know?" Kit said. "You've barely looked at him."

"Hey, no, Doc," Vince said. "Stay long enough to have a coffee."

"I don't want to interrupt."

"Interrupt? Me'n Kit been friends since police academy. She worked the Dog Squad for a while until they found out what a great sniper she was."

"A sniper?" He turned to stare at her. "A *police* sniper?"

"First woman in the T.A.C.T. squad. First woman sniper," Vince said proudly. "Best in the business. Take out a gnat's eye at a thousand yards. You ever get into a hostage situation, Doc, you better hope they send our gal Kit out to save you."

"Not any longer." Kit sat in a wing chair beside the fireplace. Kevlar immediately jumped into her lap, turned in a circle and settled down. "Men are supposed to be better snipers than women because their pulse and heart rate are slower, but mine used to be so low that every time they took it they wondered if I was actually alive."

She shrugged her shoulders as though it didn't matter, but Mac could tell it mattered terribly. "I could probably train hard enough to get it down again, but my depth perception's all screwed up." She touched the scar that bisected her eyebrow. "Besides, who needs a sniper who can't hear the order to fire?"

Mac had never registered that Kit's sardonic look came from the thin scar that raised her left eyebrow slightly. "The scar is barely visible. Good stitching."

"As good as yours?" She raised that eyebrow at him.

He lifted his shoulders. "Close."

"So how 'bout that coffee?" Vince headed for the kitchen with easy familiarity.

Adam followed his master with his eyes, but didn't rise from his place beside the couch.

When Vince came back with a mug, Mac took the coffee, which he really didn't want, and sat opposite Kit so that she could see both his face and Vince's. "Where is your daughter?" he asked.

"Upstairs doing homework."

Vince stretched out his thick legs in front of him and leaned his head on the back of the sofa. "Doc, as long as you're here, how about some advice."

Mac nodded.

"See, you're keeping Adam here going fine, but he's seven years old now and close to retiring as a police dog. The canine unit likes younger dogs." Vince reached down and scratched behind the dog's ears. "He'll be going home with me for good when he does. See, right now we either get dogs from Germany — that's where Adam came from — or from a guy in Ohio who breeds German shepherds specifically for police departments."

"Right, I know the process."

"He assesses the pups and does basic training for the first two years, then if he thinks a dog's a good candidate, he recommends we buy it. So far he's been a hundred percent on the nose. We're paying upward of ten thousand bucks a pup, then we have to complete the training and train the handlers ourselves."

"Ten thousand dollars?" Mac said. "Isn't that a bit steep even for a good shepherd?"

"Not for these guys," Vince said. "The imported Belgian Malinois cost even more. Thing is, I think with the right female, I could breed some pretty good pups from old Adam here."

"Possibly."

"I got my eye on a great big old girl from outside Leipzig in Germany — that's where Adam came from. I've got permission to breed her to him if I can get her over here. I could undercut the guy from Ohio and still make a nice profit, even if I only sold one pup a litter to a police department and the rest for pets."

"So what do you want from me?"

"Think Kit here could manage a kennel?"

"I beg your pardon?"

"I want to set up a kennel on some land I've got over in Hardeman County. If I can persuade Kit, we could go in together on the female and split the profits. I could keep working while she looked after the kennel."

"It would certainly be worth investigating," Mac said, trying to keep the dismay out of his voice. He wanted to keep Kit in his sight, not fifty miles away. "Since Kit will be working at Creature Comfort now, she should certainly be getting some excellent training." He spoke to her. "Do you have any experience running a kennel?"

"Of course not. The whole idea is crazy, Vince. Where would Em go to school? What about Jimmy's visitation rights? This house?" She turned to Mac. "Who said for sure I'll be working for Creature Comfort? Did I miss something?"

"We talked it over at the staff meeting. Nancy put in a good word for you and they agreed to hire you part-time. It's all settled. I thought we might discuss salary tonight." He glanced at Vince. He liked Vince but he wished he'd take the hint and leave.

"Hey, it's okay if you don't want to go in with me. Maybe it's too soon," Vince said. "I'm still going to try to buy that female, though. I can raise a litter of puppies in my backyard, see how it goes. I'm glad you're going to be getting out of the house more, Kit. When are you going to come down to the gym and start working out with the boys in blue again?"

"Don't forget I'm not in blue any longer."

"That doesn't matter. You'll always be one of us. You know that. Well, old Adam and me have to get home."

Vince stood and Adam came to attention beside him, eyes on his face. Vince gave him a hand signal, and he fell in beside his master.

Kit walked into the front hall with Vince.

Vince hugged her and kissed her on the cheek. "Bye, sweet thing. Come on down and see us, y'hear?"

Mac felt a jolt when Vince hugged Kit. Were they really just friends? He didn't want there to be anything between them — between Kit and anybody.

As Kit stood in the door and waved good-bye to Vince and Adam, the telephone on the hall table rang. He could see the red light blinking, but Kit was facing away from it.

Instantly Kevlar jumped up and bumped her hand. She turned, saw the light and picked up the telephone. "Just a minute, whoever you are. This is the wrong phone. Hang on." She said to Mac, "The phone I use is upstairs in my bedroom. Excuse me."

He started to tell her goodbye, but she turned and took the steps two at a time before he could. He went back to the living room to wait for her.

It was a comfortable room with bookshelves packed with current fiction on either side of the fireplace. A few pieces of furniture that his mother would probably approve of, but mostly an accumulation selected with taste but without much money. He had picked up a picture of a much younger Emma, when he heard Kit coming downstairs.

"Sorry. Jimmy wanted to change his night to have Emma sleep over. One of these days I am going to kill him."

"I'm sorry?"

"Jimmy Lockhart, Emma's father, my ex-husband. He rides a patrol car. He makes me so mad. He thinks having Emma sleep over is something he does when one of his bimbos cancels." She sank into the recliner. "I'm sorry. You don't need to hear my problems."

"At Creature Comfort we all interact like family." He felt his face flaming. Of all the stuffy, stupid things to say! "Now, I really must go. Thanks for the coffee."

"When do you want me to show up at Creature Comfort?"

"Would next Monday be too soon?"

"Not at all. We can talk about how much I can pay toward my bill out of my salary."

"Don't worry about your bill."

She put her hand on his arm to turn him to face her. "Can't lip-read your back, Doctor."

"Sorry. I said, don't worry about your bill." He loved the way she watched him, the way her lips parted and almost spoke the words as he did.

If he didn't look out, he was going to grab her and kiss her.

And probably wind up flat on his back with a karate chop to the throat.

"Uh, see you Monday."

He practically fled from the house. As he jumped into his car, he saw the curtains behind one of the upstairs windows flutter. Emma. He started the car and burned rubber getting away.

CHAPTER FOUR

When Kit opened the door to the Creature Comfort conference room early the following Monday morning, Nancy looked up from the comics section of the morning paper. "I wasn't sure you'd show up."

"Neither was I," Kit replied, taking her out-stretched hand. "I nearly lost my nerve. I'm not sure I can do this job without a good set of ears."

The early-morning mist still hadn't lifted from the Creature Comfort parking lot, although the weather was supposed to clear later in the day. About time. Everybody was sick of the unending late-February rain. Even the jonquils beside the roads looked dispirited.

Kit had dropped Emma at school, then had driven straight to Creature Comfort. Until the accident, she'd loved being surrounded by people. Now she realized that for eight months she'd seen almost no one except her doctors, the audio-clinic staff and her immediate family — if she could still consider Jimmy Lockhart family. She felt shy and out of place. These people knew one another well, worked together all the time. Could she possibly fit in? Would she see conversations around her that she couldn't interpret? The speech pathology people had warned her against becoming paranoid. It was easy to imagine others were gossiping about her.

Nancy bent to ruffle Kevlar's ears, then tilted her face up so that Kit could read her lips. "Around here you may find it a plus not being able to hear. All the barking and yapping gets to you after a while. Come on, I'll show you around and introduce you to the staff that's here. Later I can fill you in on them over lunch. Did you bring your lunch?"

"You're going to have to speak more slowly," Kit said. "I only got about half of that."

"Oops. Sorry. Did-you-bring-your-lunch?"

Kit laughed. "Not that slowly! The way it works is that I catch some of the words and fill in the blanks from what seems logical. B's and P's and M's look almost alike, but if somebody says, 'How about you blank me after work?' the chances are she's saying 'meet' me after work, not 'beat' me after work. Not unless you're talking to somebody deeply weird."

"As the Mad Hatter told Alice in Wonderland, we're all mad here," Nancy said as she shoved through the doors to the kennel. "And overworked, as you're about to see."

With Kev trotting at her heels, Kit followed Nancy to the large-animal area.

Nancy knocked on the first door on her left, waited a moment, then opened it and stood back for Kit to follow.

A pretty woman in a lab coat sat behind a desk piled high with reports. A happy baby toddled around the edges of a large playpen beside her desk.

Nancy pointedly looked back so that she was facing Kit. "Dr. Sarah Scott, this is Kit Lockhart. She's going to be working part-time with us in the small-animal area. Kit, this is Dr. Sarah Scott, head of our large-animal section."

The baby bounced up and down. "And this," Nancy said, "is Nell, known to all and sundry as Muggs."

At the mention of her nickname, the baby opened her mouth and began to make what must be crows of delight. Kit stiffened. She'd never be able to hear her own grandchild's voice — assuming she ever had a grandchild!

Sarah came around her desk with her hand out-stretched. "Hi. Welcome to the nuthouse."

"Thanks. Can't be any nuttier than what I'm used to."

"Keep that thought."

Nancy took Kit's arm and led her down the hall. At the far end a wizened elf of a man was giving the Percheron mare a shot in her neck.

"Jack Renfro. He does for Sarah and Eleanor Chadwick, our other large-animal vet, what I do for Mac." She paused. "But not half as well."

He pointed a crooked finger at her. "None of that now, missy." He took Kit's hand. His felt like old leather and twisted twigs. "Happy to meet you, lass. Nancy told me already we're to have you with us part of the day."

"We also have Kenny Nichols part-time," Nancy told Kit. "He comes in after school three days a week. He's off to Mississippi State to do pre-vet as soon as he graduates. You'll meet him and Dr. Chadwick later."

Kit learned that Bill Chumney — the veterinarian who handled exotic animals — was on assignment in the Black Hills and wouldn't be back for several weeks. And Dr.

Weinstock was off in Kentucky doing something with horses for the next month.

As she followed Nancy back through the door that separated the small-animal area from the large, she hoped she'd run into Dr. Thorn. Nancy had made a few comments about his bearish reputation, but so far Kit had seen nothing from him but kindness. He might be a little gruff, but he had been charming to Emma and had taken the trouble to make a house call on Kevlar on Wednesday evening. She wanted to thank him for giving her the chance to work again. Besides, he was the first man she'd met since her divorce who interested her. Big, competent men always had. She'd actually thought Jimmy was competent.

But she felt certain Dr. Thorn was the genuine article.

"I thought you wanted to train another surgical assistant," Rick Hazard said as he poured himself a third cup of coffee and took it back to the conference table.

"Kit's bright," Mac said. "She could learn."

"That's about the only job she *can't* do around here. She can't hear you and she won't be able to read your lips through your face mask."

85

Mac flushed. "So Nancy will train her to take over the other duties — dispensing meds, draining wounds, aftercare, checking on ICU patients. Big still gets confused sometimes and doesn't want the responsibility. Except for the occasional parrot, our clients don't generally communicate in words. I think Nancy can bring her along fast."

"I just wish you'd let me at least interview the woman before you brought her on board."

"Mark approved the expenditure. You agreed to try her at the staff meeting. Don't go back on your word now."

Rick raised his hands. "Don't get huffy. I'm sure she'll be fine. When can I meet this paragon?"

"This afternoon. According to Nancy, she had an appointment scheduled with her doctor. She'll be back for a bit after that. Nancy already had her fill out employment forms, so she can start learning her responsibilities this afternoon and really get started tomorrow."

"Fine. I've got a lunch meeting scheduled with Mark and my esteemed father-in-law at Buchanan Industries' corporate dining room." Rick crumpled up his cup and lobbed it expertly into the trash. "I can meet her this afternoon."

"Money problems?" Mac asked. He knew that Coy Buchanan was a tough old coot whose only soft spot seemed to be his daughter, Margot.

"For once, apparently not. Creature Comfort's more than meeting objectives."

"Good. Then maybe we can afford another trained vet tech on staff and a couple of clerks."

"Whoa!" Rick said. "We may be meeting our objectives, but we're still not rolling in money."

As he followed Rick out of the staff lounge, Mac said, "Kit Lockhart will be bringing her dog to work with her."

"Another one?" Rick stopped with his hand on the doorknob. "We've already got Mark's Nasdaq running around, and Big sneaks Daisy in every chance he gets. The last thing we need is another —" He stopped in midsentence. "Oh, I forgot. He's a helper dog, isn't he?" He shrugged. "I guess she needs him."

"He's well-behaved. I promise he won't eat the patients."

"Sometimes I wish the internet had never been invented."

Dr. Reuben Zales rubbed his hand across

his completely bald head and took a deep breath. "I've read the same articles you found on that site, Kit, and a great many more in medical journals. The operation they're talking about is experimental, and I mean *very* experimental. At the moment it's far, far too risky."

Kit leaned forward and put her hands on the edge of his desk, palms up as though in supplication. "But it sounds perfect for me, Reuben."

"Sure it does. And maybe in five years, or even two or three if they have good results, we'll look into it."

"But it said —"

"I said I am familiar with the internet site, Kit."

She couldn't hear his tone, but she suspected there was an edge of exasperation creeping in. He didn't like to have his judgment questioned. He admitted he was conservative. Maybe it was a good thing all she got was the words.

He ran his tongue over his lips. It was a constant gesture, almost a tic, and it drove Kit crazy because he spoke while he did it. What she read came out like some archaic Far Eastern language. "Stop that," she snapped.

He looked at her blankly.

"The tongue thing. I can't hear you when you do that."

"What tongue thing?" He dismissed her comment at once. He obviously wasn't even aware he did it. "Okay. Let's make it simple. Yes, regular cochlear implants can be miracles. For some people, not for you. You know that. We've consulted and discussed a dozen times. The operation you found on the internet is far more than a simple co-chlear implant. I can do those all day with excellent success rates and almost no complications. What you're talking about is much more dangerous with no guarantee of success. Yes, it might work. Yes, it would be wonderful, and no, not yet. You could wind up with seizures or a brain hemorrhage or throw a clot from the operation itself."

"But the success rate is eighty percent . . ."

"According to the internet. It might be eighty percent out of a total of ten patients. Even eight hundred out of a thousand means two hundred failures. Listen, there was a time when bone marrow transplants were very dangerous. They still are, but the success rate and the new techniques make them much less so. We transplant hearts and kidneys and implant pacemakers and defibrillators like garage mechanics. *Now.* But we didn't when we started. Let those geniuses practice on some other people before they work on you."

"But —"

"You are young, smart, tough, healthy, quick and you've made incredible strides in lipreading. You have closed captioning on your television. Your computer lets you talk on the telephone —"

"Only at my own computer in my own house."

"Still. And now you've got Kevlar . . ."

The little dog that lay beside Kit's chair raised his head and wagged his stumpy tail when he heard his name.

"You're functioning better than nine-tenths of my patients."

"That's because I'm working so hard at pretending this deafness thing is only a small inconvenience. Reuben, you deal with deaf patients every day, but you don't have a clue what it's really like to be locked into this silent world. If I thought it would last forever I don't know what I'd do — I can wait if you make me, but I miss hearing Emma's voice. And music. Emma hates having me like this. She doesn't say much, but she's stopped having her friends for sleepovers, and she practically dives into the car when I pick her up at school for fear some of her classmates will come over to chat with me.

Reuben, what if I can't hear her say 'I do'? What if I never hear my grandchildren laugh?"

He threw up his hands. "I wasn't aware that she was engaged. Obviously we'd better fly you to Boston for the surgery this evening."

"All right. So she's only ten years old. But all I can see is this horrible silence stretching away until the day I die. Sometimes I don't think I can take it any longer."

"By the time Emma is married and pregnant, you'll have had the operation. You'll hear your grandchildren laugh."

"Promise?"

"You know I can't do that."

"But you think?"

"Yeah. They'll probably have something even better by then. So far I'm told that with the successful procedures, the patient only gets hearing like a scratchy old Caruso record."

"Reuben, at the moment I'd kill for a scratchy Caruso." She looked at her watch. "If I don't get out of here I'm going to be late getting back to my new job."

"Job?"

She picked up Kevlar's leash. "I'm working as a grunt at Creature Comfort, the vet clinic."

"Lisa takes Biff and Shorty there. Great place."

"They saved Kevlar's life. He had to have a kidney removed."

"He's okay now?"

"Fine. Thanks to Dr. Thorn. Do you know him?"

"Lisa's mentioned him. Great with his hands — very, very bad with his bedside manner. If you're going to work there, it's probably a good thing you can't hear him."

"So I've been told. Okay, Reuben. If you're absolutely dead set against it, I won't risk that operation right this minute. But you have to promise me you'll research it and talk to the guys in Boston. Try to figure out the absolute first minute it'll be safe for me to have it."

"That, I'll do, but don't expect me to fly you off to Boston tomorrow."

In the parking garage she strapped Kevlar into his car seat so that he could see out the windows, strapped herself in and started to back out of the parking space. Kevlar put a paw on her arm. She braked and checked her rearview mirror again. A red Corvette, nearly too low to the ground to be seen, flashed by and raced down the ramp.

"Whew! Too close, Kev. Thanks. I didn't see him."

The dog wagged his tail and grinned. She drove out more sedately. She'd never realized how much she relied on sound. Before, she'd have heard that idiot's tires squeal around the corner even before she saw him. But now she had Kevlar.

"You know, boy," she said as she drove toward Creature Comfort. "I may be a risk-taker, but I've never been foolhardy. I always called for backup when I needed it, and followed my commander's orders. The screwup with the flash-bang didn't happen because I went off half-cocked."

She turned onto the interstate that led to Germantown.

"Mom taught me that the important thing for a cop is to go home alive at the end of the shift. Take as few risks as possible, but be aware that the risks are always present. Now I'm stuck in a situation where I can't even assess the danger.

"The last thing I want is to stick Emma and my parents with somebody who has seizures or is half-blind. Emma's had too much put on her as it is. No wonder she's scared. A ten-year-old shouldn't have to play momma's little helper. Momma's supposed to help *her*."

Kevlar leaned over as far as his car seat allowed and licked her ear.

"Okay, so *you're* momma's little helper."
She laughed and wiped her ear. "You better
keep your mind on your work once we get
to the clinic. Stay away from the big dogs
that could scarf you up as a morning snack."

Wednesday morning of her first week she'd
come in earlier than usual because Emma
had some sort of early breakfast thing at
school. Kit stuck her head into the first
treatment room because the light was on.

Liz Carlyle hovered over a tiny red dog
that lay on its side on the table. She looked
up when Kit opened the door and said,
"Oh, great. Come on in here, will you?
Nobody else is in yet."

Kit came in and sent Kevlar to the corner
of the room to lie down.

Liz looked up at Kit and said slowly,
"She's a Brussels griffon. Her owner
dropped her off just before midnight. She
couldn't stay. She's got kids at home. These
little folks almost never have more than one
pup per litter, but I think she's got two
squeezed in there. If she doesn't deliver at
least one in the next five minutes I'll have
to cut her."

Kit nodded. "I've never been around
anything like this."

"Just don't faint or scream," Liz said.

"Hey! I think we've finally got some action!"

The pup looked more like a wet, red gerbil than a dog. At Liz's instructions, Kit wrapped it warmly in a towel and jiggled it until it began to breathe. Meanwhile Liz gently pried the second pup out of its mother with the tips of her fingers. As Kit bundled that one against her chest, Liz began to work furiously over the little dog. Five minutes later Kit held a third pup.

"Enough!" Liz said and turned to Kit. "Can you handle all three of those guys while I carry the mother to the whelping box?"

Kit nodded again. "Sure."

"You're going to have to sit beside them and watch until everybody's suckling."

Once the pups and mother were installed in the warm box, Liz put her hand on Kit's arm. "I heard Rick come in. I'll tell him what's going on. He can take over. I've got to get some sleep." She pressed the heels of her hands into her eye sockets. "Thanks."

"You're welcome."

Liz looked down at the little dog that was already nuzzling her tiny pups into place against her nipples. "Three pups! That's practically a record."

An hour later Nancy came in and sank onto her haunches to look at the pups.

"Ooh, they're teensy." She grinned at Kit. "That'll teach you to come in early."

In the next week and a half, Kit taught abandoned kittens how to nurse from a baby bottle, sat with a Labrador puppy that had been hit by a car until it came out of anesthetic, and helped deliver a baker's dozen of puppies from a Great Dane. Whenever a small animal needed a baby-sitter, everyone seemed to turn to Kit. Even Dr. Sarah requested her services to stay beside a foal whose crooked front legs had been straightened and splinted.

"Pups from tiny to giant," Kit told her father over dinner Friday night.

"Can I see the puppies?" Emma asked. "I'd rather see the puppies than spend the night with Daddy."

"They've gone home, baby," Kit said. "But the way things are happening, I suspect there'll be plenty more. Seems like this is the season for babies. Dr. Carlyle says those three Brussels griffon puppies she delivered last week are worth at least a thousand dollars each and the Great Danes yesterday will sell for about eight hundred. The owners want good vets to deliver as many healthy babies as possible, not to mention saving the mother if she gets into trouble."

After Emma reluctantly left to spend the

night with her father, Kit sank into the wing chair in her living room opposite her father.

"So, you like this job?" Tom Barclay asked.

"Love it so far. Nice people, good hours, and nobody seems to mind that I can't hear."

"How about that Dr. Thorn who saved Kevlar? You work with him at all?"

"No, Dad. As a matter of fact, I seldom see him. He's always in surgery with Nancy." She moved uncomfortably in her chair.

"I've heard he has quite a reputation with the ladies."

"Really?" Kit tried to sound casual.

"He dated the daughter of one of Catherine's clients. She decorated his apartment."

Kit shrugged. "He's management, Dad, I'm definitely labor."

"He's not married. You ought to start thinking about dating again."

Kit put up her hands. "Please, Dad. No men in my life ever, ever again. Jimmy gave me enough problems for a lifetime. Besides, I'm a deaf woman with a kid. Hardly marketable goods."

"A good man wouldn't care."

"Find me a good man. So far I've come up empty."

Her father stood and Kevlar jumped off

Kit's lap to stand beside him. "Your mother ought to be home from her meeting by now. See you for dinner on Sunday?"

"Maybe." She kissed her father's cheek and let him out the front door. As she watched him climb into his car, she said to Kevlar, "My father, the incurable romantic. The eye of an eagle. But he can't possibly know I have a little thing for Mac Thorn. Come on, Kev, let's hit the treadmill."

Kit felt him before she turned and saw him. She didn't react to other people that way. It wasn't that she smelled him. She'd learned to identify the odor of her mother's familiar perfume and her dad's scent of wood chips and sawdust. She smelled Emma's little-girl scent sometimes, but Mac Thorn didn't have a discernible scent. No aftershave, not even that antiseptic odor that lingered around some of the doctors who'd treated her in the hospital.

Yet, for the past few weeks, it was as though he created a small disturbance in the air around her. If she weren't wearing a long-sleeved sweater, she was sure she'd have been able to see the fine hairs on her arm rise as they might in an electrical storm. An odd sensation — pleasant but disturbing.

She knelt and laid the sleeping kitten she'd been holding gently on the towel and shut the door of its cage carefully, then turned to look at him.

He'd been staring, she was certain of it. At what? The back of her head?

"Did you need something, Doctor?" She pivoted on her knees so that she could look up at him.

"Not at the moment. I've heard good things about you. Rick says when it comes to babies, you've got the touch."

She felt her stomach muscles tighten. "All I do is sit until they come out of anesthesia, then I tell Nancy."

"And Kevlar?" He leaned over to scratch behind the dog's ears.

"If you mean, is he freaking out and barking at the other animals, he's not. One of the tests helper dogs have to pass is to ignore a rabbit that literally walks across their feet. After that, this is a piece of cake."

The man was standing there making idle conversation about something he couldn't possibly care about. What did he really want? Nancy came through the double doors behind him with so much force she hit him in the shoulder.

"What the —" she read before he turned on Nancy.

She was looking right at Kit so that she was able to catch the vet tech's words.

"Zoo just called. Two emergencies. Dr. Hazard's on his way, but he needs us."

Kit stood up but she couldn't catch Mac's answer.

"You get the tigress with the bad tooth. They don't want to knock her out until you get there. Dr. Hazard's got an orangutan that's gone into premature labor. If she needs a C-section, Dr. Hazard wants you to do it."

Mac said something and shoved past her. As he went out the door he pointed a thumb over his shoulder in Kit's general direction.

"You sure?" Nancy asked.

"It's a baby, isn't it?"

Kit had never been this close to a full-grown tiger before. Just looking at those fangs sent a shiver up her spine. Mac Thorn didn't even seem to notice that his hands were deep in the open maw of the big cat, and his head was so close that if the cat woke up, he could be decapitated.

Nancy stood between him and a small table on which lay a tray of shining instruments. Beside Mac a zookeeper named Mick monitored the cat's breathing.

Mac looked up and asked the keeper,

"How long has this tooth been like this?"

Kit's head swiveled to watch the keeper's lips. She'd positioned herself so that she could catch much of what Mac and Nancy said.

"I just noticed this morning she was off her feed. I wasn't sure what the problem was, but from the way she was trying to eat with just one side of her teeth, I knew there was something wrong. Is it an abscess?"

"No. Broken tooth. Can't believe it just started hurting."

"I assure you, Doctor —"

"Keep your shirt on. I'm not suggesting . . . Oh, too bad." The cat gave a great sigh. "No choice. Our girl here needs a root canal." He shifted the instrument that kept the cat's jaws open. "This is going to take some time."

He bent over the tiger's open mouth so that Kit could no longer see his face. She moved around to the far side where she could watch as he opened his right palm to Nancy without lifting his head. Nancy handed him what looked like a cordless electric drill. She watched it begin to spin and shuddered. The screech of the dentist's drill had always given her a migraine. At least this time she couldn't hear that high-pitched whine.

She stared at Mac's arms so that she wouldn't concentrate on the tiger. The man had muscles on his muscles. His forearms were covered in fine dark hair and the skin was pale, as though he seldom went outdoors in short sleeves.

He hefted a knee onto the table as he drilled deeper into the broken tooth. The root seemed to go down forever.

Suddenly the cat stirred. Mac froze, glanced toward Rick Hazard who presided over the three hoses suspended from the ceiling. Kit had read the labels before they had brought in the sleeping cat. Oxygen, anesthetic and some other drug with an unpronounceable name.

Rick replaced the mask over the cat's face and let it breathe until it quieted again.

Mac raised his head. "Have to work fast. Let's plug this thing before we have to give her any more anesthetic."

Ten minutes later he and Nancy stood on either side of the cat. Mac's face ran with sweat and the top of his greens clung to him. He gave Nancy a thumbs-up sign and stepped back so that Rick could fit the mask back on the tiger's face. Kit watched him switch to pure oxygen.

So far as she could tell, the big cat slept on.

But when she looked at the long, limp tail that hung off the end of the table, she could see the faintest twitch at the very tip. She backed away, moving toward the double doors into the hall.

Well, at least she hadn't fainted or done anything else stupid.

Mac turned to Kit as though only now aware that she was in the room. "Have fun?"

"Will she be all right?"

"She'll hurt for a couple of days, but nothing like the pain she's been in. Can't use the normal painkillers and anesthetics on tigers. They have bad reactions. Can't even use the stuff we use on lions and leopards."

"What happens now?"

"Now she goes into one of the hospital cages until she wakes up. Then in a couple of days, she'll go back to her buddies. Please stay and help Mick get her moved."

"Then come next door," Nancy said. "If that orang hasn't delivered her baby by now, Rick thinks we'll probably have to do a C-section."

Mac and Rick walked out. Nancy packed up the instruments to take back to the clinic to be sterilized. Then she, too, slipped out of the room.

The keeper stroked the tigress's flank as though she were only an oversize house cat.

He looked up at Kit and said something she didn't quite catch.

"Sorry, I didn't get that."

Mick blinked, then nodded. "You look pretty strong. Are you?"

"Very strong."

"Think you can handle a three-hundred-pound tigress?"

"Alone? Uh, no."

Mick grinned. "I should have said half a tigress. Stay here. I'll be right back."

Kit found herself alone beside the sleeping tiger. She couldn't bear to be this close and not touch her. She put her hand on the fur to find it softer than she'd imagined, but with a tough overcoat.

Suddenly the tigress yawned mightily. Kit jumped. "Mick?"

"Right here." He rolled the gurney beside the operating table. "As a favor, you can take the end that doesn't bite." They swapped places. "All we have to do is grab the rubber sheet and slide her over. On three, okay?"

The cat's rear end was a dead weight, but Kit managed without looking foolish. "Do you need me to help get her into a cage?"

"Absolutely."

She helped Mick roll the gurney down the hall and into a room with heavy steel cages.

Mick opened the door of the nearest cage, lowered the gurney to floor level and slid it inside. Then he shut it, locked the door behind him and turned to Kit. "I'll stay here with her. You go find the doctors. Thanks. Sometimes we can get a little short of help around here, especially in flu season."

Kit turned away and saw a pair of fat, pink tummies and eight legs sticking straight up in the wire cage next door to the tiger. She touched Mick's shoulder and pointed. "What are those things?"

He grinned. "A is for Aardvark."

"I thought aardvarks were the size of armadillos."

"Nope. They're big dudes and nocturnal. They won't bother to wake up until after dark."

"Are they sick?"

"Nope. We're just finishing their new enclosure. They'll be moved tomorrow."

"Thanks. I never saw a real live aardvark before."

"Anytime. Now go find your doctors."

Kit slipped into the examining room next door to the small operating theater where Mac had treated the tigress.

Below lights in the center of the room, a large rounded lump lay under a green surgical sheet. From beneath the sheet she saw a red, hairy arm and hand strapped to the table. Dr. Hazard sat at the head end of the sheet with his mask and tubes, while Nancy and Mac bent over the green mountain as it rose and fell gently with the animal's breathing.

Suddenly Mac reached down, grasped something and pulled it from the orang's belly, then bent over and began to shake it.

Kit shrank back into the darkness. It was a baby, all right, a tiny red thing that Mac was handling like a soccer ball. He thumped it, stuck his finger in its mouth and then held it upside down and bounced it. Then he set it down on the table and bent over the mother while Rick grabbed a towel and picked up the baby. He looked over at Kit.

"Here!" He thrust the little red scrap at Kit. "She's breathing, but she needs warmth. Get her dry and hold her."

Kit took the little creature, whose large luminous eyes were open and staring at her, wrapped the towel around its little form, pressed it close to her chest and began crooning to it and swaying with it in the same way as she had rocked Emma when she was a baby. One tiny hand snuck out of the towel and reached up to her face. Kit bent down and let the little creature touch her cheek. Its hands were soft and damp.

Kit looked around and saw a pile of towels in the far corner of the room. She exchanged the damp towel for several dry ones, wrapped the baby and cuddled her close.

The baby began to nuzzle her. "She needs milk," Kit said.

From his place at the table, Rick looked at her. Neither Nancy nor Mac acknowledged her.

The baby shivered. "Nancy?"

Nancy turned toward her. "The mother's hemorrhaging. There are people outside. Take her to them."

Another shiver. The little mouth opened in a silent whimper. "Great," Kit breathed. "It's just you and me, kid."

But it wasn't. Outside the door a woman in a keeper's uniform paced for all the world like an anxious husband waiting for a human birth. The moment Kit shoved through the operating room doors, the keeper came up to her.

"It's alive!" The keeper was a short, square woman with curly gray-blond hair and a face that had seen too much sunlight.

The moment the woman touched the baby, it burrowed its face into Kit's chest and clung to her with amazing strength.

The keeper dropped her hands. "Better not fight. Come on, let's get some formula.

That, at least, we're prepared for."

Ten minutes later Kit's little charge lay across her chest suckling happily on the bottle Kit held. But her big eyes never left Kit's face. The keeper, who had introduced herself as Mary Rose Milner, sat beside the pair and petted the baby gently.

Mary Rose listened to Kit's explanation of her deafness and made certain Kit could see her face when she talked. She asked about the mother's condition. Kit longed to be able to reassure the woman, but was unable to.

The doctors had been inside that room with the orang mother for a very long time. What would happen if she lost too much blood? She'd go into shock and die. But they surely didn't keep orang blood around for transfusions. And were there half a dozen blood types?

Mary Rose touched her shoulder. "That's enough." She took the tiny bottle from the sleepy baby.

Kit lifted the baby to her shoulder. "Do I have to burp her?"

Mary Rose nodded and smiled. "You're good at this."

"It's been nine years since I did it, and I definitely wasn't good at it."

"Well, then you've learned how since."

"Shouldn't I give her to somebody who knows more about her?"

"She's happy. Let her be. Those towels are already soaked. You're going to stink." Mary Rose left for a minute and returned with a box of newborn-size disposable diapers and a stack of fresh towels.

When she tried to pry the infant off Kit, however, the baby began to squirm. And then she did what all babies do after they have been fed. Kit looked down at her jeans. Mary Rose laughed, unwound the protesting baby from Kit and laid her on a counter. "I'll take care of the little princess, here. You go clean up a little."

That, Kit thought as she looked at herself in the ladies' room mirror, was going to take more than sponging off her jeans and shirt with wet paper towels and hand soap. She did the best she could, then went back out to what she had already begun to think of as "my baby."

Mary Rose had the little orang properly cleaned up, diapered and wrapped in fresh towels. The instant she saw Kit, the baby began to wriggle. Mary Rose handed her back to Kit. The orang latched onto her hair with one surprisingly strong little hand.

"Ow!" Kit unwound the fingers. The baby decided she would rather chew on her own fist. She nestled against Kit, her soft downy head tucked under her chin, and closed her eyes.

"How much does she weigh?" Kit asked.

"Probably three or four pounds. No more. The doctors will have to go over her — what's taking them so long?" Mary Rose went over to the doors of the examining room and peered in.

"When can she go to her mother?"

Mary Rose shrugged and turned back so that Kit could read her lips. "We'll hand-raise her until we locate a surrogate mother at another zoo. Lilly did so much damage to her last baby before we took it that it didn't live a week."

"So who raises her in the meantime?" Kit realized they were speaking in whispers to avoid waking the baby.

"We've got a docent set up to babysit her for a couple of months until we can put her with her own species. The problem is that Lilly delivered early. Our docent is in Hawaii marrying off her daughter."

"Your . . . what was the word you used?"

"Docent. One of the volunteer helpers. They occasionally take home one of the babies requiring round-the-clock care."

"Oh. So who's going to look after this little one until the docent comes back? You?"

Mary Rose smiled at her and shook her head. "It looks like she's found her surrogate mom."

"Me?" Kit stared at her. "Don't be crazy. I know nothing about orangutans."

"You seem to know about babies. Even if your doctors say she's healthy, they're probably going to want her at the clinic for a while anyway so they can watch her. They've got a better incubator than we have if she needs it."

"Repeat, please. Slowly."

Mary Rose complied, then stroked the baby's head gently. "She seems to have chosen you."

"I can't, Mary Rose. Even if I weren't totally untrained, I have a ten-year-old daughter. I wouldn't be able to hear this little person if she cried, and I rely on a hearing ear corgi. I already have too many problems in my life. I can't play mommy to the princess here twenty-four hours a day. I just can't. Even if Dr. Hazard would trust me, and I'm sure he wouldn't."

The double doors swung open. "Barring major infection, the mother should make it," Mac was saying. "Now, Kit, what wouldn't Dr. Hazard trust you with?"

CHAPTER FIVE

"What you need is one of those baby carriers you sling over your shoulders," Mabel said.

Kit slipped one hip onto the other bar stool behind Mabel's high perch at the registration desk. "I had one when Emma was tiny, but I have no idea where it is now. Probably went to charity with most of her baby clothes."

"I've got one at home from when my grandkids were little," Mabel said. "I'll bring it in tomorrow night."

"Great. You can give it to whoever is going to babysit the princess for the next two weeks until that docent person gets back from Hawaii."

"Uh-huh." Mabel looked at her curiously.

"Not me! I agreed to do it tonight. But I can't after that. Mabel, I need you to make a telephone call for me."

"How?"

"Put it on the speakerphone. That way I can talk and you can relay what my mother says on the other end. Okay?"

"Uh-huh. What's the number?" Mabel clicked the speaker button. "What's her name?" she asked as she punched in the number.

"Catherine Barclay."

"Ma'am? Oh, sir — are you by any chance Mr. Barclay?" Mabel Halliburton nodded at Kit. "Your daughter asked me call you, sir. Here she is. Can you hear her okay?"

"Dad? You picked up Emma after school?"

Mabel listened and nodded. "Says she's right there with him. They were expecting you to pick her up an hour ago."

"I know, and I'm so sorry. Emma, I've got a big emergency here at the clinic . . ."

Mabel spoke quickly. "No, honey, she's not hurt. She's fine. Promise."

"Dad, can you and Mom keep Emma tonight and get her to school tomorrow?"

Mabel whispered, "Emma wants to know what's wrong."

Kit shifted the baby to her other arm. "Nothing's wrong, sweetheart. As a matter of fact, everything is great. I'm standing here holding a tiny baby orangutan . . ."

Mabel raised her hand. "Can't make out the words, but they're shouting."

"She was just born this afternoon, and she seems to have taken to me as her surrogate mom. She's really tiny, Emma, and she has to stay in somebody's arms full-time. The thing is, she's latched onto me, and I don't think it would be a good idea to unlatch her at the moment."

Mabel said, "Are you going to bring her home with you tomorrow?"

Kit shook her head. "No, tomorrow she'll be a little stronger and the clinic can work out a schedule for her, but I don't want to leave her tonight. She's so little. I don't want anything to happen to her."

"Your dad says they'll be delighted to take care of Emma. Do you need him to bring you anything?"

Kit started to ask for a change of clothes, but then decided against it. This baby needed quiet and peace and a place under her heart. She'd worry about her smell tomorrow when she went home.

"Emma wants to know if she can come see the baby."

"Not tonight. She can't have visitors for a while. I'll ask the doctors if you can come visit someday soon."

"Your dad apparently just shooed Emma away. He says he wants to talk to you privately. How do we manage that?"

"We don't. You still get to hear everything. What is it, Dad? Is Emma sick?"

"You know how much I wanted you to take this job," Mabel repeated. "And I am always glad to pick Emma up at school and look after her. But Emma's gotten used to your picking her up on time and going home with her. Suddenly it's back to the way it was when you were on night duty or called out in the middle of the night on a hostage situation. You should have phoned to say what was happening."

"I'm sorry, Dad, but I *have* been a little busy." Kit knew she sounded annoyed. That was because she felt guilty. Her father was right, of course. "Emma knows I'm not in any danger. I've been working here a month and this is the first time I've ever been late. It can't be helped. Tell Emma I love her and ask her to think happy thoughts for the baby. That should take her mind off me."

"What about Kevlar?"

"He's right here at my feet. Where's Mom?"

Mabel listened a moment, then looked up with a puzzled expression in her eyes. "This can't be right. Down at the jail? With one of her fathers?"

Kit nodded. "She must have caught a deadbeat dad. My mother is a retired cop.

She's now doing P.I. work and she's tough when it comes to men who don't support their children. Tell my dad to call me here if he needs me. I'll call Emma later to say good-night."

"He says okay. Goodbye."

"Thanks, Mabel. I have a phone at home that's attached to my computer so I can read people's answers, but it doesn't work on any other phone."

"Would one of those smart phones work?"

"Maybe. Unfortunately, I don't have one and they cost a fortune. Besides, my parents have never got the hang of texting."

The baby wriggled fretfully.

"Oops," Kit said. "I think the princess needs to have her diaper changed."

Mac had no intention of going home until he was certain that the little scrap of flesh attached to Kit like a limpet was holding her own. She seemed remarkably healthy for a preemie, but he knew that could change in a heartbeat.

He and Rick had discussed having Kit act as surrogate mother, and then Rick had begged and cajoled Kit into staying overnight at least tonight.

The baby weighed three pounds, one ounce. Hard to believe she'd ever weigh

116

nearly a hundred and fifty pounds, which is what her mother weighed. The zookeepers were watching Lilly and would call him at the first sign of trouble. Fortunately, he'd managed to control the hemorrhaging before she'd lost too much blood. But the next twenty-four hours were critical.

As for the baby, the next twenty-four hours were crucial for her, too.

With so many people out sick, the zoo simply didn't have enough personnel to monitor the baby full-time. Here, at least, one person could be delegated to babysit.

Kit was a natural choice. He'd taken her to the zoo because Nancy had told him how good Kit had been with the clinic's newborn animals. He'd also wanted to see how she reacted to stressful situations.

Maybe he'd also wanted to show off a little, to prove to Kit he didn't simply work with cats and dogs.

Kit was strong and tough, but that had been no guarantee that she wouldn't pass out at the first sign of blood. She'd actually been helpful in moving the sleeping tiger, and hadn't seemed the least bit nervous.

Once he'd pulled the baby from its mother's belly, nobody in that room had had time for anything but trying to save the mother's life. Of course Mac had wanted the baby to

117

live, but his job was to save the mother. Luckily, it looked as if both would live unless something catastrophic happened to one of them.

The orang mother might even be able to have another baby. Each surviving baby — especially a female baby — was a miracle, considering the endangered status of the species.

The baby had latched onto Kit as she would have latched onto her real mother. And Kit had reacted well. On the drive back to the clinic, she hadn't seemed worried that she smelled appalling, or that her clothes would probably have to be thrown away. She'd sat in the backseat with the baby against her chest.

On the short run from the car to the back door of the clinic, Kit had covered the baby's head with her jacket and continued to do so to shield the newborn's eyes from the bright lights.

Everyone had wanted to see the infant, of course, but they all had sense enough not to touch her. Sarah Scott, whose baby was at the age to pass on every germ with which she came in contact, wouldn't even leave her office. She simply stood in the doorway and stared as the trio passed by.

Mac had left Rick to check over the baby

and record its vital signs, while he and Nancy plunged back into their normal surgical routine, which in this case was a shih tzu with a broken pelvis.

By the time he'd finished and sent Nancy home, he was dropping with exhaustion. His stomach rumbled. He flopped down in the chair across the desk from Rick and said, "What's the status?"

"Baby's really excellent. Kit's in Mark's office."

"So you persuaded her to stay?"

"Only for tonight. She said her parents would look after her daughter tonight. What happens tomorrow night? She can't be here twenty-four hours a day."

"She can take days. Maybe Mabel can handle nights until the zoo can take over."

"Mabel's up to her eyes as it is. And that baby wants Kit."

"She'll just have to adjust. Mabel is every bit as nurturing as Kit — more, probably. She's got grandkids."

"And the records? The bills? The other stuff that Kit was supposed to do?"

"So long as that baby thrives, I don't care if we never send out another bill! Forget the records! Where are your priorities? That's a baby in there! A real, live, endangered three pounds. Keeping her alive and healthy is our job. And if Kit and Mabel manage to do that, the bills can wait until doomsday."

He stormed out and slammed the door on Rick's surprised face.

His adrenaline level collapsed. He ought to go back and apologize. Of course the bills and the records mattered. Rick's administration made it possible for the rest of them to do their jobs and not worry about things like bills and records.

He was tired, he was hungry, he'd acted like a jerk and a prima donna, and there was nobody — not a soul — in his life that he could tell that to.

He opened the door to Mark's office silently. Kit might not be able to hear, but baby orangs had marvelous hearing from the minute they were born.

Kit lay supine on Mark's sagging couch with her head and torso propped on four or five of the throw pillows that Sarah had brought in to add a little color to the drab room. Kevlar lay asleep on the rug at her feet. The instant Mac opened the door, the corgi raised his head. "It's okay, boy," Mac whispered. "Go back to sleep." The dog put his head between his paws but kept his eyes on Mac.

Mac would be willing to bet Kit hadn't had anything to eat since lunchtime.

She had, however, discarded her filthy clothes for a pair of surgical greens — his, probably, since they looked like oversize pajamas on her. Her hair was damp, and she smelled of soap, so she'd obviously taken a shower. Good thing. She'd needed one.

In the light of the desk lamp, her hair was the color of burnished bronze. Her mouth was open slightly, and he could see the gentle rise and fall of her chest as she breathed.

The little orang rode up and down against her heart. As he entered the room, she raised her tiny head and turned big black eyes in his direction. He watched until the small head dropped once more, the eyes closed, and the tiny fist went into her mouth. Kevlar continued to watch him.

He tiptoed to the side of the couch and looked down at Kit.

The baby wriggled, and without opening her eyes, Kit whispered, "Shh, baby." And stroked the tiny head.

He'd thought Kit was a handsome woman, good-looking, but not beautiful.

He'd been wrong.

She was. He longed to kneel beside her, caress her, drop his tired head onto her chest.

Hardly feasible with three pounds of orang hanging on to her for dear life.

"I don't blame you," he whispered. The large black eyes opened, but the baby didn't raise its head.

He bent and kissed Kit's open lips softly.

He pulled away and stood up. What would he do if she woke? He'd look like a complete idiot. He backed away quickly, slipped through the door and shut it behind him.

He leaned against the wall and tried to get his breathing back to normal.

This was not supposed to happen.

This was not a woman in whom he should ever be interested. Certainly not a woman to have a serious relationship with.

She was divorced, she was an employee, she had a *child!*

His job drained him emotionally. He had nothing left over at the end of the day to devote to a personal life. He was completely committed to his job. If a beagle was hit by a car on Christmas morning, he'd be in the OR instead of opening presents at home with a wife and family. How many times had he walked out on dinner or left a movie halfway through because he had a call?

Kit deserved better.

He realized with a certainty that astounded and terrified him that it might well be too late to back away from Kit unscathed.

He strode into his office and slammed the door behind him. Even if the walls hadn't been sound-proofed, Kit couldn't hear him.

He wasn't certain if it was actually a word or not, but he had the feeling that he was already "scathed" whether he wanted to be or not.

Kit stirred, blinked, and realized she couldn't sit up without disturbing the baby. What a dream! Snow White kissed back to life by Grumpy.

She touched her lips. It was as if she could taste that kiss. Had she been dreaming? Surely the good doctor hadn't stolen in and planted one on her while she was asleep. That wasn't his style. And if he had, then she wished she'd been sufficiently awake to catch him at it.

So far, he'd been polite to her, nothing more. But there was an undercurrent swirling in the air around them. With his unromantic view of the world, Mac would probably tell her that it was simply nature's way of getting the sexes together to continue the species.

Until the accident, Kit had considered herself a pretty fair specimen. Attractive, intelligent, with a good healthy body.

Her physical prowess was still there — or had been until she started getting sloppy about working out — but now she was definitely damaged goods. Anyone who watched the Discovery channel on television knew that the damaged female of any species was ignored by breeding males, and usually got short shrift and a short life. And no self-respecting male wanted to raise the offspring of a previous male.

Mac Thorn was the perfect gorilla — the dominant male, leader of the pack. She laughed. Even to his hair, which was nearly all gray and worn so short it would never need combing.

She stifled a giggle.

The baby woke instantly and started to wriggle and probably squeal, although Kit couldn't hear her.

That serves me right.

She rolled off the couch and went down the hall in her stocking feet to the makeshift nursery that had been set up in the staff lounge. She took a bottle of formula from the refrigerator, nuked it, tested it on her wrist, found it acceptable, and stuck the nipple into the baby's questing mouth.

She settled herself in one of the metal chairs by the conference table and watched the baby suckle contentedly. She discovered that tears were rolling down her cheeks.

Such a long time since she'd held Emma this way. So many times when she hadn't been there at all, and her father had taken care of Emma. He was the nurturer in the family. Her mother did not have the knack or the attention span to deal with children — even her own.

Kit's father had been the one to play Chutes and Ladders with her, to teach her how to skate and to ride a bicycle, to read the same books over and over to her at bedtime. He'd cheered her soccer games and taught her how to perfect her backhand.

Tom Barclay never lost his temper, never showed impatience, never raised his voice. He always seemed actually to be interested in the things she had to say. And he was just the same with Emma.

She and her mother had fought all the time until Kit married and joined the police department. Now Kit and Emma fought the same way. The women in the family were all too much alike.

Kit loved her mother fiercely and admired her tremendously. But Catherine Barclay had been too busy becoming the first woman police captain on the Memphis force to pay Kit more than casual attention.

And like poor Lilly, the orang, who had

never had another female to teach her how to nurture a baby, Kit had been all too willing to relinquish Emma to her father.

Or sometimes Jimmy's mother if she were forced to.

Her mother-in-law would never believe that from the day Emma was born, Kit's paycheck went to cover the electric bill and buy baby Emma new shoes. She never saw the bills Jimmy ran up at bars or on his fancy car or for new clothes.

The minute Kit instituted divorce proceedings, Mrs. Lockhart had made it clear that she held Kit one hundred percent at fault for the breakup. She hadn't been woman enough or domesticated enough for dear Jimmy. It made Kit furious, but she kept her mouth shut.

The baby spat out the bottle abruptly. Kit caught it on the fly and raised the orang to her shoulder to rub and pat.

Now, with this tiny creature warm against her shoulder, she wished she could move back the clock. If she had it to do over, she'd hold Emma against her heart night and day until she was ready to pull away on her own.

These days Kit didn't have a career to worry about. She'd been forced to slow down.

These days she had to pay close attention

to one person at a time. Before, she had always done half a dozen things at once. Move fast, do the job, cuff the perp, yell a lot. Look tough, shoot straight. Show you can play with the big boys.

She'd never been able to admit how deeply Jimmy had hurt her. He'd made her feel less of a woman. Nobody knew how insecure she felt, not even her father. Nobody ever would know.

She vowed that she'd start being a better mother to Emma.

If Emma would allow her to get close. How could she apologize to a ten-year-old for not having cuddled her enough when she was a baby?

CHAPTER SIX

"She's your full-time assignment for the next couple of weeks," Rick Hazard told Kit. He pointed at the baby. "You can't very well scrub kennels or handle ICU with that hanging around your neck."

He sat back in his plush leather desk chair, his hands templed in front of his face. He'd just finished examining the baby. He pronounced her fit and healthy and half an ounce heavier than her birth weight. She'd fretted and fussed for ten minutes after Kit picked her up again, but now she'd settled down for a snooze.

"But, sir, I can't stay here twenty-four hours a day, either. I said when I took this job that I'd drop my daughter off at school in the morning and pick her up in the afternoon. I didn't mind staying last night — as a matter of fact, you couldn't have thrown me out if you'd tried. My dad can pick Emma up after school for a while, but he can't take care of her every afternoon and evening. And how about weekends? The princess here isn't my only responsibility."

"First of all," Rick said, "drop the 'sir.' We're all on a first-name basis. I understand you have scheduling problems, and we're trying to work them out. Maybe Mabel can take over from you at night. If you could work the next couple of weekends — just days, mind you — the clinic would be grateful. Double pay, of course," Rick said hopefully. "The way the princess clung to you this morning, she obviously considers you her private nursery. She really put up a fuss for such a small person."

Kit sighed and stroked the little head nestled under her chin. "I'll see what I can do about the weekends. I might have to bring Emma with me for part of the time. She's a good kid. She wouldn't get in anybody's way."

"She's a kid. Kids get sick. A common cold or a bout of diarrhea could be life-threatening for a newborn, particularly since she didn't get any immunity from her mother yesterday. We're all primates. We tend to be susceptible to the same germs."

"At the moment Emma's healthy. Of course I wouldn't let her within germ distance if she were sniffling." The baby shifted and switched from sucking her left fist to sucking her right. Kit adjusted her so that she rode more comfortably against her chest. Her own right arm ached from shoulder to wrist. Three pounds didn't sound like much weight — certainly not for a person who used to work out every morning — but after a while it began to feel like two hundred pounds. "Have you heard how Mother Lilly is this morning?"

Rick ran a hand over his face. "I went back to the zoo and stayed until midnight. I've already been by this morning to check on her. We're hiding antibiotics in her food and so far she's taking them. She's doing as well as can be expected. No more blood loss. They're keeping her half-sedated so that she won't pull at her stitches. No sign of infection, however, and a tiny little incision. Mac really is a genius with a scalpel."

Kit's stomach gave an ominous rumble. "Sorry. I haven't had anything to eat except peanut butter crackers since lunch yesterday."

"I'm sorry. I should have thought about you and sent over a pizza last night."

"Don't worry about it. Missing a couple of meals won't hurt me. As a matter of fact, I could stand to drop a few pounds."

Rick stared at her. "From where? Oh,

sorry, that was inappropriate."

Kit smiled. "Don't apologize. It was a compliment." Her face turned serious. "But that doesn't really solve the problem, does it? And can we please find a name for her? We can't keep calling her the princess."

Rick shrugged. "Have to do for the moment. The zoo always has a contest to name its babies. Good publicity. Look, I know you need to go home, but if you could hold on until this afternoon when Mabel comes in, we can see about transferring the baby from her to you. She's a grandmother several times over."

Kit felt dog tired. Her shoulders ached from holding the baby. She had half a headache, probably from lack of food. She felt dirty — no, down-right grotty. The greens she wore swallowed her and left her feeling half-naked. She wanted a few hours' sleep in her own bed and to hug Emma. "Sure," she said. "I'll stay until Mabel gets here. I washed and dried my clothes from yesterday in the laundry, so at least I can change back to my own clothes."

"We'll get you some breakfast. Thanks, Kit. It's a lot to dump on you, but you've shown that not much throws you. And you really are good with babies."

Kit knew she was dismissed. She dragged

her weary bones out of the chair in front of Rick's desk. At least she could make a pot of coffee — strong coffee.

She opened the door to the staff lounge to find Big Little pouring water into the coffeemaker. He turned, saw her and her charge. "Awww, ain't that the cutest young'un I ever saw?" He came to Kit and reached the index finger of his immense hand toward the baby's head.

Kit held her ground. As a policewoman, she'd known too many felons to be entirely comfortable around an ex-con, even one who'd been pardoned for heroism. Nancy had told her that Big had been trying to save a dog from torture when he'd nearly killed a man. She tried to accept him as a gentle hero, but her training was against her. It would take a while to learn to trust him completely.

Big touched the baby's head softly. "Awww."

Kit expected the orang to bury her head and try to get away from the strange touch. Instead, the little animal wriggled around in Kit's arms so that she looked up into Big's face. Then she stretched out her right fist and patted his chest with her knuckles.

Big's face broke into a joyous grin. "Hey, baby. You like ole Big?"

The baby twisted and reached out toward him with both arms.

Kit was horror-struck. The orang was tiny. Big was immense. One of his hands was larger than the baby's whole body. He could probably crush a rhinoceros, much less a three-pound infant.

"Can I hold her?" Big asked, but without taking his eyes off the baby.

"Uh, I don't know whether that's a good idea."

Big reached out for the little bundle anyway. "I promise I won't hurt her." Surprisingly, the baby went to him as though Kit didn't exist. She cuddled into a ball against his chest.

"Hey, listen to that," Big said, laughing. "Oh, sorry, ma'am. I forgot you can't hear her."

"What do *you* hear?"

"She's making these little kind of 'whuff, squeal,' sounds."

Kit felt a wave of jealousy sweep over her. He, this bear of a man, could hear the baby — *her* baby — when she couldn't.

The door behind her opened. She turned her head quickly to see Mac. He held a big brown bag that smelled heavenly. "Breakfast. Sausage biscuits and orange juice. Lots of both. Thought you might be hungry." His

133

eyes took in Big and the baby with no hint of surprise or anxiety. "Morning, Big. How's our girl?"

"She's the prettiest thing. Look at these little old hands. Fingernails and everything."

The baby stuck her hand back into her mouth and sucked on it with her eyes closed.

"I hope I didn't do nothing wrong," Big said. "Here, ma'am, you take her."

Kit started to reach out, then stopped. The baby had gone to Big in complete confidence when she'd fought to stay away from Rick. Big might be nearly seven feet tall and half as broad, but those giant paws of his held that baby as gently as a feather. She curled into his hands like a little bird secure in her nest.

His face glowed as he looked down at her. There was something almost angelic about him. The baby had sensed his special quality instantly. Kit felt her eyes well with tears. Time to grow up. This wasn't some little doll, this was a real live infant. And whatever was best for her was best for Kit as well.

Besides, with the princess in Big's arms, she could finally ease the ache in her shoulders and get some food. She turned to Mac. "Do you think it would be all right for Big to hold her while I grab some breakfast, take another shower and put my own clothes on?"

He raised an eyebrow at her and said, "Of course. She'll be fine with Big."

Kit heaved a sigh of relief. A good part of the tension in her shoulders had come from the awesome responsibility of the last fourteen hours. She'd enjoyed it — relished it even — but now it felt good to be able to turn the baby over to someone else for a little while.

The baby began to wriggle, and Big made what Kit assumed were cooing noises. "She's hungry, Big. If I get everything ready and give you the bottle, do you think you can feed her?"

"Oh, my! I don't want to hurt her."

"I'll stay here with you. After she eats and poops, she usually falls asleep. I'll change her and clean her up. You could hold her then, couldn't you?"

"Yes'm."

"It's Kit, Big, not 'ma'am.' " She smiled up at him. "Now, you sit down and I'll get her bottle."

He moved as delicately as a gazelle in an elephant's body.

After she'd given him the bottle, she watched Big feed the little orang with as much concentration as the average person would use defusing an atomic bomb. Mac leaned against the wall beside the door with his arms folded. When she glanced at him, he nodded.

When the baby was finished, Kit took her from Big, showed him how to burp her, changed her diaper, rewrapped her and handed her back to him. He snuggled her down against his chest and began to rock softly. She could see his lips move and thought he must be singing. She could tell that the baby was content.

Mac picked up the bag from the table. "Let's go in my office. Nancy brought this stuff. I'm starving."

She followed Mac. She should have known Nancy would think of breakfast. Mac looked exhausted. There was dark stubble along his unshaven cheeks. If he had stayed all night, she hadn't seen him, and except for that phantom kiss, hadn't even felt his presence.

He sat at his desk, took out a couple of packets and shoved the bag across the table. "Here. There's plenty."

Kit dug in, found a sausage biscuit and a carton of orange juice, and sank back in the chair. She hadn't realized how hungry she was until she bit into the sausage.

"I wondered how long it would be before you understood about Big," Mac said. He wiped his mouth and took a giant swig of orange juice.

"Nancy tried to tell me he was amazing with animals, but I didn't believe her. He made me terribly uncomfortable. But the baby went to him without a moment's hesitation. She hasn't gone to anyone but me before. Rick and I had to practically pry her off me this morning so that he could check her over."

"Big may not have the world's highest IQ, but he's well above genius level in his AQ — his animal quotient. I don't doubt he could have walked into that tiger's cage yesterday and patted him like a big house cat. He talks to them, and they seem to understand." Mac shook his head. "When he's looking after the animals in ICU, they seem to heal faster. You've met Daisy, haven't you?"

"That yellow pit bull of his? With the scars and the torn ear?"

"She was born and bred to fight. By the time we got her from the humane-society people she was nearly dead. No one thought she'd make it, or that she'd ever be rehabilitated so she'd be safe around people. But Big took her and looked after her and trained her. She worships him. The only reason she's not with him all the time is that she frightens the clients. So she stays in his apartment during the day."

"You know, watching him with the baby, I thought maybe . . . It's not my place to say anything . . ."

"Say away." He drained a carton of orange juice quickly.

"Dr. Hazard — Rick — said that Mabel might be able to babysit the princess after I go home in the evenings."

"At least part of the time. The rest of the night, the baby would have to stay in her incubator."

"She'd hate that!" Kit almost shouted. That was another one of her problems. She tended either to whisper or to shout because she couldn't hear her own voice. This time she was fairly certain she'd yelled.

Mac blinked and sat back.

Oh, yeah, she'd yelled at him all right.

"Sorry, it's just that . . . everybody says she'll do better if we treat her as close as possible to the way another orang would treat her. As Lilly would if she knew how."

"Go on."

It came out in a rush. "What about Big?" Before Mac could answer, she raised her hands in front of her. "You saw the way she went to him. For a minute I was jealous . . ."

Mac began to laugh. She felt her face

flush. "Well, I was."

"It might be the perfect solution if Big agrees. We'd be asking him to do two jobs, you realize, because we can't do without him during the day."

"Last night I got *some* sleep. I just took it in two-hour increments between feeding and changing. So he'd be able to fit in some sleep too. But I'd be terrified if he took her back to his apartment for the night. I know everybody says Daisy is a wonderful dog, but I've seen the things pit bulls do to children." She shuddered. "I wasn't any too comfortable having Kevlar with me last night, and he's the dearest little dog in the world, and trained to help, not fight."

"Where is he this morning, by the way?"

"I put him outside in one of the big runs while I helped Rick with the baby. He deserves some time off."

Mac leaned forward. "So do you." He shoved a carton of orange juice and another sausage biscuit at her. "Frankly, you look a little worn out."

"Well, you're no Adonis, either, Doctor!"

"I didn't mean it that way. Are those my greens, by the way?"

Kit looked down at herself. Despite all her efforts, the front of the surgical top was grubby.

"They could be. Nancy gave them to me before she left. I'm sorry. I'll put them in the washer with the next load of towels and stuff."

"Actually, I think they look very fetching. Much better than they do on me."

She narrowed her eyes. His blue-gray eyes were supremely innocent, but the corner of his mouth twitched.

"If that's all, *Doctor,* I have to shower and get myself ready to face the day." She stood, realized that the cord that held the waist of the greens had slipped slightly, and grabbed at the pants with as much dignity as she could muster.

On her way out she longed to twist around to see if she could catch him laughing at her. She compromised by shutting the door to his office much more forcefully than she would normally have done.

Halfway down the hall she stopped. Mac Thorn had a sense of humor! Would wonders never cease?

Dressed in her own clean still-warm clothes, after another shower and another hair wash and even some lipstick, Kit felt ready to face the day. "Please God," she whispered, "let this one be quiet." She checked her watch, went to the front and met Alva Jean coming in. "Morning."

"You didn't stay here all night with that baby, did you?"

"There didn't seem to be any alternative."

Alva Jean parked herself squarely in front of Kit so that there would be no mistaking her words. "You listen to me, Kit Lockhart. It's great that everybody around here is so dedicated, but I swear, you give those doctors an inch, they'll eat you alive. You'll find you don't have any more of a life outside this place than *they* do."

Kit raised her eyebrows. That was the longest speech she'd ever heard from Alva Jean. "But there was no choice. This was an emergency."

"They are *all* emergencies. I'm a single mother now, just like you, and I got two kids and a daddy who hasn't paid one thin dime of child support for three months. I need this job and I downright love what I do, but I have learned to walk out of here at four o'clock in the p.m. come hell or high water. See, they don't understand about kids. Except for Dr. Sarah who brings Muggs with her every day, and Dr. Carlyle whose husband looks after their two sons while she works, nobody around here's got kids of their own that aren't already grown and out of the house. If I don't meet the school bus, nobody does."

"You were talking so fast, I didn't get nearly all of that, but I did get the gist."

"Good, because the first time you have to take Emma to the pediatrician when there's half a dozen patients in ICU coming out of anesthesia, trust me, Dr. Mac's going to look at you like you've lost your mind."

"He'll get mad at me?"

Alva Jean waved her hand. "Oh, he'll let you go, or Nancy will. But they get this kind of look like they're surprised you think there's stuff to do out there that's more important than what we're doing in here."

"I see, or I think I do. Listen, before you open up — we've got ten minutes — could you make a telephone call for me? I want to call my daughter before my dad takes her to school."

"Sure."

Kit went through the instructions as she had with Mabel earlier. When Emma came on the line, Kit said, "Hi. Just wanted to wish you a good morning and a good day at school and say I miss you and I love you."

"Is something wrong with the baby?" Alva Jean repeated.

"No, she's fine. Why would you think that?"

"I get worried when you get all mushy."

Kit closed her eyes. Oh, boy, that was just great. "Listen, I'll pick you up at Granddaddy's after school. Would you maybe like takeout?"

Alva Jean listened and grinned. "Could we have Chinese?"

"Sure. Chinese it is. Have a good day, kiddo. And I do love you, even if it does sound mushy."

After she broke the connection, Alva Jean said, "My kids want pizza or burgers."

"Those even I can do at home, but I'm not up to attempting Kung Pao pork." She looked at her watch. "Shouldn't you open the doors? I have to go get back and relieve the babysitter."

"Who?"

Kit grinned. "Big."

Alva Jean gaped, then smiled broadly. "Perfect. You ought to see him with my kids. They think he hung the moon." She peered at the glass front doors and went to open them. With her hand on the key she stopped and turned back so Kit could read her. "Go. Egg Roll and Moo Shu are waiting out there. If there's anything worse than one pot-bellied pig, it's two."

Through the glass Kit saw a frazzled woman holding two heavy leather leashes. At the end of each leash a hugely fat black pig about the height of an English bulldog strained against her.

"They need their toenails trimmed again. You just better be glad you *can't* hear. Those pigs can squeal louder'n a fire engine. Here goes."

She unlocked the door. Kit watched as the pigs pushed open the doors with their snouts and waddled in. Alva Jean jumped back behind her counter, picked up a couple of hard candies from the dish on her desk, peeled off the cellophane and tossed one to each pig. The pigs dived for the sweets, then sank onto the tile floor in front of the counter with all four legs sticking out and looks of pure contentment on their little piggy faces.

Their owner gave Kit a harried smile and began to speak to Alva Jean.

Kit slipped back through the hall doors to the examining rooms and went to find Big.

Dr. Sarah Scott found Kit in Mark's office feeding the baby. Kevlar sat at her feet and began to wag his rear end the moment Sarah stuck her head in the door.

Sarah wore surgical gloves and a green surgical mask hung under her chin. "Hi. Thought you might like to have this. Muggs has outgrown it. I sterilized it last night.

144

And I've got on fresh greens. I should be safe." She held out a bright pink checked baby sling, a little pale from many washings.

"Oh, thanks. Mabel said she'd try to find the one she used for her grandbabies, but she's not due in before I leave this afternoon." Kit rolled her shoulders. "My arms feel as if they're going to fall off."

"The carrier will take the strain. You know how to put it on?"

Kit shook her head. "The one I had with Emma was different."

"Slip the top straps over your shoulders like a backward bra and fasten the lower straps around your waist."

"And insert the baby how?"

Sarah laughed. "First, insert baby, then suspend baby. Here, I'll show you."

The baby protested vigorously at being pried out of Kit's arms and kicked to try to avoid putting her legs through the bottom holes of the sling, but eventually they wrestled her in.

"Whew! That's three pounds of sheer muscle," Sarah said. "Maybe we ought to keep her in front of you for the time being. That way at least you can lean back without crushing her."

With Sarah's help they settled the baby,

who seemed to accept the sling after only a moment. It was very nearly too big for her, and only the thick diaper kept her from sliding right out.

"There. Is Mabel taking over tonight?"

Kit took a deep breath. "Actually, I think Big is going to do night duty."

Sarah nodded. "I'd never in this world have thought of giving her to Big, but he's perfect. He comes over here three or four times a night anyway if we have animals at risk in ICU. He may not fit on this couch, however, and his dog is going to be very jealous."

"He's agreed Daisy should stay away for the time being."

"I see. Yes, that's probably right. Daisy is a dear, but she might scare the baby."

"She scares me."

"Don't let her. She's a sweetie, but she had a terrible childhood." Sarah stroked the baby's head. After a moment she looked up and caught Kit's smile. "So all right, I've been dying to touch her. It's a pity we won't have her with us more than a few days."

Kit sat up. "I thought we had at least a couple of weeks."

Sarah shook her head and sat down on the couch beside Kit so that she could hold the baby's tiny hand. "I just met Mac in the hall. The zoo called. Apparently the docent who was supposed to take her is cutting her trip to Hawaii short and coming home. As soon as Mac thinks the baby is out of the woods, she'll go to the docent until the zoo can find a barren female orang who is willing to act as surrogate mother."

"Oh." Maybe it was exhaustion, but Kit felt her eyes begin to tear.

Sarah put her hand over Kit's. "I know. We get so attached so quickly, and then if we do our jobs right we wave goodbye, smile, and then go back to our offices and cry. And a little one like this . . . well, it's tough."

Kit sighed. The baby reached out and clung to her neck. She blinked back the tears. "It's better this way. If I had her more than a few days longer I might never be willing to give her up."

"Well, with the sling, you'll be able to do some data entry on Mark's computer while the baby's sleeping. Take your mind off her."

"Right."

Sarah looked at her watch. "Isn't it about time you were changing the guard?"

Kit glanced at hers. "Yes, but before I change the guard I have to change the baby. Would you mind telling Big to come down here if you see him?"

"I'll make it a point to find him." She patted Kit on the shoulder. "You'll get over it. I promise."

As Kit cleaned up her charge and changed her, she consoled herself with the thought that at least she'd have a few more days. And Sarah was right. Better to get it over with. When Big came in she slipped out of the sling and adjusted it for his shoulders.

"I won't never fit into this thing," Big said as Kit worked the straps down to their longest.

"The belly band won't meet around you, but I think you can make do with the straps. Just keep a hand under her so she doesn't slide out. Now, are you sure you know how to take care of her bottle, and burping and changing?"

"Yes'm. I used to babysit my cousins some when they was little before . . . well, before I had to leave home."

Kit picked up her purse from behind Mark's desk and signaled to Kevlar to join her. "Call me tonight if you have any trouble — any hour."

"But you can't hear me."

"Sure I can, on my own phone at home. Kev'll wake me when it rings. Then when you talk, it writes what you say on the screen, then I talk back to you. It's great."

"I promise I'll look after her real good."

"I know you will. Now, I have got to get out of here or I'll be late picking up my daughter again."

As she walked past Mac's office, he came out into the hall. "I wish you'd warned me we have to give the baby up early," she said.

"Who told you?"

"Sarah Scott."

"I meant to tell you before anyone else did."

"I'm trying to convince myself it's better this way, so I won't have much time to become attached to her."

He touched her shoulder. "Time has nothing to do with it. You bond completely in five minutes sometimes. If you had her for longer, you'd miss the routine more when she left, notice the hole in your life more, but I doubt you'd care about *her* any more than you do now."

She was certain that if she could have heard his voice, it would have sounded gentle. Nancy kept saying that underneath that tough exterior, Mac was a marshmallow. She wished he'd put his arms around her. Instead he stepped back. "See you tomorrow," he said, and walked away.

Okay, so he'd let down his guard with Kit.

He had felt the same sense of loss she was feeling now over and over again. He tried not to let his patients worm their way into his heart, but he'd never been successful. What was that old saying? "Never give your heart to a dog to tear." Or a kitten, or a foal, or even a tiger.

It was a constant battle that he lost more often than he won. He covered his feelings by snarling. At least Kit was honest about hers.

Frustration caught him off guard. He wasn't being at all objective about Kit. He went to check on Big.

"Hey, Doc," Big whispered. "We got us a little cradly thing for the baby."

"Fancy," Mac said, and sat down beside him. The baby began to squeak and snort.

"She's kind of fussy. Guess she misses Miss Kit."

"Let me check her over, be sure she doesn't have an upset stomach."

"Can you do it without taking her off me? She sure has strong arms for such a little thing."

"I'll try." The baby snorted and whuffled and squirmed, but although her tummy was round it wasn't hard, and there didn't seem to be any real discomfort. She was, as Big had said, merely fussy.

Mac left Big sitting in Mark's desk chair and rocking the baby while he sang to her in a surprisingly sweet tenor.

He saw two more clients with minor ailments, and prescribed medication for an arthritic poodle.

His last patient was wheeled into the room in a glass cage on top of a heavy plastic garden cart. Mac sighed. Not one of his favorite clients, but one with whom he was familiar.

"Okay, Arlo, what's wrong with Janis this time?"

Arlo looked as though someone had started with a six-foot-four linebacker and squashed him down to five foot seven. Everything about him was broad. His startlingly blue eyes were a little watery, as though he'd been crying. He wore a black T-shirt with a cigarette pack rolled up in the sleeve, tight black leather jeans belted below his paunch. The silver buckle read, Born To Be Bad.

Arlo, as Mac knew from previous visits, was an accountant for the IRS during the day. At night he metamorphosed into an aging biker dude.

"I think Janis has gone blind," he wailed.

Mac slid the top of the cage open. "Okay, Arlo, you ready to help me lift her? Big's otherwise occupied, so it's just the two of us."

"Janis won't give us any trouble."

Mac grasped the African tree boa behind her head and reached down to help Arlo pick up her sixty or so pounds and put her onto the table. She was a gentle snake, not venomous, but she could bite when provoked. Usually Arlo brought her in because she'd eaten something like a tennis ball or a cat toy that she couldn't digest that had to be surgically removed.

Today, however, she looked in excellent condition. She was a beautifully patterned snake, and her skin glistened in the light over the table.

But her eyes were milky.

"I think she's got cataracts." Arlo sounded on the verge of tears.

Mac checked her eyes carefully, then ran his hands down her length. Arlo held her on the table, but Mac could see that she was becoming restive. "She looks beautiful. She just shed her skin?"

"Last week."

"Is that about the time you noticed her eyes?"

"Come to think of it, I suppose it was."

"I think I can fix her up in a few minutes, but you're going to have to hold her head.

Think you can manage her?"

Arlo nodded. Mac picked up a pair of tweezers from the tray of sterilized instruments, bent down over Janis's head and gently began to tease the corner of her eye. A moment later a thin membrane slid off the eye, and after another session of teasing, the other eye was clear.

"It's a miracle! What'd you do?"

"In the wild, big snakes have branches and twigs they can pull their old skin off with. Sometimes the skin over the eye doesn't come loose. I just gave it a little help."

"She's been shedding her skin for years, Doc. How come this never happened before?"

"I have no idea. Maybe she's getting older and lazier. Maybe she didn't find the right place to start peeling her skin. Some snakes never have the problem, but once it happens, it's more likely to happen again. You'll have to watch her the next time she starts to shed."

"I can't thank you enough."

"Let's get her back into her cage, and you can take her on home."

Together they wrestled the snake back. It took several minutes before they could close the lid on her. The eyes that had been cloudy now looked perfectly clear and very angry.

"I promise I'll watch her close the next time she sheds, Dr. Mac. Oh, girl, you can see!"

Mac closed the door behind him and leaned against the wall. If only they were all that simple. If only all his clients could walk out of the clinic with joy on their faces.

If only Kit weren't unhappy.

CHAPTER SEVEN

As Kit pulled out of the Creature Comfort parking lot the rain started again. "Oh, bother," she said, and turned on her windshield wipers and defroster. The rain sluiced down her windshield and obliterated the lane markings on the road. She slowed down, turned on her lights and concentrated on getting to her parents' house intact. Kev sat beside her.

She'd have to check the weather station the minute she got home for flash-flood alerts. If there were any in the city, Jimmy would probably be pulling extra duty trying to keep crazy motorists from driving through "a little bit of water on the road," that turned out to be five feet deep.

So far as southern natural disasters went, Kit hated flash floods the most. Anyone with half a brain took shelter at a tornado warning, but people tended to ignore the seriousness of the flash-flood warnings because the overflow came and went so quickly.

Her parents lived only a mile or so from her town house in one of the less affluent portions of old Germantown. The homes in the neighborhood had been built in the sixties before mansions began to invade the landscape and property values soared sky-high. The house was comfortable, but nothing fancy.

Except for Tom Barclay's garden, of course. He invariably won the neighborhood "Yard of the Year" prize. He had also added the woodworking workshop in a building behind the garage and had fought for the zoning variance to build it.

Kit had inherited only a portion of one of her father's skills. Jo-Jo the cat ate any houseplants she tried to grow. She didn't have time for more than minimal maintenance on her tiny front yard and even smaller patio.

She could hammer a nail into a wall without taking her thumb off, but that was the extent of her carpentry expertise. Watching her father turn an intricate chair leg on his lathe or hand carve butterflies on one of the chests he sold at flea markets never ceased to amaze her.

But he had finally taught her to cook, even though she'd never be the gourmet cook he'd become. She didn't have the patience. Her mother could nuke a TV dinner if necessary, but that was about all. Kit had at least become what her grandmother would have called "a good, plain cook." Her food tasted good, but wasn't necessarily a poem to look at.

Kit could read and follow a cookbook. Her mother could decode endless manuals full of "cop-speak" with no difficulty at all, but ask her to "fold in" egg whites and she simply stared at you blankly.

Kit had certainly not inherited her father's gene for intuition about people. Her marriage to Jimmy was proof of that.

Maybe now she should try to learn how to garden. This spring, she and Emma could at least plant a container garden for the patio. Her father could help.

She pulled into her parents' driveway, told Kev to stay, ran up to the front door through the pelting rain and rang the doorbell. She knew it worked, but it felt odd not to be able to hear the bong inside the house.

Her father opened the door, pulled her inside and hugged her. "You too macho to carry an umbrella?"

"Ha ha." She kissed her father and hugged him back. His spare frame had begun to feel whipcord thin to her, but he was still tall and straight and handsome with his heavy white mustache and steel-gray hair. "Emma ready?"

"Uh-huh." He called for her. "I ought to warn you —"

Before he could finish his sentence, Emma stalked into the front hall in her yellow rain boots, her slicker and rain hat. She carried her book bag slung over one shoulder.

"Hi, baby, ready to go?" Kit said.

"I suppose."

Emma was playing the martyr. That generally meant a temper tantrum before long. Kit pretended to ignore the warning signs and hoped they'd go away before she and Emma got home.

"Tell you what. Tomorrow afternoon I'll try to pick you up early and we can go by the clinic to see the orang baby."

"I don't give a hoot about some dumb ole monkey baby." She ran out into the rain.

"Em! Emma Barclay Lockhart!"

Em opened the front door of the car. Kit threw her father an anguished look and ran after her. "You know you have to sit in the back."

Big sigh. "Can I have Kev?" The dog was wriggling with joy at the sight of Emma.

"I need him up front with me."

"Fine."

Emma climbed into the rear seat and clipped her seat belt while Kit watched. Then she pointedly turned her head to stare out the left side of the car.

Kit went around to the driver's side and climbed in.

Ordinarily — or *B.A.,* before the accident — she and Em would have talked out their difficulties on the ride home. That was no longer possible. Kit could barely see Emma in the rearview mirror and then only if she took her eyes off the road. *She* could talk, all right, but she couldn't read Emma's replies.

So they rode in silent isolation. In Kit's garage, Emma piled out quickly, took her things, opened the back door and disappeared inside without once looking back at her mother. Kit unbuckled Kev, who immediately charged after Emma. Kit knew she could call him back in an instant, but Emma probably needed to hug him.

Should she follow Emma upstairs or let her stew for a little while, maybe calm down?

Kit sat on the steps to the second floor and put her head in her hands. "Why is everything I do wrong?" she whispered between her fingers. "And why does everybody have to be such a pill? I am *so* too tired to deal with this right now."

She realized with a start that she hadn't thought of Big and the baby since she'd picked up Emma. Should she call the clinic? Find out if they were doing all right? If Big needed any advice?

Advice? From Kit Lockhart, incompetent parent?

She called Kev and a moment later he trotted down the stairs. She picked up an empty envelope from the hall table that had contained the utility bill and wrote on it "What should I order for dinner?" She handed it to the dog and said, "Take to Em."

He trotted up the stairs with the note in his mouth and disappeared. Five minutes passed, then ten. Kit was losing *her* temper, when Kev tripped back down the stairs. On a jagged piece of paper torn from a lined notebook, Emma had written "Who cares?"

"Fine," she yelled up the stairs. "I'll order what *I* want."

She took the stairs two at a time, slammed her bedroom door, turned on the computer and sank into her desk chair while she looked up the number for the Chinese restaurant.

She ordered all Em's favorites, read the restaurant confirmation on her screen and flopped down on her bed. She'd ordered too much as usual, but she could always take the leftovers to Creature Comfort tomorrow for lunch.

Maybe she'd be calmer if she spent the twenty minutes before dinner arrived punching the heavy bag that hung in the corner of her bedroom.

Not tonight.

The house could wait to be cleaned. It was dusty, but not messy. Em's room probably looked as though it had been tossed by thugs looking for the Hope diamond, but then it always did.

Kit longed to soak in a hot tub, but she knew that the minute she slid into the water the food would arrive. Better to wait until Emma was in bed and asleep anyway.

All of her good intentions about Em hadn't worked out. They wouldn't until Em came down off her high horse and got whatever was on her chest off it.

And onto Kit's already burdened shoulders.

The only thing worse than being a single parent was being one of a pair when the other one was Jimmy. At least she was making ends meet now instead of having to fend off creditors the way she had when she was married. She and Em had a decent house, a decent car and even a little put back in Em's college fund. If Jimmy would keep up to date on his child support, they might even be able to afford a few luxuries — like riding lessons for Em.

And she was starting to love her new job. She caught her breath at the feelings even *thinking* about Mac Thorn raised in her.

Stupid. He was a big-deal doctor, a partner in Creature Comfort. He was also a bona fide hunk, one of those men who turned female heads whenever he walked into a room.

He was unlikely to be interested in a deaf woman with a kid. She closed her eyes and imagined what it would be like to have those strong arms around her.

She sat up quickly. "Don't even go there," she said.

At that moment Kev pushed her bedroom door open with his nose and bounced up against her knee. "Doorbell?" she asked. The corgi wagged his tail.

She ran lightly down the stairs calling, "I'm coming." She pulled open the door without looking through the peephole first to check that it was the Chinese take-out man.

Mac Thorn stood on her front stoop, just barely out of the pouring rain. He was holding a big paper sack under his dripping poncho.

"Oh. I thought you were the take-out guy."

"I am. May I come in? I'm getting soggy."

"Certainly." She stood aside. "What do you mean you're the take-out guy?"

"I ran into him as I was getting out of my car. Here's your order."

"You paid for it? How much do I owe you?"

"Not a thing."

"Come on, now."

"Call it payment for having done you out of your dinner last night."

"But you brought breakfast this morning."

"Correction. Nancy brought breakfast this morning. Look, I'm dripping all over your foyer." He handed over the bag. "This is getting cold while we're standing here."

"Oh, yes. Why are we, by the way? Standing here, I mean."

He ran his hand over his wet hair. "I let you get away this afternoon before I had a chance to thank you for stepping in to look after the baby the way you did."

"That's what you hired me for."

He laughed. "Hardly. We hired you to scrub cages and babysit animals after surgery and whatever else we could think of that nobody else wants to do. We did not plan to land you with an endangered species. I'm sorry I didn't tell you about the

163

change in the time we're going to hand the orang back to the zoo."

"I was tired and on edge. What matters is the baby's welfare."

"I know how quickly they sneak into our hearts." He looked down at his poncho. "I really am dripping all over your carpet. I'd better go and let you eat your dinner while it's still edible."

As he turned to go, he looked over Kit's shoulder. "Good evening, Emma."

Oh, boy, Kit thought, now she's going to pitch a fit because he's here. She wished she'd gotten that mirror for the foot of the stairs so that she could read the lips of someone coming down behind her. Maybe she'd have time to do it tomorrow after work.

Mac smiled. "Thank you, but I didn't come angling for a dinner invitation."

Kit turned her head in astonishment. Emma came the rest of the way downstairs and stood at a ninety-degree angle to her mother so that Kit could read both her lips and Mac's.

"That's okay. We've got plenty, don't we, Mom?"

Emma was smiling and exuding charm. If she'd been three years older, Kit would have sworn she was flirting.

164

"Yes, of course we've got plenty. I always order too much."

"I couldn't intrude," he said.

"You wouldn't. Please say you'll stay," Emma pleaded.

Aha. So that was the plan. Emma planned to use Mac as a buffer to keep her mother at bay. Sneaky but effective.

It might work. Kit didn't really want to get into a shouting match with Em tonight, either. Maybe a cooling-off period during which they had to be polite to a third party really would help.

"Please stay," Kit echoed. "If you don't mind eating in the kitchen."

"Not a bit. Beats taking a cheeseburger home to my apartment and eating it in front of the television."

Not going home to some femme fatale, then? Or taking one out to some fancy restaurant? Surely Mac could have his pick of all the eligible females in Memphis.

Kit was simply an employee. She couldn't even be considered a friend. She did wish now that she'd soaked in that tub and redone her makeup.

She offered him a glass of wine, but he opted for beer. He offered to help set the table, but Emma sat him down and began to act the part of the perfect hostess as she bustled around the kitchen as though she always got dinner ready. It was quite a performance.

A performance that Kit felt left out of. How quickly people forgot that she couldn't hear what was going on, nor read their lips when they looked away from her. She had a suspicion Emma was cutting her out on purpose, but she didn't think Mac was.

She sat down and said, "Serve yourselves, guys. Dr. Thorn, if you don't see something you want, ask for it."

"Did your mother tell you about our new baby?" he asked.

This time Emma propped her elbow on the table and leaned her cheek against her hand as though she was drinking in every word he said.

"I'd just love to see it."

Oh, brother. Kit rolled her eyes at Emma, who pointedly ignored her. "I loved seeing the baby horse and hearing about all the animals."

Where had Emma learned to manipulate so well? Not from Kit, who had all the tact of a rhinoceros. At the moment Em was acting like a diminutive Scarlett O'Hara.

And Mac was eating it up. Along with sizable portions of Kung Pao pork, Mongolian beef and shrimp with lobster sauce. There wouldn't be anything left for lunch tomorrow after all. She didn't begrudge him his appetite. He was a big man, and so busy explaining the process of delivering the baby orang that he probably wasn't even aware that he was on his third egg roll.

Jimmy had never talked during the few times when the whole family was together for a meal. Most of the time they ate on trays in front of the television set because if they sat around a table, Jimmy would criticize and find fault with everything.

Mac Thorn not only talked, he listened. When Emma asked questions, he answered them. If he used technical language she didn't understand, she asked him to explain and he did.

Kit began to feel that same tiny pang of jealousy as when the orang had gone to Big so fast. She ought to be delighted, but in reality she felt like a third wheel, unable to contribute, and frequently not even following the conversation. Mac spoke fast and used words that hadn't been taught in her lipreading courses. Kit was used to filling in the blanks in conversation, but that only worked when she could guess the right word to fill in.

Finally, she simply stopped trying and let

the two of them go at it. The effort to keep up was wearing her out.

Obviously Mac was a born teacher. Emma might be manipulative, but she wasn't faking her interest.

When the last of the fried rice was gone, he seemed to realize he had been speaking exclusively to Emma. "Kit, I'm sorry. Ape obstetrics is probably not the best topic for dinner-table conversation."

"I liked it," Emma said, without a glance at Kit.

"So did I," Kit said. "I suppose that means you really would like to come see our princess tomorrow after school?"

Emma was now stuck. She could say a snippy no, in which case she might score one against her mother. But it was apparent to Kit that Em really longed to see the baby, so she'd be cutting off her nose to spite her face. And probably annoying Mac at the same time.

Emma compromised by replying to Mac rather than Kit. "Can I maybe touch it?"

"With gloves and a mask, I don't see why not, but we don't want to pass along any viruses you might be harboring."

"I'm not harboring a thing!"

"We're all harboring all sorts of things," Mac said. "Schoolkids most of all."

"Okay. Gloves and a mask might be kind of fun."

"Fine. Then you can come back to the clinic after your mother picks you up from school tomorrow and see the baby. And touch her."

"Great! I can hardly wait to tell Jessica. She'll be so jealous!" She started for the stairs at a run, with Kevlar following her, and almost tripped over Jo-Jo, who was winding himself around the door frame and oozing into the kitchen looking for treats.

"Emma! How about some manners here?"

"Oh, sorry. Thank you, Dr. Mac. Come back to dinner again soon."

Kit nodded. "Send Kev down when you've finished your homework and gotten ready for bed."

"Can I call Jessica?"

Kit checked her watch. "Ten minutes."

"Oh, Mooooother." Emma disappeared up the stairs with Kev at her heels.

Kit turned to Mac, expecting him to be reaching for his rain poncho.

"I'll help with the dishes," he said.

"Don't worry. That's why we have a dishwasher. It'll take me ten minutes to clean up."

"You did say if I didn't see something I want, I should ask for it. You wouldn't happen to have a cup of decaf, would you?"

"Oh, I'm sorry! Sure."

"And while you're doing that, I'll get rid of the cartons and stack the dishwasher."

Talk about weird. The man was not what she'd consider domesticated in any way, shape or form. It was almost as though he didn't want to leave. With her back to him she set up the coffeemaker. When she turned toward him, he was wiping the heavy butcher-block table with a damp cloth. The rest of the kitchen was clean and straight.

"Thanks. If you ever need a second job, I'll be happy to hire you."

"You're welcome."

"The coffee won't be ready for about five minutes. I do have a living room, you know."

He followed her. She could feel him even though she couldn't hear his footsteps. The nape of her neck tingled.

Before she could sit in the wing chair, he took her arm and turned her toward him. "You try not to be serious, don't you?"

"Every chance I get."

"This is serious. You have a remarkable daughter."

"Because she has a crush on you?"

"Because she has an inquisitive mind. I don't have much — well, I don't have any — experience with children. Yours is refreshing. I was under the impression they all play video games when they are not knocking over liquor stores."

"Ten is a little young to knock over a liquor store, and Emma does play video games. She regularly beats me. But she also plays soccer and makes the honor roll at school. It's none of my doing."

"It's your gene pool."

"Only half. You do not want to know about the other half. Coffee's probably ready. How do you take it?"

"Black. A hangover from vet school. I learned to drink black coffee when I was pulling thirty-six-hour shifts. Now I even drink my decaf black."

She brought back two mugs and handed him one, then sat in the wing chair, although there was plenty of room on the sofa beside him. She did not want to get that close. What if she tried to kiss him? He'd spill his coffee and then where would she be? With a bill for clean upholstery and probably without a job.

"Good coffee. I have learned to enjoy Southern coffee. Boston coffee is more like dark tea."

"You're from Boston?"

"Not for a very long time, and never again if I can arrange it."

His tone was enough to cut off that particular line of inquiry. Kit sipped her coffee and wondered why he was still sitting here. Was he that lonely?

"So why did you marry him?"

"I beg your pardon?"

"The other half of Emma's gene pool. I assume since you are divorced that the marriage was a mistake, either on his part or yours."

"Why would you ask a question like that?" Kit asked.

"I am merely following a logical line of inquiry. I apologize if you think it rude."

"Actually, I do think it's rude, Doctor. But if you really want to know, Jimmy and I were in the academy together — the police academy. Everybody was under a heap of pressure." She shrugged. "Jimmy is charming, likable and street-smart. And I thought we had the same goals and were in agreement as to the way we were going to reach them. We were both wrong. He thought he was marrying a woman who'd put in her eight hours filling out reports and spend the rest of her time staying home while he drank with the boys in cop bars, played a little poker and flirted with a few women on the side."

"And you thought?"

She looked away from him. "That he would no more be content to remain a patrolman and put in his twenty than I would. I've always been ambitious. I think we both knew we'd screwed up big time within six months. Neither one of us was about to change. But by that time I was pregnant. We tried to keep it together for Emma. Jimmy adores her, even if he can't manage to show up on time to pick her up for the weekend and never has taken her horseback riding, the way he's always promised her. Finally, we both gave up. The divorce was fairly amicable. Jimmy didn't want custody of Emma except on alternate weekends. Funny thing, he butts into my life a whole lot more now than he did when we were married."

"You're right. I shouldn't have asked."

"Maybe if I talked about it more, I wouldn't keep feeling like such a failure."

"You didn't fail."

"Oh, Doctor, anytime a marriage breaks up, especially a marriage with a child involved, it's a big failure."

Kevlar trotted into the room and put his front paws on Kit's knee. "Emma must be through with her homework and ready for bed." She stood. Surely he'd get the message now.

He did.

"Thank you for allowing me to share your evening," he said with a formality she wasn't expecting. "Tell Emma good-night for me. I'll look forward to seeing her tomorrow at the clinic." He walked into the hall.

"Did you have a hat? It's still pouring."

He shook his head. "Only the poncho."

"Let me get you an umbrella."

"Don't bother. It's only a step to my car." He tossed the still-damp poncho over his shoulder.

She opened the door and stepped out on the porch after him, hugging herself against the chill damp.

"See you tomorrow," she said.

"Right." Without warning he took her in his arms and kissed her.

It was the last thing she'd expected from Mac. But it felt right, and good, and sweet — until she realized she was kissing her boss.

She broke away and tried to draw enough breath into her lungs to say something — anything.

Before she could, he turned and ran through the rain to his car.

Without a word. He backed out of her driveway without even switching his lights on. Good thing. He'd have seen her flopped

174

back against the doorjamb, still trying to catch her breath.

Like a big old flounder who'd just been dropped into the bottom of a johnboat.

She backed into the house and shut the door, then leaned her forehead against the cool wood.

How on earth was she ever going to face him in the office tomorrow?

CHAPTER EIGHT

Mac knew he was out of his mind for kissing Kit that way. She'd been at Creature Comfort a while now, but until the baby orangutan's arrival, he hadn't had much to do with her directly.

He'd found reasons to speak to her, of course. Nancy had noticed the way he looked at Kit, the times he checked patients while she was in the ICU or the kennel. A week ago, she'd said over a necrotic bowel, "So, ask her out, why don't you?"

He had pretended not to understand. They were employer and employee. The last thing he wanted was for Kit to feel pressured.

Tonight in an instant all his good intentions had blown up in his face.

But Kit had definitely responded with enthusiasm, he thought with a secret grin.

A car horn blew on his right. He hunched over the wheel. His windshield wipers made a valiant effort to keep his line of sight clear, but he could feel the tension in his shoulders. This was the sort of night when Sarah or Eleanor might call him to assist in pulling a stuck calf. The cow in labor would be two pastures away from the nearest dirt road and over at least two swollen creeks.

Lightning slashed the sky in front of him and was followed almost at once by a rumble of thunder. Close, very close. As a kid in Boston he'd enjoyed storms. His first summer in Montana had changed his perception radically. Lightning was supposed to hit the highest point, which was why only an idiot stood under a tree in a thunderstorm.

On the plains, however, a horse and rider frequently *were* the tallest point for fifty miles in any direction. He'd seen lightning hurl a cow twenty feet, and sometimes had hunkered down in an arroyo with the other boys to avoid lighting up like a Christmas tree himself. He remembered the first time he'd looked down at his forearms and seen the hair standing straight up. He wasn't exactly afraid of thunderstorms, but he sure had a healthy respect for them.

He pulled into his carport and turned off the engine, but didn't start for his apartment door immediately. At the moment the rain was pouring down like water from a tap. The cloudburst wouldn't last long. He'd wait it out.

He leaned his head back against the seat and tried to think of anything besides Kit.

The problem was that he was surrounded by happy families at Creature Comfort. It was like being the only kid without an ice-cream cone in a bunch of kids licking away at triple scoops of Rocky Road.

Sarah and Mark Scott were sappy about each other, and now about Muggs. Eleanor and Steve Chadwick still flirted like honeymooners.

Liz Carlyle's juggling act included a career, a marriage, a pair of rambunctious sons she referred to as "the hellions" and study for an advanced degree in veterinary ophthalmology. None of that would have been possible without the enthusiastic support of her husband.

Vet tech Jack Renfro was still besotted with the Arkansas belle he'd married some forty years ago. He'd left England for her and had never regretted it. Even stubby little Bill Chumney with his thinning hair and his paunch was still a hunk in his wife's eyes.

Rick Hazard and Margot acted as though they took one another for granted, but in a crisis, they functioned as a perfect unit.

Margot was still crazy about Rick, and he doted on her.

Mabel Halliburton and Sol Weinstock had both been happily married a long time before they lost their spouses. Even young Kenny Nichols had a steady girlfriend.

Now that Big Little was dating Alva Jean, Mac and Nancy were about the only two single holdouts. Sometimes he wondered why they'd never gotten together. They meshed so perfectly in the operating theater that they almost shared a single mind.

Bells and whistles had never rung between them. He didn't think he had a closer friend, but he and Nancy could never be more. Maybe they knew one another *too* well.

So what was it about Kit Lockhart?

Could it be because she could evade him by simply turning her head?

She was a challenge, of course, but he'd won over plenty of challenging women. She was contradictory. Flip and confrontational one minute, then warm and nurturing the next. Still, he'd known women who changed character completely from one sentence to the next. They usually irritated him. He liked knowing where he was in a relationship. He always felt off balance with Kit.

Something about her resonated in his psyche.

It didn't hurt that she had knockout emerald eyes.

As a veterinarian he'd witnessed too many animal mating rituals to believe in love. He believed in chemistry, in the hardwired need of the female to reproduce and the male to pass on his genes to as many sons and daughters as possible.

Human beings were only animals. Swans mated for life, but he couldn't think of a single primate that did. The human male was not monogamous by nature.

And yet if they were lucky enough to find that person worth giving up every other opportunity for, human beings seemed to be monogamous by *choice.* Only a remarkable woman could make Mac pledge to be monogamous. If ever he did, he'd keep his vow.

If Kit actually was his soul mate, he didn't want to know. Commitment to a woman who came with all sorts of baggage was too much. Mac had enough baggage of his own. He'd break under the weight of anyone else's.

He could never be a stepfather. Granted, Emma seemed delightful and hung on his every word, which was quite an ego boost.

But was he capable of handling the day-to-day drudgery of parenthood? Dealing with the ex-husband? In-laws? He knew that Kit had a father who picked Emma up from school, but he knew nothing about the man. Did Kit have a mother? Brothers and sisters? Aunts and uncles and cousins all integrated into a dysfunctional, intrusive little clan? He'd walked away from his own family because they intruded. They had brandished *ought* and *should* against him like weapons.

He didn't even know how Kit had lost her hearing.

Time to back off. One kiss did not make a relationship. Better walk away now while he still had choices.

Or did he?

The rain had slackened to a steady drizzle. He ran the ten steps from the carport to the front door of his ground-floor apartment and let himself in.

He could smell the emptiness. He flipped on the lights in the living room. Maybe he should get a cat. He checked his answering machine and gave thanks that there were no messages. The after-hours calling system from Creature Comfort would have paged him on his cell phone for an emergency, but sometimes clients called him at home with their problems.

He dropped his keys onto the counter

between the living room and the galley kitchen, then draped his poncho over the back of one of the four chairs around his glass-and-wrought-iron kitchen table.

He hated that table.

He hated the room, too. It had been a mistake to let Claire decorate it for him while they'd been dating. She'd called it "eclectic English gentleman's club." He called it depressing. Why had he let her paint the walls that nasty shade of yellow green that she swore was "this year's color"? Actually, it was the color of dog vomit.

He sat down on the maroon leather sofa that had so many buttons stuck all over it he felt as though he was sitting on a pincushion. It was too short from back to front and hit his legs midthigh.

He pulled off his sodden boots and wet socks, dropped them onto the varnished wood floor, and put his damp feet on the antique leather trunk that served as his coffee table. It felt clammy. He flicked on the television without sound.

He watched it for a moment, then dug into the top drawer of the antique side table for the instructions that had come with it. He hunted for a moment, read and then began to program his remote.

He messed up something on his first attempt, but on his second, he saw that the lines of dialogue from the sitcom on the screen were running across the bottom of the screen.

This was what Kit would experience when she watched TV.

He tried to decipher the words the actors spoke and check them against the written dialogue.

"Wow, this is impossible," he said aloud.

Either the person who was speaking was standing with his back to the camera, or in shadow that covered his mouth, or the speeches went by so fast that by the time Mac checked the bottom of the screen, the characters were halfway through another scene. He fought his frustration, sat forward, moved his own lips to try to match the actors', and found himself getting worse, not better.

"I'm tired. No wonder I can't do this stupid lipreading thing."

He shut off the television, flung the remote onto the coffee table and pulled himself to his feet.

He stripped, brushed his teeth, yanked the fancy silk damask coverlet off his immense Jacobean bed, climbed in and wondered how he and Kit would meet in the morning.

The bed was the size of a small yacht. He beat one of his king-size pillows into submission, rolled over on his side and, as he fell into sleep, replayed his kiss with Kit in his mind.

He'd really have to look into adopting a cat.

At ten forty-five, long after Emma was asleep and Kit had soaked in her whirlpool tub to ease her sore shoulders, Kev bounced off the bed and ran to Kit's computer. She dragged herself to a sitting position, saw the blinking red light on the answering machine that was attached to the monitor, turned on her bedside lamp and the computer. This time of night it had to be something bad. Big and the baby? "Hello?"

"Hey, Kit, it's Jimmy," the screen read.

She couldn't hear the slight slur in his speech or the bar noises in the background, but she would be willing to bet they were there. "Jimmy, it's nearly eleven o'clock. I have to get up early tomorrow even if you don't."

"Listen, I can't take Emma this weekend."

"What? Jimmy, this is your weekend. I have to work."

"So get your folks to look after her."

"Why can't you take her?" She tried to

smooth out her voice.

"Something came up."

"What came up, Jimmy? It had better be good."

"I got an invite from a guy who has a cabin over in Arkansas. Bunch of us are going duck hunting."

"Duck hunting? I have to work, Jimmy, and I have no idea whether my dad can look after Emma or not. It's Tuesday, for Pete's sake, and you throw this at me in the middle of the night? You'll just have to cancel your fancy duck-hunting thing."

"No way. This is a big hunt. Important people. Tell Emma I'll bring her some duck."

"Big poker game you mean. The only bird you'll see is Wild Turkey."

"Hey, babe, that's not fair."

"I am not your babe, Jimmy. I have to work."

"So Emma can go to Momma's. She's always complaining she never gets to spend time with Emma."

Kit felt her stomach lurch. "And have her regale Emma all over again with what a lousy wife and mother I am? No thank you, Jimmy. I've discussed that with you. Besides, I don't want her driving Emma all over town."

"There's nothing wrong with Momma's driving. I warned her after the last time she had to wear her seat belt and make sure Emma wore hers. And Momma's promised not to bad-mouth you. Listen, tell Emma I'll pick her up Friday night next weekend and keep her till Sunday afternoon. I'll talk to Momma and call you tomorrow night."

"Jimmy!"

She saw the flashing dot that indicated he'd hung up on her. She dropped her head in her hand. Now what? She'd promised Rick to work both Saturday and Sunday. She simply couldn't keep dumping Emma on her parents, although they seemed to enjoy it. And she would not let Emma stay with Mrs. Lockhart.

The door to her bedroom opened. Kev jumped off Kit's bed and pushed it farther. Emma stood there barefoot in her pj's. Her eyes squinted against the light. "Did Daddy get hurt?"

"He's fine." Kit opened her arms and Emma climbed into her lap. "I'm sorry I woke you."

"He doesn't want me this weekend, does he?"

She leaned back against the headboard, and Emma snuggled against her. "Of course your daddy wants you. He's just had an important meeting come up this weekend so he has to switch. He's asked to have you Friday night and Saturday next weekend."

"Some dumb ole poker game," Em said sleepily.

Now Kit cussed *herself*. She'd had no idea Emma was listening. She'd probably been talking much louder than she should. She ran her hand up Emma's forehead and brushed the soft damp hair away from her face. Emma cuddled closer. A moment later her soft breathing showed she'd fallen asleep.

Jimmy had never allowed Emma to sleep in their bed when they were married. Now Emma was long past the age when little children climbed between their parents. Kit could easily lift Emma and carry her back to her room and probably should.

Instead she slid herself out from under Emma and watched her snuggle deeper. Kev squirmed his way up the bed until he was close to Emma's chest.

"Why not?" Kit whispered. She leaned across Emma, turned out the light and caressed Emma's cheek where the moonlight touched it.

The hot tub had eased some of her aches, but Kit stood under the shower the following morning in hopes of finishing the job. She smiled at the difference between dream and reality. Letting Emma sleep with her had been her first try at being a warm and nurturing mother. Actually, it had been a nightmare. Emma snored, she kicked, she wriggled, she talked in her sleep, she flung her hand across Kit's face at least a dozen times and dug her elbow into Kit's ribs too often to count. Then she had woken up in a strange bed with no idea of where she was and a look of terror on her face. "Oh, well," Kit said as she massaged her sore shoulder. "I should have started cuddling her before she had so many bones."

Since neither mother nor daughter were morning people, they ate breakfast and drove to Emma's school without speaking. As Emma started to get out of the car, she turned to Kit and asked, "Will you pick me up this afternoon? Dr. Mac said I could hold the baby."

Kit nodded and hoped she could keep her promise. She remembered Alva Jean's warning. An emergency at the clinic meant everybody's schedules got thrown out the window.

As if hers weren't already messed up enough. If she ever got involved with somebody again, she hoped it would be with a *man* and not an over-grown child like Jimmy. Mac was a man. Unfortunately, he was a self-centered, irascible one who was just as selfish in his way as Jimmy was. She shook her head, trying not to think about how long it had been since anyone had kissed her the way Mac had.

She stopped by her parents' house on her way to the clinic. Her mother opened the door. She was already dressed in a business pantsuit. Her briefcase lay on the hall table. "Morning, darling. Want some breakfast? I think there's some bacon left."

Kit shook her head and walked past Catherine and into the kitchen. Wearing paint-stained jeans and an oversize sweatshirt, her father was closing the dishwasher on the breakfast dishes. The kitchen was immaculate, but then Tom Barclay never made a mess when he cooked. Kit eased a hip onto the stool in front of the breakfast bar. "I need a favor."

Her mother leaned against the doorjamb with her beautifully manicured hands folded across her stomach and one eyebrow raised. Kit wished her mother had left for work a little earlier. She'd always had an easier time talking to her father. "I really hate to ask you, but —"

"Money or Emma, which is it?" Catherine asked.

"I'm all right for money now that I've got this job."

"Jimmy's late on his child support again, right?"

"Only a couple of weeks. He always catches up. It's not that. I promised to work at the clinic both Saturday and Sunday, and now Jimmy says he's going out of town and can't take Em Friday night or Saturday."

Her mother shoved away from the door. "The child is not a soccer ball. She needs structure, routine, a schedule she can count on. Parents she can count on."

"I know that, Mom."

"Of course we'll take her," her father chimed in. "Catherine, stop talking like a watch commander and go to work. Catch some other deadbeat dads."

"At least when you were on the job, Kit, you knew when you were supposed to work," Catherine said.

"Not when I got called out on T.A.C.T."

"And Jimmy was on nights when you were on days," her mother continued as though Kit had not spoken.

"So I should have stayed married to Jimmy so he could babysit?"

"Not at all. You shouldn't have married

him in the first place, and as much as I love the child, you should certainly not have had Emma when you did."

"She wasn't exactly planned, Mom, but I couldn't live without her now that she's here."

"Precisely the way I felt about you." Her mother's face softened, and she touched Kit's cheek. "You're a good mother. Unfortunately, you don't have a good man like your father to take up the slack." She smiled up at him. "But then very few women are that lucky."

"Get on with you, Catherine Mary," her father said. Her mother went to him, and he gathered her in for a kiss.

"We'll take Emma if we have to," her mother said. "But you might try to rearrange your schedule so you can spend some time with her this weekend. She needs that."

"Yes, Mother," Kit said wearily.

She waited until they heard the back door slam. "How do you put up with her? She's so sure of everything. It's all so simple for her."

"Simple?" Her father laughed. "Want a cup of coffee?"

"I can't stay long. I'm due at the clinic in twenty minutes."

"You think it's simple for Catherine?" Her father shoved a steaming mug across the bar. "You've heard her stories all your life."

"Yeah, yeah, yeah. First woman captain on the police force. Then head of Internal Affairs, the most hated group on the job. I know."

"When that first group of six females graduated from the academy and were assigned, the wives of the other cops picketed every precinct. They didn't want their men spending eight hours at a time in a squad car with a home wrecker."

"Some of them still don't."

"The first day, her training officer drove off without her and left her sitting outside the lieutenant's office. He would have done it again, too, if the lieutenant hadn't forced him to take her. Then he literally did not speak a word to her for three months."

"I know all the tricks, Dad. My favorite is not stopping to let you take a bathroom break. When the guys need to go, they drive into an alley, get in front of the car and go. They think we ought to be able to do the same thing. It's not that different today."

"Of course, it's different. And it's different because Catherine Mary Barclay and women like her went before you. Your mother looks tough, Kit, but I've held her in my arms many nights when she cried herself to sleep and swore she'd never go back again. Most cops today are willing to work with a female so long as she proves she's as good as they are."

"Willing. Not happy."

"More than they used to be."

"But she had you to hold her, Dad." Despite her good intentions, Kit felt her eyes begin to tear. She hated feeling sorry for herself. "She wasn't alone, like me. I am *so* alone. You can't conceive of what this endless silence is like. When I was in East Tennessee learning how to work with Kevlar, one of the guys in my class who was blind told me that every morning before he opens his eyes he hopes that he'll be able to see, if only for a few seconds. He's never even seen his wife's face."

"You hope the same thing? That you'll be able to hear, if only for a few seconds?"

"Of course I do. I'm surprised Beethoven wasn't more of a nutcase than he was. At least he could hear his symphonies in his head. I'm not that good. I've even forgotten what Emma's voice sounds like."

Her father came around the end of the breakfast bar and wrapped his arms around her in a bear hug. She tucked her head under his chin and hugged him back. She could feel his Adam's apple moving and raised her head. "What? I know you said something."

"I said, 'Poor baby.' " He grinned down at her. "Everybody needs a 'Poor baby' sometimes."

She sniffed and grinned back. "Okay. The pity party's over. I'm going to be late for work."

She checked her makeup in the car mirror before she went into the clinic, then pasted on a cheerful face. How would Mac greet her? Eight to five, he'd ignore her.

She found Big perched on one of the metal chairs in the conference room. The baby lay in his arms with her dark little hands wrapped around the bottle in her mouth and her wide black eyes on Big's face. He rocked gently and his lips moved. Kit was certain he was singing to the baby. When Kit opened the door, he looked up and grinned. "Hey, Miss Kit. We done fine last night. She didn't hardly miss you at all."

Lovely. Just what Kit needed to hear.

"I already washed her and changed her, but she's gonna poop again once she gets through with breakfast."

The baby suddenly pushed the bottle away from her mouth, grabbed it with one hand

and threw it across the room so hard it bounced off the wall. She began to squirm.

"Hoo, boy, missy, you got you a temper! I think she wants her momma." He grinned and began to slide the carrier off his broad shoulder. As Kit reached for her, the baby lifted her arms, rolled her lips back over her teeth in a wide grin and burped right into Kit's face. Milk dripped off Kit's nose. That seemed to amuse the baby, who began to bounce up and down in Kit's arms.

She felt the air stirring as the door behind her opened. She turned and came face-to-face with Mac. For a moment no one spoke, then he said, "Uh, good morning. You need to wipe your face. How's our girl?"

She caught Big's interested glance at each of them, and the tiny nod of his head. That man was entirely too intuitive for anybody's good.

"She done real good most of the time," Big said. "She got fussy about midnight. Think maybe she had her a little gas. I turned her over on my knee and rubbed her back like I used to do my cousin Beau when he was little. She quieted right down after that."

"Did you get any sleep?" Kit asked him.

"Oh, yes'm, but that old couch in Mark's office sure could use some new stuffing."

195

"Right."

"So, let me have her, Kit, and we'll go do our morning examination," Mac said. The baby snorted and burbled, but she went to Mac willingly enough. "You take some time off, Big. You can't work all day and all night, too."

"Shoot, last night wasn't work. I was gonna run the tractor over the paddocks out back this morning, but it's too wet. I swear, I have never seen a spring like this in all my born days. We all gonna be floatin' soon if the rain don't stop awhile."

"So far it's only flash floods and the occasional closed road," Mac said as he cuddled the baby against his shoulder. "Come on, Kit, let's do it."

He didn't meet Kit's eyes as they worked over the baby. When they put her down into the pan on the scale, she refused to lie still until Kit offered her index finger as a pacifier. Mac recorded her weight on the chart beside the scale, checked Big's notes from the previous night about how much milk she drank and how she behaved, then finally looked up. "Well, time I got to work." He walked out without another word.

"Thank you, Doctor," Kit breathed. Okay, so last night's kiss had never happened. Did the good doctor usually hit on his staff? Or could she put it down to the rain and too much Chinese food.

She really knew nothing about Mac except that he was a good surgeon and apparently an interesting teacher.

Time to talk to Alva Jean.

Rick Hazard called a meeting of the professional staff for 4:00 p.m. so that both Sarah Scott and Eleanor Chadwick would be available.

Even Liz Carlyle showed up, although this was her day off. "I dumped the hellions on Big," she said as she slid into a seat and popped the lid on a can of diet soda. "Hal won't be home for another couple of hours. Man, I hate these meetings. Does anybody know why Rick called this one?"

"I dumped Muggs on Jack," Sarah said. "And I have no idea. Probably one of his morale pep talks, or a lecture about some client we've ticked off, although I can't think of anybody offhand."

"If it's money, Sarah," Eleanor said as she poured herself a cup of coffee, "you ought to know. You're the one who lives with the business manager."

"We do not generally talk business," Sarah said with a grin. "If we did, we might not still be married."

The door opened and Mac strode into the room. "What is this all about? I've got a French bulldog with a cleft palate scheduled for surgery in fifteen minutes. I hate these meetings."

Everybody laughed.

"What?"

Rick slid in behind Mac. "Sorry I'm late, people. I know you hate these meetings . . ."

More laughter.

"But unfortunately there are occasions that require them. This is such an occasion. We have a problem."

Groans.

"What now?" Eleanor asked.

"I spent an hour last night and another this morning on the phone to Bill Chumney."

"I thought he was still running after black-footed ferrets," Sarah said.

"He is."

"So what's the problem?" Mac asked. "Cut to the chase. I'm due in surgery."

"He's decided he wants to spend the rest of his life chasing black-footed ferrets," Rick said.

"Come *on,*" Liz said.

"What I mean is, he's been offered a job at a wildlife refuge in some remote corner of North Dakota and he's accepted the job."

"You're kidding," Liz said. "He hates snow."

"Not as much as he likes working on wild animals, apparently."

"The first snowflake, which probably comes in August, by the way, and he'll be begging to come back south," Sarah said. "Believe me, I know. I was born and raised in Minnesota. You couldn't get me through another Minnesota winter with a barge pole."

"I told him that. I told him a bunch of things. He's adamant."

"What does Becky think of all this? She's never been farther than five minutes from a mall in her life."

"What Bill wants, Becky wants. Or at least that's what Bill says."

"So when is he leaving?"

"Okay, here's the other shoe. He's not planning to come back at all except to pack up his stuff and put his house on the market. For all practical purposes, he's gone."

"Can he do that?" Eleanor asked. "I mean, I know he's not really a partner, but surely he has to give notice, give us time to find a replacement."

"Actually, whether he can or not, he's going to, and there's precious little we can do about it," Rick answered. "He's never really been happy here. He's always thought the exotic animal section was being short-changed in equipment and personnel." He sighed. "Maybe it was, but I don't think so."

"It's because of me, isn't it?" Sarah said quietly. "He's always thought the reason Mark bought the equipment I needed was because he was trying to buy *me*."

"Nonsense," Rick said. "Mark may be nuts about you, but he's still the most hardheaded and hard-nosed financial manager I've ever had to work with. No, I think Bill simply doesn't want anyone telling him what to do or asking him to be part of a team. In North Dakota he'll be running his own show."

"Frankly," Liz said, "I always thought he was a good vet but a whiny jerk. I'm not sorry he's gone."

"Tell us what you *really* think." Sarah laughed.

"I'm glad you feel that way," Rick said, "because his leaving is going to complicate all our lives. Until we find a top-notch exotics man to replace him, we're going to have to take up the slack. And that means more work for everybody."

Groans all around.

"We're all going to have to hit the books,"

Mac chimed in. "I don't know about the rest of you, but the last time I read anything about the anatomy of wildebeests and sea lions was in vet school, and I'm not certain I was awake that day."

"Fortunately, we've got access to the same internet connections and the same international vet networks Bill had," Rick said. "That'll help. At least we can call an expert if we get in a pickle, but Mac's right. An aardvark may look sort of like a pig, but whether or not its intestinal system works the same I have no idea. The good thing is that by and large the zoo runs a tight ship and manages to keep the animals healthy. The keepers are the first source of information on their animals. Most of them can recognize a sick animal just by looking at it. But it's up to us to diagnose, treat and hopefully cure."

"You and Mac did fine with the tiger and the orang," Eleanor said. "That was more than dumb luck."

"A tiger is simply a big cat and an orang is a big primate a lot like human beings," Mac said. "I also had time to do some quick reading and make a couple of phone calls to the experts before I tackled either one. If we're going to stay on top of this, it seems to me that the best way to split up the work is to try to stick as closely as possible to the same kinds of domestic animals we're used to treating."

"Makes sense," Eleanor said. "Sarah and I can handle the ungulates, the hooved animals. I don't have a clue how many stomachs a Bactrian camel has, although at one time I knew. I do know how to read up on the subject, however."

"Liz," Rick said, "you take anything to do with eye problems, and you'll be swing man for after-hour emergencies."

"When I'm not in class at Mississippi State," Liz said. "And when and if Hal can keep the boys. Sorry, Rick, but my family does come first."

"Same with Sarah," Eleanor chimed in. "She can't schlep Muggs with her if she has to check a hippopotamus. I, however, can. Steve and I don't have a family yet, and he's working such long hours getting the new plant up and running that I've got nothing but time on my hands."

"Thanks, Eleanor," Sarah said, and squeezed her arm. "I won't take advantage, I promise. Mark and I have about decided it's time to either hire a nanny or put Muggs in a day-care center a couple of days a week. At this point she probably thinks she's a cow — that's all she has to talk to."

"You've got the primates, Mac, since you're so good with them."

"One successful surgery on an orangutan does not make me good with anything, but it's the obvious choice."

"Plus, either doing or assisting at surgery anywhere in the place?" Sarah asked hopefully.

Mac shrugged. "It's what I do. Where do you fit in, oh mighty leader?"

"I fill in the cracks. And remember, we're not just talking zoo animals here. We still have to take care of any llamas down the road who've gotten tangled up in a barbed-wire fence, or the eagles somebody wounded up at Reelfoot Lake, or the possum babies left alive in momma's pouch after she becomes roadkill."

"And I thought Bill had it easy," Liz said.

"Thank God we've still got Kenny coming in after school three afternoons a week, and Big full-time and now Kit Lockhart," Rick said. "She really stepped up to the plate on that orang. Got to hand it to her, she wasn't scared when we left her with that tiger, either."

"I vote we push her into doing as much as possible with the babies on both sides of the clinic," Liz said. "She's got good instincts."

"And she's strong," Sarah added. "I think with some training she could handle a tough stud horse."

"She's got a daughter," Mac found himself saying. "If we try to run her into the ground, she'll be forced to leave."

"Limited number of things she can do under the circumstances," Rick said. "I mean, she's remarkable at reading lips, but there aren't a lot of places where she could bring her dog and be on her own as much as she is here. The animals don't much care whether she can hear them or not."

"Even so, if we want to keep her, we're going to have to cut her some slack with her family responsibilities," Mac said.

Eleanor stared at him for a moment before she said, "When did you turn into Dr. Understanding? It's not like you to consider anyone's responsibilities outside this place."

"Yeah," Sarah echoed. "Are we talking a kinder, gentler Mac Thorn here?"

"No, we are talking a Mac Thorn who doesn't want to be left without help again," he said. "Call it enlightened self-interest." He felt the skin of his cheeks flush. "She's picking her daughter up after school today and bringing her back here. That's what I mean by slack."

"I see," Sarah said, and glanced at Eleanor.

Uh-oh, Mac thought. Those two women were entirely too perceptive.

"Okay, okay," Rick cut in. "The main thing is we're going to have to schedule somebody to meet with the head keeper every morning at eight-thirty to tour the zoo and see if any of the animals look as though they need veterinary care."

"Eight-thirty in the morning?" Liz groaned. "Hal would kill me. He'd have to take the boys to school."

"Mark would kill me, too. He's always in the office by eight-thirty. And he'd have to fix breakfast for Muggs."

"That leaves Eleanor and Mac. How about it, people?"

"I'll do it," Mac said grumpily. "Eleanor already works late. She shouldn't have to work a split shift."

"Bring Nancy with you. You'll need somebody to take notes."

"No way!" Liz said. "She does half the simple procedures by herself. If she's not here, we'll be totally backed up with vaccinations and toenail clipping. Can't he take Kit or Big?"

"How's she going to hear what he's telling her to write down?"

"Well, you can't have Jack, either," Sarah said. "If I'm off vaccinating somebody's Angus herd or dipping a bunch of sheep, I need him here."

"And I'm not sure how well Big can write," Rick said. "Alva Jean is out too. No receptionist and the place falls apart."

"Kit can do it," Mac said quietly. "If the time schedule works out for her to drop her daughter off at school and go directly to the zoo instead of coming here first. Don't worry about her understanding what I'm saying. If she simply puts down the gist of my comments, I can correct them when we get back. I'd probably have to do that with Alva Jean or any other nontechnical assistant. Nancy's been teaching her the lingo. She's a very quick study."

"What about the baby?" Rick asked.

"Big can handle the baby until she gets here. He did fine last night. And we're through with that responsibility early next week."

"Fine. You want to ask her, Mac, or shall I?"

"You're the manager, Rick, it's your job." Mac set his cup down on the sideboard with a thump. "And up her salary while you're about it."

"What?" Rick said. "Why? She hasn't been

here long enough. This is just that 'other duties as assigned' thing in everybody's job description."

"It's extra gas, extra time and extra responsibility. Give her more money," Mac said quietly.

"He's right," Sarah said. "I don't imagine she's exactly rich on whatever pension or insurance money she's getting, and who knows if her ex-husband is paying enough child support. Besides, she's a real find."

"I agree," Eleanor said.

"So do I," Liz chimed in.

"Oh, well, nobody ever listens to me anyway," Rick said. "But Sarah, it's up to you to deal with Mark when he starts yelling about expenses."

She smiled sweetly. "Don't you worry."

"That's it, then?" Mac asked. "We're adjourned, right?"

"I guess . . ." Rick started to say, but chairs were already scraping, individual conversations had started, and Mac was walking out the room and into his surgery.

CHAPTER NINE

An anemic sun grimaced from behind grimy clouds as Emma left the gaggle of girls outside her school and planted herself in the backseat of Kit's Jeep. She leaned over the front seat so that Kit could see her face. "You came! Are we going to see the baby?"

"Absolutely. Say hello to Kev. He's about to have an accident waiting for his scratch."

"Hey, boy," Emma scratched the corgi's forehead.

"Seat belt."

"Right."

Kit edged through the trucks, SUVs and sedans double-parked in front of Emma's school. "How was school?" She glanced into the rearview mirror. "Never mind. Tell me later. I can't see your mouth."

Sure, Emma thought. Later. Only what was the point? When they did talk her mother seemed to understand the *words* she said, but who knew for sure? It was a whole lot easier not to try to tell her anything. Her mother could care less anyway. She just asked because she thought she was supposed to. She always had this big wall around her that Emma couldn't see over.

Emma hated the way her mother stared at her when she talked. Nobody else's mother stared at them like some kind of alien from another planet. Her friends all thought it was weird. They didn't want to come over any longer.

That was cool. Emma didn't want them at her house. At least when she went to Jessica's, *her* mother could actually hear how loud the music was. And she yelled at them when they stayed up talking too long. At home Emma could scream and her mother couldn't hear.

How can your mother look after you if she can't hear you scream?

She might as well not have a mother.

She sure didn't have a daddy any longer. She was just in everybody's way. She might as well be an orphan.

Kit hated the fact that she couldn't even have a normal after-school conversation with Emma. She remembered the times her mother had taken *her* to school. From time

209

to time they'd actually seemed to connect on those trips, maybe because neither one had had to look at the other while they talked.

Kit had decided to become a cop during those trips, not because her mother tried to point her in that direction, but because she *hadn't*. Her mother had tried to make the job seem mundane, boring, never dangerous. To hear Catherine Mary Barclay tell it, she spent her days doing paperwork and drinking coffee. Never doughnuts — she was much too disciplined for empty calories.

Would Emma want to be the third-generation female cop in the Barclay clan? She'd seen Kit wounded on the job.

She checked the rearview mirror and saw that Emma's head had slumped against the car door. Asleep. Not enough rest last night, obviously.

Would she want Emma on the job? She shuddered. Gangs, terrorism, Ecstasy and heroin, and even worse politics than in her mother's time. No. Emma would be a corporate lawyer or a teacher or a doctor — something professional that paid well and was clean.

Kit turned into the parking lot at Creature Comfort and saw that the area in front of the clinic was full of cars. Good. That meant plenty of clients.

When she saw Mac's Suburban in the staff parking area, her heart lurched. She was acting like a schoolgirl herself. She hadn't felt that jolt of expectation at the sight of a boy's car since high school. This was not supposed to happen to mothers. "Em," she said into the rearview mirror.

Emma opened her eyes and stretched. "We there?"

"You want to snuggle down and sleep a little longer?"

"I'm awake." Emma blinked. "I want to see the baby."

"Okay, come on. But be quiet and try not to get in anybody's way. Bring your books. After we check out the baby you can do your homework in the conference room for a few minutes until I can leave."

"Can I have a soda?"

"I guess one won't hurt you."

In his little orange helper-dog cape, Kev trotted between Kit and Emma through the staff door beside the big overhead door where the cattle trucks could be unloaded, and turned right toward the door that led to the main part of the clinic.

Kev stopped so quickly that Emma nearly fell over him. She touched Kit's arm. "Somebody's calling you, Mom." She pointed to Sarah Scott's partially open door. "She wants us to come in."

Sarah came around from behind her desk. "So this is Emma. Hi. We've heard a lot about you." She stuck out her hand. "I'm Sarah Scott. I handle the big animals."

Emma glanced up at her mother, but shook Sarah's hand, then looked around her, saw Muggs in her playpen and dropped onto her knees beside the toddler, who immediately began to grin and jump up and down. Sarah turned back as well. She and Emma began to talk, but because both backs were turned to her, Kit couldn't read what they were saying. She felt that left-out feeling again. After a minute she said, "Emma, we can't waste Dr. Scott's time."

Sarah looked back at Kit. "Oh, I am so sorry. We were just saying that maybe when Emma's a little older she can babysit. It's never too early to line up a good babysitter."

"Can I, Mom?"

"Not for a few years yet, but after that I don't see why not. Now, come on, we've got another baby to visit."

Emma stopped at the door and turned back to say something to Sarah, who replied, "Nice to meet you, too."

Kit stopped at the supply closet and picked up a mask and surgical gloves for

Emma, then helped her put on the gloves. "Leave the mask hanging until you're actually holding the baby. That way I can see you talk."

Emma nodded. Putting on the gloves had apparently brought home to her that this was a special event.

Kit peeked in at the door of the conference room expecting to find Big. The room was empty. She opened the door to Mark's office. Big lay sprawled on Mark's couch with his legs hanging off the end and the baby riding up and down on his huge chest as he breathed. From the way his mouth moved, Kit suspected he was snoring. If so, it didn't seem to bother the baby.

"Shh," Kit said. "She's asleep."

In an instant the round black eyes popped open and the baby began to move her mouth in the way that Big said meant squeals and whuffles. Big opened his own eyes, saw Kit and Emma, and sat up so fast he hit his head on the lamp at the head of the sofa.

"Ow!" He rubbed his head and grinned broadly. "We was just taking us a little nap. This here's Emma, right?"

"I'm sorry, Big, we didn't mean to wake you."

"Just a little snooze. My momma used to

say with little ones you have to sleep when you can, 'cause mostly you can't."

Kit wondered what Emma's reaction to Big would be.

"Come on over here, young'un," Big said. "Princess here wants to meet you."

Emma pulled the mask up over her mouth, went to him, leaned against his huge knee and touched the baby's leathery little hand in awe.

It would seem that Big's ability to charm animals extended to children.

Emma turned to Kit and slid the mask down far enough to show her mouth. "Can she walk?"

"I . . . Emma, I have absolutely no idea," Kit said.

"What say we see?" Big said, gently dislodging the baby from its carrier. "Want to sit down on the floor, baby?"

Kit sat cross-legged in front of Big and extended her arms. The baby slid down Big's leg as though it were a tree trunk and wound up on her bottom with her arms raised for Kit to pick her up.

"She's the sweetest thing," Emma said as she slid down to sit beside her mother and pulled her mask back into place.

The baby turned her head, rolled her lips back from her teeth, then pursed them and blew a big Bronx cheer straight into Emma's face. "Hey!" Emma wiped her hand over her face.

"That's not nice, Princess," Big said.

The baby twisted her fat little body and reached her long arms up to slap Emma's cheeks. Emma pulled the mask from the side of her mouth with her index finger. "Mom, I don't think she likes me."

"Sure she does," Big said. "She ain't never seen no young'un before. She probably thinks you're just like her. She wants to play."

The baby did a slow somersault right into Emma's lap, wrapped her long arms around Emma's neck and slurped a big kiss on Emma's cheek. Emma made a face and drew back.

Kit expected her to freeze or to squeal and maybe frighten the princess, but after a moment Emma began to laugh into the baby's face as she clasped her bottom. The baby grabbed Emma's hair in both hands and began to pull herself to her feet. Kit didn't need to see Emma's mouth to know she'd said ouch or ow. The baby could really pull with those little arms of hers.

The door to the hall opened and Mac walked in. "What's going on in here?" he demanded.

The baby buried her face in Emma's neck and clung to her in obvious terror. Equally scared, Emma clung back.

Kit was certain Mac would blow up at them all. After a moment, he said quietly, "Good afternoon, Emma. I see you've met our girl."

Kit could see Emma's sigh of relief and would probably have heard Big's if she'd been able to hear.

Because Emma didn't turn to face him, Kit could continue to read what she was saying.

"Dr. Mac, she wasn't doing anything wrong," Big said. "Princess wanted to go to her, didn't she, Emma?"

"Emma asked if she could walk. I had to admit I don't know," Kit said.

"She'll start crawling first. She won't walk for a while, and then only if she loses her ride," Mac answered. "I suppose if she were frightened enough she might try to walk on all fours, but she won't stand erect for some time, and even then it won't be her first choice."

He sank to his haunches beside Emma. "I think you can safely lose the mask if you don't sneeze into her face."

Emma yanked it down over her chin. "Whew. How do you breathe in those things?"

"Strong lungs. Did you know that they don't normally swing through the trees using their arms like gibbons? They prefer to use those long arms to balance themselves while they walk from one tree limb to another. They learn from their mothers which limbs are strong enough to hold them. In the wild they move through the very top of the jungle canopy. Plenty of people have lived among orangs for years and never seen one."

"But they're so red — like Mom's hair."

"In the canopy when the sunlight hits them they disappear. Or so I've been told. I've never been to Borneo or Sumatra."

"She's so little." Emma stroked the baby's head.

"In four years she'll weigh as much as your mother. But she won't be half as tall."

"When can she have her own baby?"

"Not till she's fourteen or fifteen, and then only once every few years. That's why they're so endangered in the wild. That and the fact that in the wild the princess, here, would be completely dependent on momma for five or six years. It's pretty hard to carry on a courtship with a kid hanging around your neck." His eyes widened, and he glanced at Kit, then quickly away as though he'd just realized what he'd said and hoped Kit had missed it.

She hadn't. Mac no doubt agreed with the male orang's definition of courtship. She didn't think that meant roses and perfume or long candlelit dinners. Even those were tough to arrange with a child around. Last night's take-out Chinese at the kitchen table was as close to a romantic tête-à-tête as Kit was likely to be able to manage.

"Mom," Emma said. "I think she needs changing." She wrinkled her nose. "Eeeew, gross, gross, gross."

"So were you, but I got through it," Kit said, and reached for the baby. For a moment the little orang clung to Emma, then as if she realized who was reaching for her, twisted her body completely around and held her arms up to Kit. "Come on, Princess, let's get you cleaned up and then you can have some dinner."

"Emma, since you are so grossed out, how about I show you the animals we've got in today?" Mac said.

"Aren't you busy?" Kit asked.

He shrugged. "It's almost time for me to leave. Barring emergencies, I'm through for the day. Big, you want to stay here? Have you had dinner?"

"Brought me three of those TV dinners

they say feed a big man. Then Alva Jean brought me some cupcakes. I'll eat in a while after things quiet down. Then me'n the princess here can check things out and catch us another nap until feeding time."

Mac nodded. "Come on, Emma."

"Mom said I should sit in the conference room and do homework."

"Which would you prefer? Animals or homework?"

Emma grinned. "Dumb question."

The door closed behind the two of them. Big came over to Kit and touched her shoulder. "Nice little gal," he said. "I think Dr. Mac's smitten."

Kit cleaned and powdered the baby. "She's got a crush on him. I don't know whether that's a good thing or not."

"Good for him, maybe. Don't know about her. He's a right peculiar man. I feel sorry for him."

"Why?"

"Don't know what kind of people he come from. He don't never talk about 'em. Don't have any friends, not even any lady friends far as Alva Jean knows."

"And she *would* know."

Big nodded. "Yes, ma'am, she would. Sometimes when he's worried about a creature he's worked on, he'll sleep all night

219

right in the ICU so he can be there in case anything goes wrong. He's got a kind heart, but it sure is buried down deep where it's hard to get at."

"Are you warning me off?"

"Oh, no, ma'am. Somebody'd have to do a heap of diggin', though, to get through. You never know. Might be worth it, or you might find nothin' but hurt."

"There." Kit fastened the last piece of tape on Princess's clean diaper and picked her up. She didn't want to pursue the subject of Mac Thorn's heart any longer.

"Why don't you let me feed her? You go on home, spend some time with Emma."

Kit realized she was dog-tired. "Thanks, Big. There should be enough formula made up for tonight and tomorrow morning. I'll mix up another batch when I get in."

He took the baby, who went to him readily. "We'll do fine. Good night, Kevlar."

As she closed the door of Mark's office behind her, she thought how typical it was of Big to remember Kev.

She poked her head into the ICU. No Mac, no Emma. Not in the conference room, either. She walked into the large-animal area with Kevlar trotting beside her. Eleanor Chadwick had taken Sarah's place.

"Have you seen a ten-year-old girl?" Kit asked.

"With Mac? Last I saw, they were headed to the exotics area with Kenny."

"Thanks."

She was too tired to chase Mac and her child all over the clinic. She jogged down the long central hall and turned right at the end into the exotics area. So far as Kit knew, its only residents at the moment were a fat hedgehog with a recurring case of quill rot and a scarlet macaw who needed his wing feathers clipped.

She found Mac, Emma and Kenny looking down at something on the steel examining table under the lights. Emma saw her and ran to her. Mac and Kenny didn't look up.

"Mom, we have to whisper," Emma said, and drew her mother outside the door. "Kenny found a beaver that had been hit by a car. They're trying to save it. Come on."

"No, Emma, we'll be in the way."

"I want to watch, Momma. Dr. Mac said I could. They think it's got a broken hip and they're going to have to operate." Emma's eyes were shining. "Poor thing's all bloody and Kenny says it may go into shock and just die — they do that sometimes because they're scared — but Dr. Mac'll save it, I know he will."

"Dr. Mac doesn't need us underfoot while he's doing it."

"But Mom —"

Kit knew the tone of that whine even if she couldn't hear it.

"We've got to get home, baby. It's dinnertime and you've got homework. I promise I'll let you know about the beaver tomorrow afternoon."

"But —" Emma was gearing up for tears.

"We're going home, Emma. I mean it. I'm too tired to argue."

"You're always too tired. But I have to say goodbye, don't I? That's polite."

"Don't interrupt Dr. Mac when he's working. He won't even notice we're gone."

At that moment Kenny looked their way. Kit pointed at Mac and mouthed, "Tell him we're going home."

He smiled, nodded at Emma, and turned back to the table.

Kit started down the hall. For a moment she thought Emma wasn't following, but when she turned, Emma was dragging her way down the aisle as though she were being taken straight to the guillotine. Her lower lip stuck out far enough to rest a potted plant on.

At home Emma took her stuff upstairs

without a word. It was a repeat of last night's performance, but this time Kit didn't suppose Mac would show up to alleviate the tension. She brought the groceries she'd bought at lunchtime in from the back of the Jeep. So long as the weather stayed relatively cold she could get away with leaving everything but frozen stuff in the Jeep for a few hours.

Come spring, she'd have to shop once a week on Saturday. She used to plan better, but since she'd been home all the time, she'd gotten into the habit of going to the grocery almost every day to break the monotony and the silence.

Tonight she'd fix Elfo special shrimp — a mixture of shrimp and fettuccine that used lots of pasta and few shrimp, so that it was a fairly economical dish. It was one of Emma's favorites. All she'd need to go with it was a green salad and a Granny Smith apple for Emma's dessert.

Kit decided she might even have a soda to go with it.

Emma kept up her silent treatment during dinner, then went upstairs to finish homework and get ready for bed without a backward glance or a reply to her mother's good-night. Kit was too weary to make an issue of it.

She cleaned up the kitchen, took her own apple into the den, stretched out on the couch and flicked on the television. Kevlar hopped up beside her and snuggled into the curve of her legs.

She was half-asleep and trying to keep up with the plot of a badly written cop show, when Kevlar raised his head, jumped down from the couch, trotted to the front door and came back again. "Great," Kit said as she swung her legs off the couch and went to answer the door.

This time she checked the peephole and her heart began to thud. Mac again. What could he possibly want this time? Another kiss?

"Hey," she said as she opened the door.

He stepped in without invitation. "Sorry to keep dropping by this way, but you're right on my way home, and I know the telephone's not that easy for you."

"No, that's fine. Come in." She pointed to her apple. "Can I get you something?"

Now that he was in, he seemed hesitant, almost embarrassed. "Actually, I came to see Emma. I heard the music and figured Emma wasn't in bed yet."

Kit raised her eyebrows. "You could hear it from your car?" She turned to the stairs. "Emma Barclay Lockhart, turn down that music and get down here this minute. Kevlar, go get Emma."

"Actually, I was stopped outside and had my car window down," Mac said. "The music wasn't that loud. I didn't mean to get Emma in trouble."

"Don't worry about it. Emma! Now!"

Emma appeared at the top of the stairs. She still wore her school outfit — jeans and a sweater. "What?" she said, then she saw Mac and her face lit up. "Oh!" She nearly tumbled down the stairs.

"Sorry to disturb you. I promised you I'd let you know about the beaver."

"Is he going to be okay?"

"I've pinned his hip. If he avoids infection and doesn't die of fright, he should be all right, although he may never be able to live in the wild again. He may have to go to an educational program at the zoo. We'll have to see."

"I knew you'd save him!"

Mac flushed. "Mostly luck and Kenny's quick thinking. Well, I'll let you get back to your evening." He turned to Kit. "And I'll meet you at eight-thirty tomorrow morning at the zoo."

"I beg your pardon?" She looked at Emma. "Scat. It's time you took your bath and got to bed."

"But Mom . . ."

"I'll be up to tuck you in."

"Mother, I do not need tucking in like some baby."

"Go."

Emma flashed a smile at Dr. Mac and ran up the stairs.

"Now, what's this about eight-thirty in the morning?"

"Didn't Rick talk to you?"

"No. Why? Was he supposed to?"

"Maybe we should sit down."

Halfway through Mac's explanation of Kit's new responsibilities, the front doorbell rang again. Kit didn't react until Kev alerted her. "Now what?"

A moment later Vince Calandruccio and his German shepherd, Adam, walked into the room. Vince came over to shake hands with Mac. "Hey, Doc, thought that was your car. Kit, do you have anything to drink for a poor dry man?"

"Sure, Vince. Have a seat. Adam, you want a biscuit?" Adam wagged his tail and nearly knocked a stack of magazines off the coffee table.

"Give Kev one too," Vince said. "On separate sides of the kitchen."

"Sure."

When they were settled, Vince said, "You still haven't come down to the gym, so I thought I'd check up on you. Sorry I haven't come over sooner. You still like your job?"

"You expect her to answer that with me sitting here?" Mac asked. "She can't very well say she hates it."

"Since I don't hate it, that's not a problem," Kit answered. "It's a bit like police work — paperwork, quiet times, and occasionally something really crazy happens."

"Still not ready to go into the kennel business with me?"

"We've been through that, Vince. Emma doesn't need even a small change in her routine right now. But I'm beginning to think I might find something to do with animals in the long run. I really do like working with them."

Vince glanced at Mac. "Saw Jimmy last night."

"He called me. It was nearly midnight."

"Yeah. Well, you know Jimmy. We were at the bar after work, and this trip came up. Next thing I knew he was on the phone to you."

"I knew he was in a bar. I just knew it!"

"He knows you're mad."

"He sent you over here to placate me. Give me a break!"

"I should go," Mac said, and stood. "See you tomorrow, then?"

"How much more money?" Kit asked him.

"You'll have to take that up with Rick. Vince, nice to see you."

"Hey, Doc, I didn't mean to break up the party."

"No party. Say good-night to Emma for me, Kit. I can find my own way out."

After the door shut behind him, Vince said with a grimace, "I'm sorry. You and him got something going?"

"Of course not. He's my boss."

"Hey, he's been here twice when I've been here." He peered at her. "And you're blushing."

"And twice he was here on business. I'm on his way home, that's all."

"And Emma, that's business, too?"

"Are you here spying on me for Jimmy, because if you are —"

"No, no. But you're still kind of like family, Kit. We all worry about you."

"Well, stop. I'm fine, Emma's fine, the whole world's fine."

"Whoa! Time for old Vince and old Adam to mosey along, podner."

Kit held up her hand. "I'm sorry, Vince. Sometimes it gets to me, that's all. I can't seem to blink without having somebody reporting it to somebody else. And you can tell Jimmy Lockhart this for me the next time you see him. What I do is no longer any of his business. We are *not* married any longer. I am not his property."

"Okay, okay. Sorry I asked. I'll never do it again. Cross my heart and hope to die." He crossed his heart. He put the can of cola she'd given him down on a magazine in front of him and walked to the door with Adam at his heels. With his hand on the knob, he turned to look at her. "Look, um, before, you were Jimmy's wife, and then we worked together, but now . . . maybe we could have dinner sometime? Go to a movie?"

"Are you asking me for a date, Vince?"

She could have sworn he blushed. "Okay, so, yeah. Maybe. Is that so crazy?"

"No, it's sweet." She leaned over and kissed his cheek. "I just don't know right now . . ."

"Hey, I can wait."

"You really are sweet." She held the door open for him. "Good night, Vince. Good night, Adam." She scratched the dog's ears and watched as the pair walked down the driveway and climbed into Vince's pickup before she shut the door.

She picked up the empty cola can from

229

the coffee table and sighed. Why did Vince have to show up when he did?

She longed for Mac to come back, to sit beside her, drink another glass of wine, kiss her the way he had last night . . .

But at least she'd see Mac in the morning, even if only to follow him around with a notebook while he discussed the digestive processes of giraffes.

Chapter Ten

The morning news reported that rainfall in the Alabama-Mississippi-Arkansas tristate area was nearly twelve inches more than normal for this time of year, and the snow-melt from the north was only now starting to swell the Mississippi River. Already, low-lying areas in Arkansas were disappearing under water. So far the levees in Mississippi and Tennessee were holding, but with every new weather front, flash floods closed roads for hours. Sudden heavy thunderstorms normally drained off after four or five hours, but if the levees were ever breached, there could be some long-term flooding in northern Mississippi that would isolate communities for weeks.

Now that she was no longer a policewoman, Kit didn't have to worry about being called back to duty to direct drivers around flooded streets or to rescue people who wound up in creeks or stalled hood-deep in runoff.

If this weather kept up, days off for the police and rescue units would be curtailed. Jimmy might find his little duck-hunting expedition to Arkansas canceled after all. And wouldn't that just be too *dreadful?*

This morning found the zoo clouded in a fine cold mist that seemed to penetrate not only clothing but skin as well. Kit wondered whether lack of sunlight depressed the animals the way it did some human beings. Most of the animals looked dispirited and were hanging around their dens trying to get out of the wet.

Kit and Mac strode along beside the head keeper, Brian Neely, a grizzled veteran who had been with the zoo over thirty years and knew every animal as well as he knew his own family.

She might not be able to hear what was being said, but from time to time Mac turned his face to her to give her a note.

"Schedule tuberculin testing for the primates. Female camel slightly lame on near foreleg. Check Chester, the male meerkat, to make sure the females aren't beating him up again."

"I swear," Neely said. He'd already learned to turn his face so that she could be included in the conversation. "Poor ole

Chester spends so much time in the infirmary he's started acting like he's glad to see it." He grinned. "Probably is. Least in the hospital he's safe from those witches he lives with."

"But they're so cute!" Kit said.

"They're *territorial*," Neely replied. "And Chester keeps blundering in where he's not wanted."

Kit was glad she was still in fairly good shape, because Neely's legs were as long as Mac's, and both men strode as though they were starting a marathon. In thirty minutes she and Mac were ready to leave for the clinic.

"I'll enter your notes and give you a copy as soon as I get the princess down for her nap," she told him as she climbed into her car.

He put a hand on her open door. "I apologize if I intruded last night," he said. "Next time I'll call your telephone — Alva Jean explained how it works."

She wished she could have heard whether he was simply imparting information or whether he was being cool and aloof. Words didn't mean much without the emotion behind them. She made a vow to call Dr. Zales for an update on that operation.

"You didn't intrude, I promise you. If

anything, Vince did. You see, I'm not only a former cop, I'm also a cop's ex-wife and the daughter of a retired cop. When they talk about taking care of their own, they mean every word of it. It's worse with me because they also feel guilty that I'm not on the job any longer."

"Should they?"

She brushed the mist from her eyes. "Good grief, no."

He seemed to come to a decision. "Can you talk about it?"

"Sure. It's no deep, dark secret. My disability pension proceedings are a matter of public record."

"Then follow me. I'll buy you some breakfast before we check in to the clinic."

"I'm supposed to be relieving Big with the princess, remember? And don't you have surgery scheduled?"

"This zoo visit took much less time than I thought it would. I'm not scheduled until ten, and Big's not expecting to be relieved until about nine-thirty."

"So where are we going? In case I lose you."

He named a diner famous for its grits and red-eye gravy and, without waiting for her reply, climbed into his Suburban and drove off.

"You know, Kev," Kit said as she pulled out of the parking lot after him, "I have always — well, usually — been able to tell if a man is interested in me. With Mac, I haven't a clue. He hires me at the clinic, then he practically ignores me for weeks, then he drags me off to an emergency at the zoo and lands me with the baby. He gives me an amazing kiss, and then he's Mr. Cool, and now he's acting as though he'd like to be friends." She beat her hands on the steering wheel. "I'd give almost anything to hear what his voice sounds like!"

"You could have asked Nancy or Alva Jean about me," Kit said. "They got the whole story the first week I came to the clinic."

"Would you rather I asked them?"

"I told you I don't mind talking about it. If I had to get hurt, I just wish I'd been doing something heroic at the time. It sounds so stupid to say I walked into a flash-bang."

"A what?"

"Flash-bang." She made a neat sandwich out of her country ham and biscuit and took a bite. "I thought everybody had seen enough cop shows on television to know the lingo. Anyway, here's what happened. I was part of a T.A.C.T. team that was serving a warrant on a suspected drug house.

We always go in very early in hopes that the people inside are all asleep and unarmed. The first team hits the front door with a battering ram at the same time we kick in the back door — it's usually not so heavily reinforced.

"Both teams come in yelling, and frequently the front team tosses in a flash-bang. It's a small concussion bomb that explodes with a lot of smoke and noise and light but isn't supposed to do any permanent damage to people. Then the team spreads out all over the house and rousts anybody they find. If we do it right, we drag out a bunch of sleepy dealers in their undershorts who haven't brushed their teeth yet."

"What went wrong?"

"The guy with me at the back door was new. He was supposed to kick in the back door on the count of three, at exactly the moment the battering ram took out the front door. Then he was to go left down the hall toward the bedrooms while I went through the kitchen to the front hall to meet the guys who were coming in the front.

"The guy was so anxious that he kicked in the door at one and a half. I had no choice but to cover my partner."

"But you weren't shot. Was your partner?"

236

"He was fine. Turned out the dealers had abandoned the house." She shrugged. "It happens."

She drank some of her coffee. "What's that old saying about when things start to go wrong they just get worse?"

Mac nodded. "That's certainly true in surgery."

"At that point nobody knew we were looking at an empty house. The guys in front battered the door down and came pouring in just the way they should have. By that time I should still have been in the kitchen, but because my partner jumped the gun I was already in the front hall trying to head off a possible ambush from the living room. The sergeant tried to call off the flash-bang. Too late. It went off right at my feet."

"You could have been killed. Or blinded."

"It's not supposed to blow up people the way a land mine does. It's designed to blind and deafen anybody around it for a short time — long enough so they can be disarmed and taken into custody. Usually the blindness and deafness goes away in a couple of hours, but there have been injuries. After all, it's still a bomb. Firecrackers aren't supposed to kill people, either, but they do. My helmet protected my skull, but the goggles aren't designed to take a direct hit. I got a few pieces of plastic and a sliver of coffee table in my forehead and eyes, but no real damage to my sight. My hearing's another story. Popped my eardrums like birthday balloons and damaged the auditory nerves."

"If this thing wasn't supposed to cause long-lasting damage . . ."

"It literally blew up in my face, so I'm one of the unlucky ones with a permanent injury. At first the doctors thought it *would* be temporary. Then they said I'd get partial hearing back at least in one ear. They kept saying that for two months. Then they spent another month investigating cochlear implants. We've got some of the best ear guys in the world right here in Memphis, but even they gave up in the end. So did I, for now."

He narrowed his eyes at her. "What do you mean, for now?"

"My doctor's investigating a new operation that might give me at least partial hearing, but he's not willing to let me try it until the kinks have been worked out."

"So at some point in the future you might be able to hear?"

"I can't live on hope. You're the first person I've told about the procedure, except my doctor, of course."

"Your lipreading ability is remarkable after such a short time."

"I pick up a lot less than you think I do, but I've learned to fake it. As long as I answer the question you actually asked and don't send the conversation reeling into left field, you assume I've understood every word. Wrong."

"I tried it the other night."

"What?"

"I enabled the closed captioning feature on my television and turned off the sound. I was hopeless at reading lips."

"Because you knew you could turn up the sound whenever you wanted to. I don't have that luxury."

"Have you started learning sign language?"

She looked away. "Not yet." She avoided his eyes. "That's admitting I'll always be this way. And the only people who could understand me are other people who can sign. Could you read me? Could Big? I'd have to drag around an interpreter. Nope, I'll stick with lipreading for the moment." She looked down at her watch. "We'd better get to work or they'll fire me. You, they'll keep."

She started to get up, but he reached across the table and covered her hand with his. She sat down again.

"That kiss the other night . . ."

She drew in a quick breath.

"It wasn't a fluke or a brainstorm. I wanted to kiss you. I've wanted to kiss you since the first time I saw you in the clinic."

She gulped. "And snarled at me."

"I'm being serious. You might try it sometime."

"I don't dare. Serious scares me. You can't take back serious. It hurts."

"Not with me."

"Oh, right. Like I believe that."

"Stop it, Kit. Stop it or I'll come around this table, drag you to your feet and kiss you again right here in public."

"Nuts. You wouldn't dare."

The instant the words left her mouth she realized her mistake. She didn't even have time to brace herself against him before he swept her out of her chair and into his arms.

It was like the flash-bang all over again. She couldn't breathe with his arms around her, couldn't do anything except kiss him right back. The restaurant fell away, the people watching ceased to exist. She couldn't hear the pounding of her heart, but she could feel it. She didn't even have sense enough or strength enough to put her arms around him. She simply hung in his arms like a semiconscious captive.

The kiss seemed to last forever and to be over in a second. When he released her, she could only gasp.

His eyes bored into hers.

And then he began to laugh. She could see it, feel the laughter in his belly. She was starting to feel offended, when he swung her around with one arm. Behind her, the stuffy brokers, the power-suited corporate mavens were applauding.

She realized Kev was bouncing up and down against her knee and trying to warn her about the hubbub. She closed her eyes. When she opened them, she saw Mac toss a twenty-dollar bill onto the table. He put her jacket around her shoulders and fairly dragged her out the front door.

"I have never been so embarrassed in my life," she said as he opened the door of the Jeep for her. She cuffed him on the chest.

"And I have never *done* anything like that in my life. Actually, it feels good." He smiled down at her and touched her cheek.

She leaned her cheek against his hand. "It does," she whispered. Then she looked behind him. "Oh, good grief!" Two empty patrol cars were parked several spaces from the Jeep. She stared into the restaurant. Two broad blue backs sat hunched over the counter. She hadn't seen them come in and had no idea who they were, but they must have been there during the kiss and the applause.

"What?" he asked.

"Do you have any idea what you've done? The entire police force, city, county and suburban, will have some crazy version of what just happened within an hour." She leaned back and shut her eyes. "Oh, great — my mother!"

"You're not a teenager, Kit. It was just a kiss."

"Yeah, and now I have to deal with the fallout." She touched his cheek again. "It's not your fault. It was wonderful and crazy, and I loved it. I've got to stop by the house to make a couple of calls before I come to work. Is that all right?"

"Certainly." He looked puzzled.

"I'll be there as quick as I can." She shut her door but rolled down the window. "And for Pete's sake, drive *very* carefully."

Kit was beautiful. Somehow he would have to get some time alone with her. Emma's father took her alternate weekends, didn't he? Was he scheduled for this week or next?

Mac wasn't certain he could wait a week. In the meantime, he'd have to keep his cool at the clinic. All the females in the place were too perceptive, as far as he was concerned.

He saw the flashing red and blue lights behind him before he heard the squall of the siren.

"What the . . ." He checked his speedometer. He wasn't speeding. He hadn't run a stop sign or jumped a yellow light.

He pulled over and stopped. A gray-haired patrolman with a paunch climbed slowly out of his car, hitched his belt, used his index finger to shove his mirrored sunglasses back up to the bridge of his nose and sauntered over to peer in Mac's window.

"Seat belt check. You wearing your seat belt?"

"Yes."

"You got proof of insurance?"

"Yes."

"May I see it, please, sir, and your driver's license?"

Puzzled, Mac rummaged in his glove compartment, came up with his insurance papers, and then opened his wallet to extract his driver's license.

"Here you are, Officer."

The man took the papers, moved away from the car, seemed to take an eternity to read them and then brought them back to Mac.

"These seem to be in order, sir. You're a doctor?"

"A veterinarian."

"Uh-huh. You know those car tags expire in three months?"

"Yes."

"You be careful they don't expire on you. Big fine for that."

This was starting to get weird.

"I know."

"Well, Doc, have a nice day, and don't forget that seat belt."

The man sauntered off, climbed back into his patrol car and drove off.

Mac crossed the city line from Memphis to Germantown, stopped at the stoplight at Poplar and Forest Hill, and realized that there was a Germantown patrol car right behind him.

He knew enough not to speed in Germantown. The city was notorious for handing out speeding tickets for cars doing no more than three or four miles over the speed limit. He drove slowly, carefully, his eyes on the rearview mirror. The patrol car hung behind him and made no attempt to pass him. When he pulled into the Creature Comfort parking lot, the patrol car sped up and went on its way.

Inside he found Jack Renfro and Sarah Scott positioning needles to let the air out of a cow's bloated stomach.

"Morning," he said, started to walk by, then stopped. "Can you listen and work?"

"Sure," Sarah said.

"The oddest thing just happened to me. A cop stopped me to see if I was wearing my seat belt, then checked my insurance and registration and driver's license."

"Were you speeding?"

"No, thank God. I had the feeling that if he could have found even a broken taillight I'd be in the city jail calling a bail bondsman. And that's not all. A Germantown squad car followed me all the way from Forest Hill."

"Interesting," said Sarah. "Okay, Jack, here we go."

Mac went to his office. Apparently Sarah and Jack didn't think his experience that strange.

Five minutes later, Rick stuck his head in. "Hi. How'd it go at the zoo this morning?"

"Fine."

Rick backed out.

"Hey, Rick," Mac called after him.

"I'm really busy, Mac. Can it wait?"

"Get in here. You were supposed to discuss

Kit's new duties with her yesterday."

"I got busy, and when I looked for her, she'd already left for the day. So I guess she didn't meet you at the zoo this morning, huh?"

"She met me all right. I stopped on my way home yesterday to tell her daughter about . . . never mind. I discussed it with her then. She was very surprised."

"Oh, good. Well, that's it, then."

"Wait just a minute, *Doctor*. I told her to take up the increased salary with you."

"We did talk about an increase, didn't we?"

"We didn't talk about it, we agreed on it. And when I check with Kit later, she better know about it, too. And it better be good."

"Yeah, okay. I'll do it now."

"I don't know whether she's in yet or not."

"Why wouldn't she be? You're here."

"She had to make a telephone call. She can't do that in private except from her house. I told her to go ahead. She'll still get here sooner than I thought we would."

"Look, Mac, I know you've got a thing for her . . ."

"Do not go there, Rick. I'm not cutting her any slack because I like her. I'm cutting her some slack because she works her tail off."

"Okay, okay. Now can I go get some work done?"

"What are you doing about finding a replacement for Bill?"

"It just happened. I'm not a miracle worker. If I could get back to my office, I might start putting out some feelers."

"Be my guest."

"I called Sol Weinstock in Lexington. He's going to cut his trip short. He'll be here the middle of the month. He's no zoo man, but he can relieve some of the pressure on the rest of us until we find someone who is. He wasn't happy about it. He went on and on at me about how he's supposed to be semiretired and how his research grant helps fund this place. Sometimes I wish . . ."

"You wish you didn't have to put up with the rest of us."

"You said it. I didn't. And this afternoon I'm going down to Buchanan Industries to meet with Mark about the new business projections for the practice."

"Bill's resignation should save us some bucks in the short haul," Mac said.

Rick shook his head. "We'll probably have to up the ante significantly to get somebody else. And we'll have to pay relocation expenses. Maybe even offer a junior partnership. I hate money."

"But you love the wheeling and dealing. Admit it."

"I do not love the wheeling and dealing. I started out to be a veterinarian, not an administrator."

"Opening this practice was your idea, Rick, yours and Margot's. Her father's money got us started, her father's business manager has kept us honest, and if it weren't for you the rest of us wouldn't have as much time to do our jobs. We're grateful to you."

Rick grumbled, but he looked happier. He thrived on praise, needed it the way some people needed caffeine. He didn't often get it from his colleagues, Mac thought. He'd have to speak to Liz and Sarah and Eleanor. See if they could make Rick feel appreciated.

And since when, he asked himself, did Mac Thorn care whether anybody felt appreciated? He must be going soft.

As Rick left, Nancy came in. Rick said in passing, "Watch it, he's grumpier than usual."

"Not with me, he's not," Nancy said. "Morning, Doctor, ready for your morning session of cut and paste?"

Upstairs in her bedroom, Kit switched on her computer phone and put through a call to Vince Calandruccio. When she was told he was unavailable, she left a message for him to call her at home that evening. She gave the heavy punching bag a smack and ran down the stairs with Kev at her heels.

She was already in her car with the ignition on and Kev on his seat beside her when Jimmy's Mustang screeched to a stop behind her. Jimmy jumped out and started toward her.

"Jimmy, I'm late for work."

"What do you think you're doing embarrassing me that way?" he said. "Look at me! Read my lips."

"I have no idea what you're talking about."

"Get out of the car, Kit, and come inside. I don't intend to discuss your behavior out here where everybody can see us." He turned his back on her, then spun around. "No, make that everybody *else.* The ones who don't already know what you've been up to."

She knew she should stay in the car, lock the doors, back out over the lawn if necessary and go to work. "Nuts," she whispered, and climbed out. "We'll talk here, Jimmy. Out in the open. Now, what are you yelling about?"

"I've had half a dozen phone calls already telling me my wife was practically screwing some guy in public over breakfast this morning."

"Your wife? Your *wife?* I am not your wife. It was one kiss, and even if I'd been rolling around naked on the linoleum, it wouldn't be any of your business."

"What kind of an example are you setting for my daughter?"

"Don't you dare speak to me of examples, Jimmy Lockhart. I pay my bills — and yours, too, half the time. I spend my nights at home looking after my daughter, not playing poker or getting drunk in some cop bar. I keep my promises to Emma. I don't dump her for a stupid duck hunt!"

Jimmy had never lifted a finger against her, but for a moment Kit thought he might slap her. She almost wished he would. She'd haul his butt off to jail so fast . . .

No. Emma would be devastated.

She'd be devastated to hear her parents snarling at each other like a pair of wolverines, too. Kit took a deep breath. "I'm sorry people called you, Jimmy. I knew when I saw those two squad cars that you'd hear about it. I just didn't expect it to be so quick."

"So you admit you embarrassed me."

"I didn't do a thing to *you.* Stop thinking of me as your property. Stop thinking that I owe you fidelity, or that if I date another man or even sleep with another man I am committing adultery. I am not. I will not do anything that will upset Emma. You might consider making the same resolution."

His eyes narrowed. "Ever think what it's like for Emma to live in the house with a handicapped woman? How maybe you can't really take care of her the way you should? Ever think what a judge would say if I went back to court and asked for custody?"

Kit froze. She tried to control her breathing. She must not show Jimmy that he frightened her. "You don't want custody, Jimmy. You never wanted it. You don't take her the times you're supposed to now."

"Yeah, but my mother could."

"What?"

"She'd love to move in with me. She's a great cook, keeps a neat house. Sews, quilts. Cans her own vegetables. We could buy a house with a big yard. A dog that belonged to Emma, not like that mutt of yours. Momma doesn't work. She'd be home every day. When was the last time you baked a cookie? Emma would have a stable environment with a full-time caregiver. One who could hear."

Kit fought the urge to vomit. It was a bluff. He was angry and so he said the most hurtful thing he could think of.

"Don't even think of using Emma to punish me," she said. "I've tried to keep things amicable between us for her sake, and I haven't ever said a word against you to her. But I warn you, if you ever try to take Emma away from me, I'll destroy you. And you know I can do it."

She saw his eyes widen and realized the quiet fury in her voice must have gotten through to him, even if she couldn't hear the tenor of her words herself.

He backed up a step. "I don't want to hurt Emma, either." His face looked a little gray. "But you just watch your step, you hear me? I don't like being laughed at."

He jumped into his car and roared away.

Kit leaned against the side of the Jeep while she tried to get her breathing under control. Surely he couldn't take Emma. He wouldn't even try. She knew where the idea had originated. Mrs. Lockhart was strong-willed enough and angry enough at Kit to encourage Jimmy. A custody fight would be devastating to Emma. Kit felt nearly certain she'd win, but the battle would get nasty.

She opened her car door and crawled in behind the steering wheel. She didn't want to go to work. She wanted to cry on her father's shoulder.

But, as much as she hated to do it, she had to warn Mac about Jimmy — and the local cops. Jimmy's buddies and hers. She probably had more friends on the job than Jimmy did, all of whom would butt in to protect her. Add to them her mother's pals, men and women who had known Kit all her life and considered themselves her uncles and aunts.

Kit prayed Mac had never had so much as a parking ticket, because she suspected somebody at the main precinct was already running his name through the national crime database.

CHAPTER ELEVEN

When Kit read Vince's name on her phone that evening, she almost didn't answer it. But it would do no good to avoid the issue, and Vince was a good friend.

"Hey, babe," she read. "Guess I know now why you weren't that interested in going to the movies with me."

"Please, Vince, not you, too. Is there anybody in the department who isn't snickering?"

"A few, but they're mostly detectives. You know they're always out of the loop."

"Ha, ha. Very funny. Jimmy is furious. He came flying over like a husband who just caught his wife cheating on him. How come it's all right for him to do whatever he wants, but I share one simple breakfast with a man and it's the end of the world?"

"More than a simple breakfast the way I heard it."

"Okay. One kiss. An overenthusiastic boss

celebrating a successful surgery. Nothing else."

"Tell me another one."

"Do me a favor and pass that story along. Do you know that some Memphis patrol car stopped him for a seat-belt check?" Kit heard her voice rise.

"Did he get the badge number?"

"Of course not. Then a Germantown patrol car followed him all the way to the parking lot of the clinic. Were you all expecting him to stop off along the way and commit an ax murder?"

"Leave me out of it, babe."

"You know it's against the law to check a name on the national crime computer for nonofficial purposes."

"Who told you somebody did that?"

"I knew it! I've a good mind to call the chief and tell him my boss is being stalked."

"Don't you want to know what we found?"

"No, I do not." She waited a second. "Nothing, right?"

"Wrong. The good doctor has a juvie record."

"Juvie records are sealed." Her heart had begun to beat faster. What had she gotten Mac Thorn into? She couldn't believe he was anything but a solid citizen.

"Yes, sweet pea, ordinarily they are sealed,

but at fourteen he got himself sent to a reform school in Montana. That's a matter of permanent record. It doesn't go away when you reach eighteen. It would seem he got drunk, stole his daddy's new BMW, and drove it into a light pole."

"I don't believe you."

"Have I ever lied to you?"

"I'll bet there isn't so much as a parking ticket since," Kit said, hoping it was true.

"There you got me."

"So you're telling me that because he *borrowed* his father's car at age fourteen, he's a criminal? Get real."

"Hey, I'm just telling you. He's my hero, remember. I love the guy. He saved Adam's life. But I'm not a woman with a daughter to protect."

"Vince . . ."

"Bye."

She hung up the headset on her telephone so hard it bounced off the cradle and hit Kev on the head. "I'm sorry, boy. Come on, let's tuck Emma in."

Emma, however, had tucked herself in and was fast asleep. Kit wondered why she'd gone to sleep that early. When she checked her messages after talking to Vince, she found one from Emma's teacher.

"What now?" She dialed the number.

She explained to Mrs. Hicks the system by which she used the telephone, then asked, "Is anything the matter with Emma's schoolwork? I've been checking her papers and . . ."

"No, no. Emma's grades are fine, although they've slipped a little since first semester."

There was a long pause during which the cursor bounced rhythmically on the screen.

"Mrs. Hicks?"

"Yes, yes, Mrs. Lockhart. I'm sorry. I was trying to decide how best to put this."

Emma had done something wrong, or was doing something wrong. Surely to God it couldn't be drugs. Not Emma. She knew ten wasn't too young to start where there were gangs, but Emma's small school . . .

"Emma turned in a very disturbing essay today, Mrs. Lockhart."

Kit expelled her breath. An essay. So she made an F.

"I would like to speak to you in person tomorrow after school if possible. I think you need to read what Emma wrote. Normally, I wouldn't share a student's work that way, but . . ."

"What time? I'd have to arrange for my father to pick up Emma. I don't imagine you want her there."

"No, no, I don't. Leave word at the school

office tomorrow if you can come. Say, four-thirty?"

Kit gulped. "Four-thirty. I'll be there."

"Good. And don't worry too much, Mrs. Lockhart. It's nothing really bad, it's merely . . . worrisome."

Next Morning, Mac leaned against the hood of his Suburban and watched as Kit arrived at the zoo in her Jeep. He pushed off and sauntered over. "Good morning." He reached for her.

She ducked. "Don't you dare!" She looked around furtively.

He laughed. "Don't tell me there's an actual law against kissing in public."

"Only when it's me."

"Then let's break it together." This time she let him wrap his arms around her and pull her against his chest. He had planned to give her a simple good-morning kiss — kind of a joke to break the tension between them.

But she felt so good in his arms that their kiss quickly became more than just an easy greeting or joke. He pulled back first. "Kit, I . . ." His voice sounded hoarse. He was glad she couldn't hear the passion in it.

"Morning, people. Having a good time?"

Kit saw the change in his expression. She

looked over his shoulder and saw Brian Neely. Instantly she moved away. "Morning, Mr. Neely."

"Call me Brian, please, Kit. Well, how about we get started. Don't want to keep y'all from whatever it was you were doing."

Mac heard his snicker. Thank God Kit couldn't.

The camel was back to walking soundly on all four legs without treatment.

Chester, the meerkat, perched on a rock at the very top of his enclosure. No signs of blood.

"We're due to have a Grant's zebra foal in a week or so," Brian said. "Might ask your large-animal vet to check the mother to see if she's started to bag up with milk. We'll bring her in tonight in case she foals early."

The rest of the animals seemed to be in perfect shape.

As Mac was saying goodbye to Brian, Kit's Jeep burned rubber out of the parking lot.

"Nice girl," Brian said. "Pity she can't hear. Most animals compensate for their problems, though. She's doing well with hers." As Mac closed the door of his Suburban, Neely held up a hand. "Almost forgot to tell you. Mrs. Harlow, the docent, is due in this afternoon. If you think she's ready to leave the clinic, Mrs. Harlow can pick up the orang tomorrow morning, take some time to talk about her with your people. Of course, she'll be bringing her into the clinic a couple of times a week to be checked, but at least you won't have to look after the baby around the clock."

"We'll be sorry to see the princess leave."

"Princess, huh? Good name. We'll keep calling her that for now until we have the contest to give her a permanent name. You can always visit her. Tell your people they're welcome here anytime."

Being able to visit the baby was not at all the same as raising her yourself. Big would be every bit as sad as Kit.

"At least I won't have to work all weekend," Kit said. She stroked the baby's head. "I was going to have to park Emma with my parents. Now that there's supposed to be a break in this gosh-awful weather, maybe we can go to the park." She hunched in the chair across from Mac's desk. He'd hated telling her the princess would be leaving even earlier than planned.

"Brian said Mrs. Harlow will come by to pick up the baby tomorrow morning. Think your parents can keep Emma until noon?"

"They were expecting her to be there the whole weekend." Kit stroked the baby's back. Her small hands stroked Kit's cheek in return.

Mac felt near as miserable as Kit did.

"Look, I've got an idea. Eleanor has a client with a big cattle ranch. Since the weather is supposed to be warmer than normal and sunny, how would you feel about taking Emma on a picnic and letting her ride a horse?"

"Are you serious?"

"J. K. Sanders won't mind. I could put Emma up in front of me and show her what riding a horse feels like."

"I couldn't ask you to give up your Saturday afternoon."

"What would I be giving up? Solitary football on television?"

"Then yes, we'd love to. I'll bring the picnic."

"You'll be here with Mrs. Harlow all morning. *I'll* bring the picnic. It won't be fancy, but it should be filling."

"I can't wait to tell Emma. She'll be thrilled."

What had he gotten himself into? Emma was a pleasant child to have around for a short time, but he'd only seen her on her best behavior. Now he planned to spend an entire afternoon with her and Kit. And since she wouldn't be going to her grandparents'

261

to spend Saturday night, maybe the whole evening as well. Just what did he think he was doing?

"Mrs. Hicks? I hope I'm not late." Kit could feel her pulse racing. The chalk smells, the odor of child sweat permeated Emma's classroom.

Mrs. Hicks turned from cleaning the blackboard with a smile. Kit had met her at parents' night and at the fall teacher conference, but didn't feel she knew her. She was an apple of a woman with iron-gray hair and a bright smile — the sort of teacher that any child would like. Kit had liked her at once. Now she loomed like a dragon.

"Please, Mrs. Lockhart, have a seat. I managed to scrounge a full-size chair so you won't have to squeeze in."

Kit sat with her knees carefully together and wished she'd had time to change out of jeans. She glanced around the walls at the maps and posters.

"Here, Mrs. Lockhart. I'll let you read this first, then we can discuss it. We're working on anger management. The way things have been going, the school system as a whole decided to devote time in every grade to teaching kids how to handle anger. Each essay was to start with 'I get angry when' and

262

then suggest ways to manage the anger better."

"As a former cop, I think that's a great idea." Kit looked down at the lined notebook paper. Emma was proud of her handwriting, so there was no chance for Kit to misunderstand the words.

I get angry when nobody listens. My mother reads lips real well, but sometimes she turns her head and I yell and she doesn't hear.

Kit felt the hair on the back of her neck stand up.

My daddy can hear fine, but he talks to his girlfriends or watches television and sometimes he doesn't even know I'm there. He thinks I'm supposed to like what he likes and not what I want.

I told Meemomma not to say bad stuff about my mom, but she called me snippy. Meemomma says my mom and dad didn't want to have me. Maybe if they didn't have me they'd still be married.

I never know who's going to pick me up at school or where I'm going to go for the weekend. Half the time I look for my mom and see my granddaddy's car. My daddy says he'll pick me up, then he doesn't. Or he shows up sometimes when I want to go to Jessica's.

I try to look after my mom, but she doesn't really need me. Nobody does.

I play Frisbee with my mom's dog Kev. Sometimes I feel like that Frisbee. I try not to mind. I know my mom's trying to do the best she can, but sometimes I feel like they'd all be happy if I wasn't there.

By the time she finished reading the essay, Kit was shaking. She handed the paper back to Mrs. Hicks. "I don't know what to say. I didn't know . . ."

"I know you didn't. That's why I called you. I spoke to your husband at parents' night, remember?"

"He's my ex-husband."

"Of course. I'm sorry. I thought if I showed him this he'd get defensive."

You bet he would, Kit thought.

"Mostly Emma's the same happy, hard-working child she's always been. But I think your divorce and your accident coming so close together have been tougher on her than you realize."

"So what do I do? Take her to a shrink?"

"No, I think you need to sit down and talk

to Emma. When anything happens to a family or a parent, the child always feels as though she's somehow responsible."

"Emma in no way caused my divorce or my accident."

"Did you ever tell her that?"

Kit sighed. "Not in those words. I tried to show her —"

"Remember show-and-tell? The showing part isn't worth much without the telling part. Children need words. She already doesn't believe her grandmother . . ."

"I will kill that old woman."

Mrs. Hicks grinned at her. "Anger management?"

Kit smiled sheepishly. "Okay. I'll tell Jimmy that Emma shouldn't be left alone with his mother for any reason. Until she shapes up."

"Better."

"And he and I had better come to an understanding. Barring real emergencies, we don't change Emma's schedule. Maybe I should give up my job."

"No. You have a life, too. You have to make a living. Emma understands that."

"And I need to listen to Emma more."

"Hug more. If you start staring at her every time she opens her mouth, she'll think you're nuts."

"Will you keep me up-to-date? Let me know if you get any more of these things?"

"Absolutely. All children go through rough periods, Mrs. Lockhart, just like all adults. Healthy children — and Emma is basically healthy — get through them. With your help she'll get through this one quickly." She stood. "Now, I've got to pick up *my* son at soccer practice."

Kit didn't know whether to speak to Emma at her parents' house or to take her home. She finally decided home was best even though it gave Emma an escape route — she could slam the door to her room.

The minute they got home, Emma started up the stairs. Kit called her back.

"What?"

"Come on into the kitchen. I'll fix you a soda. We need to talk."

"A soda? This soon before dinner? I must really be in trouble."

Kit couldn't hear the sarcasm, but she knew it was there. She couldn't hear the fear, either, but Emma had to be at least a little worried at the gravity in her mother's tone.

At the kitchen table, Emma took a few tentative swallows of her soda with her eyes just above the rim of the glass and fixed on her mother.

"Did Mrs. Lockhart tell you Jimmy and I never wanted you?"

Emma slammed down the glass and got up. "That's it."

Kit grabbed her arm. "Sit. If you run away, I'll follow. Answer me."

Emma threw back her head. "So, all right. Yeah. You trying to say she was wrong?"

"Not exactly. We *didn't* want a baby."

Emma's eyes widened. This was not what she'd expected to hear, obviously.

"We were very young, very poor, working long hours at dangerous jobs, and we were already having problems keeping our marriage together. The last thing we wanted was a baby."

Emma's chest had started to heave. "Then why'd you go ahead and have me?"

"We didn't want a baby because we were scared we wouldn't be able to feed and clothe it, or that we'd screw up its mind. I guess all parents feel that, too. You'll probably feel the same way."

"I'm not having any babies."

"You may change your mind. The thing is, Emma, we didn't want *a* baby. For about a week after I found out I was pregnant, we worried ourselves sick. And then I had my first ultrasound. Jimmy was right there holding my hand. Suddenly you weren't *a* baby, you were Emma, our daughter-to-be — a whole new person that had never been in the world before."

"Bet you wanted a boy."

"I wanted *Emma.* So did Jimmy. So did my parents and his mother. We talked about nothing but Emma, Emma, Emma for six months while I started looking more and more like a hippopotamus. I wanted Emma when my ankles swelled and I couldn't sleep on my side and I had to go to the bathroom every ten minutes. When the contractions started I could hardly wait for Emma. It was like Christmas and birthdays all rolled into one. The best present any of us ever got."

"Yeah. Then I started to grow up."

"Listen, sweetheart, you were Emma and nobody else the minute you came out and you've been Emma ever since. There are times when you pull those tantrums I could cheerfully throttle you, just like I'm sure there are times when you could cheerfully throttle me. But you're my Emma. I loved you then, I love you now and I'll love you when we're both old and crotchety. And Jimmy loves you, too. So do your gran and granddaddy. In her own way, so does Mrs. Lockhart — she wouldn't be so angry at *me* if she didn't love you."

"Maybe if it wasn't for me, Daddy would have stuck around."

"Jimmy and I didn't get a divorce over you. We got it over *us*. And just in case you've got some crazy idea about my accident, you can forget that, too. You were wonderful when I was in the hospital. I'm sorry I embarrass you now —"

Big tears had begun to roll down Emma's face. "It's okay, Mommy."

Kit realized there were tears on her own cheeks as well.

Emma slid off her chair, climbed into her mother's lap and stroked her cheek. "It's okay, Mommy."

They clung together and wept together, trying to wash away the insecurities and the misunderstandings.

Kit knew they'd resurface again and again, and next time Emma might be too big to crawl into her lap. But maybe — at least for tonight — they could both sleep in peace.

CHAPTER TWELVE

Kit expected to spend hours talking to Mrs. Harlow on Saturday morning when she came to pick up the princess. Kit and Big waited for the woman with the baby snuggled in Kit's arms. They were like adoptive parents facing a birth mother who wants her baby back.

"That poor woman," Alva Jean said when she came into the conference room to tell the pair of them that Mrs. Harlow had arrived. "I sure wouldn't want to face the two of you when I've got jet lag. Big, I can't tell whether you're mad or about to cry."

"Both," Kit answered. "At least I am. What does she look like, Alva Jean? Is she nice? If she's some tough old harridan, I swear Big and I will run away to Brazil with the princess."

"Judge for yourself. I'll send her on back."

"We can't run away, Miss Kit," Big said. "Wouldn't be right."

"I know. I didn't really mean it. Have we got everything together so we can load it for her? How's she going to get the baby home alone?"

The conference room door opened. "Hello. I'm Imogene Harlow. You must be Big and Kit." She came forward with a broad smile on her face. "And this must be the princess." She started to reach out to her, then glanced up at Kit and stopped. "If I were you, I'd probably shoot me about now."

"Oh, no, ma'am," Big said.

"I considered it seriously," Kit said. "Maybe now that I've seen you, I won't have to."

"Let's sit down, shall we? My, she does hold on to you, doesn't she? Poor baby, it's not going to be easy for her the first couple of days, but we'll be all right, won't we, sweetie pie?"

The baby blew half a cup of regurgitated formula straight into Mrs. Harlow's face.

Now, we'll see, Kit thought.

Mrs. Harlow burst out laughing, pulled out a linen handkerchief bordered with homemade lace and wiped her face. "Oho, you've learned that one already, have you?" She turned to Kit. "She's not my first baby. I raised a dwarf anteater last year. He's

another one that likes to spend all day cling-
ing to his mother. Unfortunately, she re-
jected him. A lot of zoo animals do."

"We hate to give her up."

"I fully understand. Brian told me you
were hearing impaired, and I see that you
have a helper dog. It must take a saint to
raise a dog for a year, then give him up to
be trained for somebody else's use."

"I get your point. I knew we were going to
have to let her go. I just thought we'd have
another week."

"Trust me, my dears, it's much easier this
way in the long run." She reached out her
arms. "May I hold her?"

The baby ducked her head under Kit's
chin. Mrs. Harlow slid out of her chair onto
her knees and began to speak to the baby.
Kit assumed she was whispering. After a
good five minutes, the baby turned to her,
and when Mrs. Harlow held out her arms,
went to her.

"That's a good girl," Mrs. Harlow said,
rising to her feet with the ease of a much
younger woman. "Now, if you'll help me
carry her things to the car and give me a
hand strapping her in her child seat, I'll get
out of your way."

The baby wasn't thrilled to be riding
backward in the rear seat of a car all by

herself strapped into a baby seat, but Kit knew it was the safest way to transport her.

"Now," Mrs. Harlow said, "Brian has my address and telephone number. You both are welcome to come visit anytime you like. I'm not going anywhere for the next few months."

"Mrs. Harlow, how does your husband feel about what you do?"

"He's used to it. He did get a little upset when the cheetah kit chewed up his favorite loafers, but he knows better than to try to stop me. I love being a docent. I don't get to raise many babies, you know. Most of the time I take tours of schoolchildren around the zoo or visit schools with some of the tamer animals." She glanced at the backseat.

Kit saw that the princess was wriggling in her seat.

"Better get her settled before her next feeding. Thank you both so much for what you've done for her. Try not to cry, either of you. Now, we're off." She climbed into her green Jaguar with its cream leather upholstery and drove off with a wave.

"She's gonna be fine. That Mrs. Harlow's a nice lady," Big observed.

"She is. And now I am going to cry."

"Me, too," said Big.

"Can you really ride a horse?" Emma asked.

Kit began to pack the remaining fried chicken and chocolate cake in the fancy picnic basket Mac had brought. It looked very new and very expensive. "Mac's lived in Montana," she said, and nearly bit her tongue.

When she glanced up at Mac in apprehension, he didn't seem to have noticed her gaffe. No way was she supposed to know he'd lived in Montana.

"Not only can I ride a horse, I'm good at it," he said.

"Prove it!"

"Fine. I'll show *you,* young lady, I am not just a pretty face."

Emma giggled. "You're not pretty, either."

"You are speaking to the man who just fed you lunch. No insults, please."

"Can I ride?"

"That's what we're here for. First I'll give you a demonstration of my prowess as a horseman, then I'll haul you up in front of me and gallop off into the horizon with you. How about that?"

"Wicked."

A Mexican ranch hand brought a fat sorrel quarter horse out of the stable. He handed Emma a white helmet, then stepped back. The horse was saddled and bridled. Mac took the reins and prayed that after all these years he would not make a complete idiot of himself in front of Emma and Kit.

"This is a good horse," the man said. "Turn fast. Watch out."

Mac nodded his thanks, picked up the reins in his right hand, settled himself in the saddle and walked off toward the fenced arena. "Got a calf I can work?" he asked over his shoulder.

"*Sí, señor.*"

Now he *was* showing off. He hadn't cut a calf in years. He hoped it was like riding a bicycle.

It was. When the calf ran out of the chute, Mac's horse hunkered down and began to keep the animal from running past him to the end of the arena.

Mac whooped. He'd forgotten how much fun this was. He and the sorrel pushed the calf back into the round pen behind the arena. Then he loped easily over to the rail where Kit and Emma stood. He knew he was grinning like a lunatic.

"Wow!" Emma said. "That was so cool."

"Put on your hard hat and climb aboard. I won't let you fall, but just in case, it will protect that pretty head of yours."

"Mac," Kit said, "are you sure?"

"Very sure. I won't try any funny stuff with Emma. I'll hold on to her. Climb up on the rail, Emma. I'll pull you aboard from there."

He avoided Kit's worried eyes, wrapped an arm around Emma's waist and pulled her into the saddle in front of him. She was small enough so that he didn't feel too cramped. He walked around the arena, then moved into a jog trot, and then into a slow, easy lope. Emma held on tight to the saddle horn.

He knew she was scared. He also knew she was loving every minute of it.

After about ten minutes in the arena, he asked the ranch hand to open the gate into the pasture.

"Watch out for mud, *señor. Mucho* rain lately."

"Will do."

"Mac, don't you think that's enough?" Kit called.

"No, Mom, no!"

"We'll be back," Mac called.

The sorrel moved off in an easy lope. When they came to an area that looked well drained, Mac let the horse open up into a gallop. Emma yelled, but with pleasure.

He pulled back down to a walk and let her take the reins for the walk home.

When he let Emma down into Kit's arms, she cried, "Can I have a horse, Mom?"

"We can't afford a horse. You know that."

"Then lessons, Mom. I'll bet Gran and Granddaddy would pay for them."

"I'm not going to ask them."

"M-o-o-o-mmm."

It was the first time Mac had heard Emma whine.

He realized with a jolt that she must be exhausted. Did kids her age take naps?

"Let's go, Em," he said. "We'll come back again, I promise."

"Everybody promises stuff," she said under her breath. "Nobody delivers."

One of the few problems about Kit's hearing impairment was that Mac and Kit couldn't talk when they were riding in a car. So the ride home was silent. From time to time he smiled at her, but a few smiles were a long way from a conversation.

When they reached Kit's house, he turned to Kit and whispered, "Do you want me to carry her in for you?"

Kit smiled and shook her head. "If I let her sleep any longer, she'll never go to bed tonight." She leaned over the backseat and touched Emma's shoulder. Kevlar took his cue and licked Emma's face.

"Yuck!" Emma groaned sleepily. She sat up, rubbed her eyes, stretched and yawned. "Are we home?"

"Sure are."

Emma climbed out of the Suburban slowly, dragged herself up the stairs to the front door and leaned against it.

Kit took her by the shoulders and gently moved her away from the keyhole, then opened the door and slid Emma into the house, and watched her daughter slowly climb the stairs.

"Combination of chilly weather and adrenaline, I suspect," Kit whispered. "I can't thank you enough. Did you mean it about taking her riding again?"

"Absolutely." He considered telling Kit that *he* would teach Emma to ride, then he thought better of it. This wasn't the time. "I had a wonderful time, too. I like Emma. She's very adult."

"Oh, no, she's not! She's a preteen, and pretty soon she's going to be a teen. I'm already dreading it."

"She's levelheaded."

"Were you surrounded by booze and Rohypnol and Ecstasy and gangs and kids with their own SUVs at sixteen?" She gulped, and her eyes widened.

Suddenly he remembered her remark about Montana. "How did you find out I lived in Montana?"

"I . . . don't know what you mean."

"Look, I'm not going to stand here like this and discuss my wild youth. Who checked me out? Vince or your mother?"

"My *mother?*"

"Ex-cop, ex-captain of cops, private detective. Don't tell me she doesn't have all the resources to check out any man her daughter is dating."

"Who says we're dating? Who says my mother even knows you exist?"

"So which one of your blue protectors? Or was it Jimmy making certain I'm not some kind of child predator?"

"You might as well come on in. It's starting to rain again anyway. Would you like a coffee? Soda?"

"I could use a glass of water. Straight from the tap, please, no ice. My mouth is dry."

"Mine, too."

He glanced toward the ceiling.

"If you're worried that Emma will come down, don't be. She's either asleep or on the telephone to Jessica, her best girlfriend at the moment, telling her all about the picnic and the riding. She'll talk for hours if

279

I don't stop her."

"Actually, I was thinking that the music might be a bit loud."

Kit went into the front hall. "Emma! Turn that mess down. And don't stay on the telephone too long."

She turned to Mac. "Well? Did she do it?"

He listened for a moment, then nodded. Kit handed him his glass of water, poured herself one. They stood on either side of the kitchen counter swallowing as though they'd been stranded in the desert for months.

"You want to talk here or in the living room?" Mac asked.

"You don't have to do this."

"Of course I do. I'd rather you heard my side of the story instead of the versions you've been handed already. Are your cop friends this protective of everyone?"

"Unfortunately for me, I *am* special. First female T.A.C.T. squad member, first to be permanently disabled on the job. Then there's my mother. And Jimmy. And Vince. It just goes on and on. Normally, I'd be grateful. If you were a child predator or an abuser you wouldn't have a chance to get close to either Emma or me. But I didn't ask them to check you out. It may be nice to be protected from the hyenas by a pride of lions, but you're never quite sure when you'll turn into dinner for the lions."

"Remind me never to kiss you in public again." Mac followed her into the living room. She quickly took the wing chair on the far side of the fireplace. He was left with the sofa.

"All right, if you're going to tell me, then tell me," Kit said.

"First you have to know about my family." He held up his hands. "I know, I know — every crook blames his crimes on his terrible parents. Mine aren't terrible, they simply didn't understand me."

Kit started to laugh.

"God, that sounds even worse, doesn't it?" Mac grinned sheepishly. "On paper it sounds as though I had the perfect upbringing. My father is a thoracic surgeon with an international reputation and the money that comes along with it. My mother is beautiful, charming, and works unceasingly on charity committees. My younger sister, Joanna, was the kind of child who goes to a birthday party looking neat and comes home with the ribbon in her hair still tied."

"What about you?"

"According to my mother, I was born wild. My parents still live in the suburban mansion I grew up in. Plenty of land to roam. I started bringing squirrels and snakes home with me as soon as I could catch them."

"So you always wanted to be a veterinarian?"

"Certainly not. I planned to be a trust-fund bum. Skiing in Switzerland in the winter, surfing on Maui in the summer. Maybe a little apartment in New York. Nothing fancy, just a place to stay while I went to Broadway plays."

"Nice life if you can get it."

"Looking back, it sounds like an awful life. But it was as far from the life my father planned for me as possible. From the day I was born he started grooming me to be the third generation of Thorn surgeons. My grandfather was a general surgeon."

"You didn't want that?"

"Maybe if he hadn't pushed so hard I might have gone along with him. The man had me sewing up cuts in bicycle inner tubes when I was eight years old! If I even tried to talk about becoming a banker or a lawyer or a teacher, he would shut me down before I got two sentences out. I was to be a Boston surgeon in practice with my father. Period, end of discussion."

"So you rebelled."

"Of course I rebelled. Meanwhile, Joanna was dying to become my father's third-generation surgeon, but because she was a female and wouldn't be able to carry the Thorn name if she married, he brushed her off."

"She could keep her own name."

"Not the same in my father's book. Besides, her sons would be called after their father. Not acceptable."

"Where was your mother when all this was happening?"

"My mother tied my father's shoelaces every morning."

"Excuse me?" Kit said. "I must have read that wrong."

"Shoelaces. To protect his precious surgeon's hands. They lived completely separate lives, but when Dad did come home, he was the sun in the center of his very own galaxy."

"Sorry? I didn't get all that."

Mac repeated himself slowly. Kit nodded.

"I never once heard her raise her voice to him, not for herself, and definitely not for me or Joanna."

"He sounds like a monster."

"No. He's merely a genius with a scalpel. And a very hard act to follow."

"So you didn't try?"

"I began drinking when I was Emma's age."

Kit started. "Ten? You started drinking at ten?"

"After school. The liquor cabinet was never locked and always full. Joanna knew, I think, but didn't tell anybody. Even when my father discovered his twenty-five-year-old brandy was largely tea, he thought one of the servants had done it."

"You let him think that?"

"He didn't fire anybody over it. But he started locking the liquor cabinet. Lousy lock. Took me maybe five minutes to pick it."

"This doesn't sound one bit like you. What changed you?"

"Two days after my fourteenth birthday I downed a bottle of scotch, called a couple of my friends and stole my father's new car to joyride. I hit a light pole and wound up in jail. My father refused to bail me out until my mother had hysterics. Not because her baby boy was locked up with a bunch of very scary people, but because it might make the local papers and embarrass her.

"He did bring his lawyer down when I was arraigned. The judge, who had a low tolerance for bratty rich kids, sentenced me to six months of juvenile detention and a hefty fine. It's the only time I've ever seen my mother faint. I almost joined her. This was not supposed to happen. I was supposed to be as big a jerk as I liked without having to pay any consequences. It wasn't fair."

"Boy, have I heard that tune before," Kit said.

"Dad's lawyer talked to the judge, and somehow got him to agree to send me to Jake Galbreath's ranch in Montana for the following two summers. It was a boot camp for juvenile offenders. Fifty miles from the nearest bar or liquor store or grocery.

"I was determined to run away as soon as I got there — just get off the plane and disappear. No such luck. Jake plucked me off that plane and locked me in his pickup. Before I knew it, I was looking at a lumpy bunk in a shack with a tin roof and an outside latrine."

"How many boys did he take at a time?"

"Anywhere from five to twenty. That summer there were fifteen of us." Mac shook his head and grinned at the memory. "I was already near six foot four, but skinny. I was a fourteen-year-old terror. I figured I could outfox some old cattle farmer and get out of there in a week."

"I take it the old cattle farmer was a lot smarter and tougher than you thought."

"And then some. I thought I was *bad*. I didn't *know* bad. The only other suburban kid that summer was an apprentice wise guy from New Jersey. The others were Latinos from L.A. and gang members from Chicago and Philadelphia. Some of them already had prison tattoos. After five minutes in the bunkhouse with them I was scared to death. Jake kept the mayhem to a minimum. He didn't actually have guards, but he had enough big, tough ranch hands to head off any trouble. At least two of them were with us every minute of the day and night.

"The first morning the gang bandannas disappeared. By lunch we'd been introduced to the finer points of breaking cow ponies. Trust a horse to lower your self-esteem radically. I knew how to ride, of course, that being one of the sports my mother considered appropriate for a gentleman, but I'd never ridden like *that.* I had an easier time of it than some of the city kids.

"We were too stiff and sore and tired to fight. Reveille was at five-thirty in the morning, and by six-thirty we were back at the corral with those hardheaded mustangs. I considered sneaking down to the barn, stealing a horse and riding off in any direction at all just to get away from the place, but decided against it after Jake warned us about the rattlesnakes and the scarcity of water holes.

"By the end of the second week, Jake had us learning to work cows from the saddle. I think I'd probably put on fifteen pounds — all muscle. I was still considered a rich wimp, and I took some punishment when the ranch hands looked the other way. I was still the outsider.

"Until one day when we were out learning to cut cows. One of the horses tripped over loose barbed wire that some idiot had left lying out in the pasture. By the time we got him up, he had a ten-inch gash on his shoulder that was so deep you could see the muscle underneath.

"The nearest vet was four hours away. The kid who had been taking care of the horse was really upset. He was afraid Jake would shoot the animal.

"For the first time in my life, my father's sewing lessons paid off. While Jake called the vet on his cell phone, I got the medical kit out of the supply wagon, and cleaned that wound and stitched up that cut like a pro. That's when they decided I might not be such a jerk after all. From that moment on I was 'Doc.' I had never had a nickname before. I gloried in it.

"When the vet showed up, he checked the wound, gave the horse a shot of antibiotics and told Jake I'd done a fine job. He asked if I might like to ride along with him one day. I sure did. I wasn't certain I'd keep my promise not to run away if we came within sight of a convenience store, but at least it would get me off the place for a few hours.

"Jake always said he knew right that minute he had me. He believed that once you find the thing a kid wants bad enough to behave in order to get it, you've got him. I knew if I broke the rules, I'd forfeit my rides with the vet. Jake became my real father that summer. I didn't want to leave. I don't think any of us did, even the Chicago hoods. I knew I'd be back the following summer for my other three months of detention, and I looked forward to it. When I got on that plane back to Boston, I knew I would be a vet."

"What did your father say when you told him?"

"I *didn't* tell him. He was thrilled at the rise in my grades. I took every science course my high school offered, and all the math. He thought I was preparing for med school. I let him think that. The next summer when I went back to Jake's, I was considered a sort of junior counselor. I knew I'd graduate a year early with all the extra work I was doing. My father wanted me to go to Harvard or Johns Hopkins for premed. I wanted to go to LSU or Auburn for prevet.

"Jake said I had to tell my father about my plans. When I did, Dad threatened to disown me, to cut me off without a cent. That was fine with me if only he wouldn't stop me from going. Fortunately, he couldn't do anything about the small trust fund my grandmother had left me. I got control of it the day I turned eighteen. It wasn't enough for Switzerland or Maui, but it was enough for the University of Wyoming if I worked part-time. When Jake agreed to front me my first year's tuition, I drove away from my house in a secondhand pickup truck and never expected to go home again."

"Surely you did."

"Yes, I did." He sighed. "My mother convinced my father that if I kept coming home, seeing life in Boston, living the good life, I'd give up the stupid notion of veterinary medicine in the Wild West. Marrying me off to a Boston debutante would forge the final link in the chain to medical school."

"Say again."

Mac repeated himself. Kit nodded. "Sometimes your sentences get a little complicated."

"Sorry. I'll try to stick to simple stuff."

"Just keep going. I'll stop you if I need to."

"Every time I went home for Christmas or to see my family between the end of the spring semester and the start of summer school, my mother arranged dates with every beautiful, brainy girl who was used to having an unlimited Visa or MasterCard. I had ski dates, golf dates, tennis dates, sailing dates, dinner parties, beach parties . . . Took me a little while to catch on. Who doesn't like to date beautiful women?"

"But you never fell for any of them?"

"Only my mother would dream such a crazy scheme might work. Once the young ladies found out that all I had to offer was a studio apartment in Alabama and three years of vet school followed by a lifetime of dog and cat surgery, they wrote me off the eligible list fast."

"So you went off to Alabama on your own."

"Rick Hazard and I roomed together for a while. Jake ended up paying most of my expenses at vet school. I planned to go back to Montana when I qualified, but my last semester Jake died suddenly of a massive stroke."

Mac looked away so that Kit wouldn't realize his eyes were tearing up even after all these years. "He'd set up the ranch as a foundation and endowed it well. I'm still on the board of governors. He left me enough money so that I could set up in practice and eventually buy into Creature Comfort."

"He sounds like quite a guy."

"Yeah. I've kept up with some of the people I worked with at the ranch. Most of them have gone on to become solid citizens. A couple of them are working at the ranch now, doing for other kids what Jake did for them."

"Why would he start that kind of program in the first place? Seems odd for a Montana rancher."

"His son died of a drug overdose. He always said he was expiating some heavy sins —" He broke off, fighting down the lump in his throat.

Kit dropped onto her knees in front of him and caught his hands between hers. "Hey, it's okay."

"Sorry." He took a deep breath. "So now you know the story of my misspent youth. Think Vince would buy it?"

"Yes." She grimaced. "But Jimmy wouldn't." She squeezed his hands, released them and sat back on her heels. "Yesterday he came over here and we had a real sling-ing match. He even threatened to try for custody of Emma."

"For Pete's sake, why?"

"I'm hearing impaired. Plus, I work for a living."

"So does he."

"But his mother doesn't."

"Any judge would toss him out of court."

"That's what I keep telling myself. He doesn't really want custody anyway. He's embarrassed and jealous. It's fine for him to date, but I'm supposed to be alone for the rest of my life."

He leaned forward and touched her cheek gently. "That would be a terrible waste of a beautiful woman."

"Come on. Beautiful? Puh-leeze."

"Stop arguing and come here. I'll prove it to you." She stood up and joined him on the sofa. He touched her cheek gently and traced the line of her lips slowly.

He began to kiss her eyelids. Her eyes closed, her head lolled back into the palm of his hand.

"You can't see my lips or hear my voice," he whispered, and kissed her eyelids again. "I think of you every minute of every day." His lips trailed across her forehead and down her cheek to her ear.

She opened her eyes, those incredible soft emerald eyes. Her lips parted.

"Shh," he whispered. "Close your eyes."

She obeyed.

"I've heard you laugh and seen you cry. When you walk into a room I can't take my eyes off you. I walk the halls at the clinic hoping I'll run into you. I think up reasons to talk to you. I brought you with me to the zoo just to be with you."

"Mac?" she whispered. "Why are my eyes closed?" She opened them.

"The better to kiss you with." He touched her lips gently with his. She returned the kiss just as he heard the click of Kevlar's toenails on the stairs. He pushed Kit away from him.

"What?" Kit turned her head.

Emma stood at the foot of the stairs with one hand on the banister. Her face was expressionless. A moment later she turned, raced up the stairs and slammed her door.

CHAPTER THIRTEEN

Kit fell back on the sofa. "Oh, no."

"Kit, I'm sorry. I've done it again, haven't I?"

"You weren't in this alone." Kit's shoulders slumped. "I'll have to speak to her." She started to get up.

"Let me."

"No! Definitely not you. Not now."

"I kissed you, you kissed me back. It's not a crime."

"In Emma's book it may be."

"She must have realized there's something between us."

"Subconsciously, maybe. That's not the same thing as finding her mother in the arms of a man who is not her father."

"You're the one who keeps saying you're divorced."

Kit put her head in her hands. "You don't understand. I've been trying to convince Emma how important she is to me — to all of us. This just shows her she's — I don't know the word — peripheral."

He tilted her face so she could see his lips. "I know nothing about children. All I know is I like Emma, I enjoy her company. Watching her is fascinating."

"Fascinating? As in an interesting specimen?"

"Maybe that's not the right word."

"You used it. We had a great time today. You gave Emma the thing she's longed for all her life — a ride on a real horse. But this is not a rent-a-kid service so you can enjoy the fascination of seeing a family in action."

"That's not fair. And it's not accurate."

"You're a great teacher, Mac, and Emma is the perfect student because she's half in love with her professor. But underneath she's still scared and angry because I can't hear her and Jimmy and I are divorced. Most kids hope their parents will get back together, even if one of them is a homicidal maniac. Emma doesn't much care about Jimmy's bimbos of the week because she knows he's not serious about any of them. So long as I wasn't interested in anyone else, there was a chance we might be a family again."

"She likes me. We enjoy each other's

company. Why shouldn't we go on doing it?"

"You don't get it, do you? You've only seen the good side of Emma. See how you feel after you live through one of her moods. And what happens when you decide you've had enough and you move on to your next challenge? I can survive. But I don't want Emma hurt any more than she has been already."

He had kept the lid on his temper so far, but he could feel the heat rising in his face. "Why are you so all-fired certain I'll move on to what you call the next challenge?" Mac said.

"Because men *do!* Half the calls I used to work when I was riding a patrol car were domestics where a guy had moved in with a woman and her kids and was drinking and beating them. And then he disappears. Most men do not step up to the plate, Doctor. When the going gets rough, they walk away either physically or psychologically."

"Your father didn't."

"My father is the exception that proves the rule. He came home from Vietnam with two purple hearts, a silver star and a hunger for peace. But even he's no saint. He and my mother used to have some real screaming matches. Dad was always the one who threatened to leave, who said he'd known marrying a career woman was a mistake."

"He stayed."

"Sure. Because my mother, bless her, is the most secure female I have ever known. She *knew he loved her.* She trusted his love completely."

"And her love for him?"

"That, too."

"And you don't trust love."

"You bet I don't. My mother is extraordinary. I am not. If I had been, Jimmy wouldn't have needed the liquor and the bars and the other women."

"Your mother is extraordinary, all right. Not because she trusted your father's love, but because she was smart enough to pick a man who could give it to her. You weren't. You got what you expected to get all along."

"So it's my fault? Because I'm stupid?" Kit's green eyes snapped at him.

"Because you were naive. We all look at our parents and think that's what marriage is. I saw in my parents a woman whose husband neglected her, who demanded complete control of our lives, who was never wrong about anything, who never suffered because of his tirades and his temper tantrums and his rudeness, and I thought, 'I don't want to be like my father.' Then I looked at myself and I thought, 'My God, I *am* my father.' You looked at your parents, and you thought, 'No matter what she does he's there for her. That's the kind of husband I'll have.' You married Jimmy because you thought he was that kind of man."

"He was, or at least I thought he was until we got married."

"You saw what you wanted to see. So did he, probably."

"So you're telling me you're different?"

"I care about you and Emma."

"For how long?"

"You're just as likely to kick me out as I am to leave. I promise you this. I'll stick it out as long as you do."

"After what happened, it may be tough."

"Can we work it out, do you think?" Mac asked.

"I don't know. Now, please, go home. This is my problem."

Mac tried to speak to her as he left, but she'd turned her head away.

Kit climbed the stairs slowly, dreading her encounter with Emma. She had felt after their talk yesterday that maybe the air between them was a bit clearer. Now things were messed up again.

She knocked at Emma's door, then tried

the knob. It was locked. "Emma. Please open the door." Emma could be howling curses at her. So long as that door stayed closed, Kit had no way of knowing. She kicked the bottom of the door in frustration. "Emma Barclay Lockhart, you open this door right this minute or I swear I will break it down!" How was that for anger management? Mrs. Hicks would be proud.

The knob twisted, and the door opened only wide enough to accommodate the width of Emma's mouth. "Go away." She started to shut the door, but Kit knew how to block doors. She'd done it a million times in domestic disputes. This was certainly one of those. She stuck her shoe in the door. Emma banged it against her foot three or four times, then gave up. By the time Kit came into the room, her daughter was lying facedown on her bed with a pillow covering the back of her head.

"Please turn over, Emma. I can't read you if I can't see your face."

No movement.

"Please, Emma. We have to talk."

Emma sat up and whirled around. "Again? I thought we talked. How come you didn't tell me about you and Dr. Mac?"

"There is no me and Dr. Mac."

"Yeah. Right." Emma's eyes blazed with

jealousy and anger. "I thought he was *my* friend. I thought he liked *me*."

"He likes you very much."

"He's nice to me so he can be with you."

"He likes you for you. He likes me, too, but I'm a grown woman . . ."

"And I'm a snotty little kid."

"I know you're angry, and I'm sorry."

"You're not going to marry him, are you?"

"That's not the issue . . ."

"I don't want a stepfather. Jessica has a stepfather, and they hate each other."

"Mac doesn't hate you . . ."

"I hate *him*. And I hate you, too. Get out of my room." She dived back under her pillow.

Defeated, Kit watched as Kevlar crawled up beside Emma and cuddled against her back. She turned her body only enough to let her arm fall over the little dog. Kit left the room quietly and went to dial her parents' number.

When her mother answered, she said, "Mom, remember what you said about giving Emma a stable environment? Well, I've done something really stupid."

Mac hated Sundays. He generally went out for breakfast, then to the clinic where he checked patients, did paperwork and secretly hoped for an emergency to give him something to do. He really hated this particular Sunday. He'd been waiting for Kit's call. It hadn't come.

He hesitated to leave a message on Kit's answering machine in case Emma intercepted it.

The everlasting rain didn't help his mood, either. The rain gauges now read some twenty inches over normal for this early in the year. Every day there were reports of more houses being flooded. Piles of wet carpet lined some of the low-lying streets waiting to be picked up by the garbage trucks.

Mac remembered a French song that he had heard a long time ago. Something about "It rains in the streets the way it rains in my heart." Apt.

After he threw the newspaper across the room and knocked over one of Claire's bronze lamps, he decided he'd better get out of the apartment before he destroyed the place. He drove to the gym and worked out in the weight room for an hour.

A blonde in a skintight workout suit smiled at him in the health bar while he was downing an electrolyte drink. Under normal conditions, he'd have smiled back and struck up a conversation.

But he was no longer interested in blondes — or anyone, except one special redhead with green eyes.

He took a shower at the gym, pulled on fresh sweats, picked up a cold chicken-sandwich plate from the bar and drove to the clinic.

Since the clinic had found that they could save money without compromising care by opening on Sundays only for emergencies, Mac assumed he was alone in the building. He didn't know who was on call this weekend, but whichever vet had the duty would already have checked the animals on-site.

Big wouldn't feed and water again until evening.

Although they were not his patients, he checked the large animals. A couple of foundered walking horses and a mare recovering from colic surgery. Nothing new or interesting.

In the exotics area the beaver with the pinned hip was grunting and gnawing away at the leafy branches Kenny had provided for him. He did not look happy. They'd have to get him a kiddie pool to swim in.

He listened to the echo of his footsteps as he walked back through the large-animal section toward his office.

The yelps and meows started as he opened

302

the door to the kennel area. He checked the patients. Everybody seemed fine. The English mastiff whose hip joint he had replaced opened one eye and drooled at him. No fever. Good.

He couldn't seem to concentrate or settle down.

He wanted to speak to Emma, to try to explain to her that his feelings for her mother did not interfere with his special feelings for her.

Oh, sure, that would fly.

He needed some good advice. From whom? Rick? Hardly.

Big? Ordinarily he was both sensible and practical. He had won over Alva Jean's kids.

Mac didn't think Big would understand the problem.

If Jake were alive, he'd know how to handle Emma.

There simply wasn't anybody else.

He propped his feet on his desk. He was starting to get a headache. Low blood sugar, probably. Too much exercise, not enough liquid.

He knew one person who had experience handling both Emma and Kit, but might not want even to talk to him. He dropped his feet to the floor and opened the right-hand drawer of his desk to find his phone book, looked up a number, pulled his telephone to him and dialed.

A man answered on the second ring. "Hello?"

"Mr. Barclay?" Mac said. "My name is Mac Thorn. I don't know whether you've heard of me."

"I've heard a great deal about you from both Emma and Kit. I'm glad you finally got Emma up on a horse."

"Did Kit tell you what happened after I took them home?"

"Yes."

"You're Emma's grandfather. How can I convince her that I haven't betrayed her?"

"I'm not certain you can. At the moment I'd say give her some time to get used to the idea of you and Kit."

"Could I send her a present, maybe? A stuffed horse?"

He could hear Tom Barclay's chuckle. "Not unless you want her to burn it on the front lawn. In time she may accept the situation or she may not. You see, Emma thought you liked her for herself and not because of Kit. Now, she thinks you were simply using her."

"I do like her for herself."

"Do you?" Barclay asked. "Think about it carefully, Doctor. I don't want either of my girls hurt. Now, if you'll excuse me, I hear my wife's car in the driveway."

Mac hung up the telephone. Barclay had been deliberately neutral. That was better than hostile.

He called Kit and left a message, then waited. She didn't call back. He stalked the halls of the clinic and walked around outside until he was soaked. Then he left another message on Kit's machine.

He got into his car and drove by Kit's house. The Jeep was not in the driveway. She was probably at her parents' house. Emma might be there as well, unless she'd gone to one of her friends' houses. He'd written down the Barclays' address, now he cruised slowly past their house. Kit's car was not in the driveway, but a sedan that probably belonged to the Barclays was. He pulled into the driveway behind it. If he couldn't get Kit to call him by leaving messages, maybe he could leave a message with her parents. He had to reach her some way.

He sloshed through the rain and rang the front doorbell. He heard a female voice say, "I'll get it, Tom."

The woman who opened the door was older than Kit, but she had that same deep red hair and those emerald eyes. She was shorter than Kit, too, but still slim.

305

"Yes?"

"Excuse me —" He felt awkward.

"Catherine, who —" A tall, spare man came out of what must be the kitchen, wiping his hands on a dish towel. "Ah, you've got to be Dr. Thorn."

Catherine Barclay raised her eyebrows. She wasn't smiling.

"Gran, was that Mom?" Emma ran down the hall behind the Barclays and skidded to a halt the moment she saw Mac. "What're *you* doing here?"

He tried to smile. "I wanted to tell you I had a great time with you yesterday."

"I hate you!" Emma flew back down the hall. He heard a door slam.

"That went well," he said.

"Give her time," Tom told him. "She's hurt and angry, but she's also enjoying playing the tragic betrayed queen. She'll get over it."

Mac forced himself to smile. "Anything I can do to speed up the process?"

"She has to find a way out that won't leave her feeling like either an idiot or a quitter. That's going to take time."

Mac nodded. "Thanks. Sorry to have bothered you." He didn't hear the front door shut until he climbed into his car.

"Kit warned me Emma was more complicated than I thought," he said to himself as he pulled out into the road. "Kit said men didn't step up to the plate when the going got tough." He shook his head. It was time to prove that in his case she was wrong. Aloud, he said, "Watch me, Kit, I intend to hit a home run."

When Mac stepped out of his Suburban in his carport, the rain had slowed to a cold drizzle. He lowered his head and started running. He had to do something to tire himself out so that he could sleep. If he caught pneumonia in the process, who'd care?

By the time he rounded the last corner of the apartment complex, he was soaked with a combination of rain and sweat. At least his headache was gone. He should be hungry, but he wasn't.

He brushed the rain out of his eyes and ran up the sidewalk toward his entrance. A black mass huddled in the doorway under the porch light. As he came closer, it moved.

"Kit, what are you doing out here?"

"I didn't want to miss you in the dark. It's okay. Kev and I are all covered up under my poncho. We're not wet." She looked up at him. "But you are. What have you been doing?"

"Trying to wear myself out and give myself pneumonia."

"Lean into the light more. I can't read you. Pull me up, I'm stiff."

He pulled her up and then backed away and unlocked the door. "Come in. I'll make some tea. Can I get you some dry clothes? Something to eat?" He knew he was babbling. He sounded like his mother.

She hung her wet poncho on the hook beside the door and came to the center of the room. She stood with her arms wrapped tight around her chest. "My dad told me you saw Emma. I'm sorry she treated you that way."

"You warned me. She says she hates me."

Kit shook her head. "She doesn't mean that. She wouldn't be so angry if she didn't care about you. She's staying over there tonight, and Dad will take her to school tomorrow. Maybe I should have dragged her home with me, but I couldn't face it. I guess I let her get away with a lot."

"She's a good kid. You didn't have to come apologize for her."

"I didn't come because of her." Kit still stood in the center of the room. Kevlar sat beside her, his eyes on her face. "I wanted to see you." She dropped her eyes.

He went to her and lifted her chin. "Open

your eyes," he said softly.

"I'm so tired of trying to please everybody."

"Then let me please you." He kissed her softly, felt her arms slide around his waist. "I want to be with you, Kit. I want to try this."

"You do?"

"I do," he said, kissing her again. "You are so beautiful, you know that?"

"What? I didn't catch that."

"I said, you are so —" Her grin made him stop midsentence.

"Okay, so maybe I did catch that. But I just like when you say it," she said, reaching up to kiss him again. He pulled her into his arms.

"I'd stay like this forever if I could, my love." He caught his breath. His love? He'd never said that to a woman in his life. It scared him more than he wanted to admit.

Kit hadn't heard him because of the way he'd been holding her. She didn't know he'd used the word. He wasn't certain he'd be able to repeat it when she could read his lips. It seemed to stick in his gullet.

He kissed the top of her head. For the first time, he wished they both knew sign language.

She pulled back to look him in the eye. "I

should go," she said. "Especially since I'm supposed to meet you at eight-thirty at the zoo, remember?"

"Stay a little longer," he found himself pleading.

"But Kev needs a walk."

"Then we'll walk him. I'm not about to have you walking around this complex by yourself at midnight."

Her eyebrows went up. "I'm a cop, remember? Well, an ex-cop. And this is a very safe area."

"No area is safe at midnight."

"I really ought to go home. What if somebody sees us here together?"

"What if somebody does? Does it matter?"

"Jimmy might be able to use it to prove I'm not a fit mother."

"Forget Jimmy."

She raised her eyebrows. He smiled his most charming smile at her. "Okay, let's walk Kev. Is it still raining?"

"Isn't it always?"

But it wasn't. The chill still felt damp, and the skies remained overcast, but for the moment the seemingly endless rain was taking a break.

Mac tucked Kit's arm through his. If anyone had ever told him he'd enjoy waiting for a dog to relieve himself at midnight he would have told them they were nuts. Walking in the dark beside him, Kit couldn't read his lips, so they moved silently through the night.

Mac was surprised to discover he was happy. If he'd ever known happiness before, he'd forgotten what it felt like.

New or not, he identified the feeling immediately. Whatever happened with Kit in the future, he could look back on this perfect moment and remember what it felt like to be happy.

When Kit met him for their walk-through of the zoo, she was unusually quiet. She kept her distance as they walked back to their cars in the parking lot. Before she could get into her Jeep, he touched her arm and turned her so that she could read him. "You never answered me about giving this a try."

Kit took a deep breath. "It won't work, Mac."

"Why? Because of Emma?"

"Mostly. I haven't always put Emma first, but for now I must. I have to work things out with her and I didn't make much headway yesterday."

"Your father says she'll work it out for herself."

"I hope he's right." She closed her eyes and leaned against her Jeep. "But I have to help if I can. How did things get so complicated? I can't be with you unless I hide from my own daughter."

"I want to mend fences as much as you do, but I'm selfish enough to want to see you any way I can."

She shook her head. "Please don't ask me to choose between Emma and you."

"I'm not asking you to choose. You said you didn't think men stuck around when things got tough. Maybe in the past I wouldn't have, but you and Emma mean too much to me. You and I caused this problem together. We should solve it together."

"All I know is that I can't be in the same room with you without wanting to kiss you. The only way I can think straight is if I avoid you. I don't want to quit my job . . ."

He took her arms. "You mustn't quit!"

"Then please give me some space and time, Mac. It's easy enough to avoid each other at work when we're both busy."

"How much time? A day? A month? A year? Do we speak in the hall? Acknowledge each other when we're both at the coffee machine?"

"I don't know how much time. You think

this is easy for me? I've never acted this way in my life, but I've never felt this way, either." She touched his cheek. He saw that her eyes brimmed with tears that threatened to spill over. "She's my daughter, Mac."

"You win. But I don't intend to let you go — you or Emma."

"Right now you have to."

"Fine. We both know where we stand." He climbed into his Suburban. For the first time in years he felt completely powerless.

CHAPTER FOURTEEN

For the next several weeks Mac seldom saw Kit alone. She seemed determined to avoid him. She went straight from her Jeep to meet Brian at the zoo and usually left for the clinic while Mac and Brian were still chatting in the parking lot. Once at the clinic, they were both busy. Kit happily accepted more and more responsibility.

Both Sarah and Eleanor had begun to use her as a backup for Jack Renfro. Jack was a Cockney ex-racehorse jockey who knew how to handle the most difficult horse, but he made no secret of his dislike for cows and sheep. Besides, although he was still tough, he was over fifty.

With Bill Chumney gone, Big had to spend more time checking on the few exotics that were in-patients. Kenny, who still came in faithfully three afternoons a week after school, cared for the exotics to the best of his ability. He'd learned a great deal, but he was still a senior in high school and needed help.

The zoo animals remained blissfully healthy, while the tuberculin tests on the primate population had been put off until the rains cleared, if indeed they ever did.

"Saw some guy with a big wooden boat loading a bunch of animals two by two," Neely had joked one morning in mid-March. "Might consider joining him on the ark if this doesn't stop."

The ground had long since reached saturation point. Even the animals were grumpy from lack of sunlight and the never-ending dampness. Mac could not remember an early spring this wet since he'd moved south to go to vet school.

When he did manage to catch Kit alone, he tried to quiz her about Emma, but she put him off. "Give her time," she kept saying.

He wanted at least to speak to the girl again, take her riding, anything to re-create the bond they had been developing. Privately, he thought Emma was manipulating Kit. If so, it was working. Kit refused to let her parents babysit even long enough for Mac to take her out to dinner.

Maybe it was time for him to take steps. When a new feature-length cartoon opened in movie theaters to rave reviews, he suggested that he and Kit could take Emma.

"I think it's too soon. I don't think she's ready."

"Look, I've got to do something. This can't go on."

That afternoon he picked up a funny friendship card and addressed it to Emma. All he added to the printed text inside was, "When are we going riding again?"

The next day he sent her a photo of a brand-new hippopotamus baby at the zoo with a note that said, "I miss your company."

He assumed she received them, although Kit didn't mention either card. He even considered sending her flowers. Bad idea.

He even met Tom Barclay for coffee just so he could check on Emma. He liked Tom. He seemed such a gentle, laid-back soul, but a certificate on the wall of his workshop said that he had received the silver star in Vietnam.

Tom wasn't much help about Emma, either. Everybody said to give it time. But he was running out of patience.

"Jimmy still plans to take Emma on Friday night," Kit said with a shy glance at Mac.

"Please say that means you'll have dinner

with me."

She actually blushed.

"When is he picking Emma up?"

"I told him to pick her up from Mom and Dad's after school Friday. I'll pack her things and drop them by there during my lunch hour Friday. I don't want to see Jimmy's face, much less put up with his mouth. I've asked him again not to take Emma to his mother's. He swore he'd talked to her and told her not to fill Emma's head with garbage. I'm not certain I believe him, but what can I do? The court set up the visitation schedule."

"Tell me you'll spend Friday evening with me."

"What if I have other plans?"

"Cancel them. I'm about to go crazy without seeing you."

"Boy, are *you* turning into a tyrant."

"I was always a tyrant. Since I met you I've mellowed. But there is nothing easy about this."

"I promise we'll talk to Emma together."

"When?"

"Soon . . ."

He sighed. "Give it time. I know."

Rick stuck his head into the conference room. "Staff meeting in five minutes, people. Everybody, that includes techs and clericals."

"Kit, did you get that?"

"Staff meeting. Rick talks very fast. Take good notes, I may have to ask you what happened afterward."

"There's not a soul up front," Alva Jean complained as she sat down by the conference table. "What if somebody walks in with an emergency?"

"This won't take long," Rick said. "We may have a problem, people."

"What now?" Nancy said under her breath.

"You know we agreed to join the National Animal Rescue Coalition last year."

"So did half the vets in the county," Sarah said. Muggs sat on her lap cheerfully chewing on a soda cracker.

"It just so happens that our name is at the top of the roster."

"So?" Mac asked.

"I just got a call from National. At least two of the levees in the Mississippi Delta are in danger of breaking. If that happens, we'll have a major disaster on our hands."

"We've had flooding for the past two weeks," Sarah said. "Nobody's mobilized any rescues that I'm aware of."

Rick looked at her and at Muggs, who had

begun to toss crumbs at him. "You're from Minnesota, Sarah. You know about snow emergencies? Well, down here we get flood emergencies. A real flood is a whole different ball game from flash floods that rise in minutes and are gone in hours. When the river breaches a levee, we're talking several feet of water that stick around for a month or more. Evacuations, shelters, Red Cross-aid stations, FEMA, national guards, cops from county mounties all the way to the feds. Evacuees have to leave their pets behind when they're moved to a shelter. It's up to us to set up a database, rescue pets and reunite them with their owners, and to handle any medical emergency required to save lives. The beef cattle and other livestock are a real problem. You can pick up a cat. You can't pick up a Charolais bull who's standing neck deep in ice water."

"I guess livestock is my problem," Sarah said. "Mine and Eleanor's."

"We've got safe locations already arranged where we can assemble livestock, and some livestock trailers on call. But we may have to swim the livestock out to dry land before they can be picked up."

"With one boat?" Sarah asked.

"Once the human beings are rescued, we'll have help from the local people and their boats. But they need supervision. We'd prefer not to have anybody drown trying to save a cow."

"Are we certain this is going to happen?" Liz Carlyle asked. "Because if you're expecting me to take off for a week or so, I have to know now. I can't leave the kids alone."

"Nothing's definite," Rick said. "We've been alerted, not called up. In the meantime we need to inventory the mobile clinic and replace whatever supplies we're missing. We should bring out all the portable cages and collapse them so that they can be loaded quickly. Mabel, you need to update the evacuation computer program on the laptop and make certain we have all the connections we'll need to print out forms."

"Do we have any idea when it will happen if it does indeed happen?" Mac asked.

"Not a clue. Sorry to add to your jobs, but we all voted to join this alliance. Now we have to put our money where our mouths are. That's all, unless anyone has any questions?"

Alva Jean raised her hand. "Do I have to go? I mean, somebody has to stay here."

"Good question. I plan to take the people without young children and leave those of you with family responsibilities here to keep the place running. Alva Jean, you plan on working regular hours. And I've talked to Eleanor. Steve isn't happy to have her go, but he understands the seriousness of the situation. Kenny can probably give us a weekend, but he can't miss school." Rick turned to Big. "How about you, big man? You game?"

"I been running a johnboat since before I could walk."

"Good. Mabel, can you come with us?"

"Sure."

"I'm planning on staying here to keep the clinic functioning, but I'll relieve Mac as soon as I can. Jack, Sarah's going to need you here."

Jack nodded.

Rick turned to Kit. He immediately began to speak more slowly and carefully. "Kit, I assume you want to stay here. If you do, you'll be responsible for postop care as well as cleanup and anything else that needs to be done. Think you can handle it?"

"I'll have to, won't I?" She grinned at him.

"Great. Okay, people, let's hop to it." He clapped his hands at them and fled back to his office.

The rest of the assembled staff slouched in their chairs in silence for a moment, then Liz said, "That man is the biggest disaster junkie I've ever seen."

"That's because he's so good at them," Sarah answered. "He gets bored with the day-to-day stuff. This sets his adrenaline pumping. Muggs, put that pencil down — you'll poke your eye out."

"Got *mine* pumping," Nancy said. "I'm scared of floods. You get snakes in the kitchen cupboards." She shivered.

"I doubt we'll have to go," Mac said. "But in case we do, Nancy, we'd better start making that list of the things we'll need to take along." He stood. "And I would suggest that everybody bring in a couple of changes of clothes tomorrow. Bring old things that you won't mind throwing away afterward. Give Alva Jean your shoe sizes, and we'll send Big out to buy us all gum boots so we can slog through the mud."

"Don't forget to pack any medicine you take and deodorant and toothpaste and things," Mabel said. "We may not have access to the local discount store."

When everyone left, Mac kept Kit behind. The moment the door closed, he reached for her.

"Nuh-uh," she said, and eluded him. "Somebody could walk in."

"Did you get all that?"

"The gist of it. The way Rick talks to me is hysterical. It's like a seventy-eight record played at thirty-three."

"He means well."

"If you have to go, will it be dangerous?"

"No. I can operate in a van as easily as I can operate here. Mabel and Big will have most of the burden taking information and getting people reunited with their pets. I'll probably only have the occasional cut or abrasion to look after." He took her arms. "I don't want to leave you. Not for a minute."

"From the way Rick talks, I won't have time to miss you."

"Maybe after this weekend, you'll miss me anyway."

Emma had started to act nearly normal around Kit again. So long as they talked about homework, Emma's friend Jessica, and which teachers were obviously out to get the entire class, they could converse politely.

Kit knew Emma had received two cards from Mac, but the girl had taken them up to her room without opening them. Kit didn't find them in Emma's trash, so she assumed Emma had read them and kept them.

After dinner on Thursday night, as Emma was heading upstairs to do homework, she suddenly turned to her mother and said, "If this stupid rain doesn't quit, I'll never get to ride again."

Kit kept a straight face, but inside she was cheering. It was a small but significant breakthrough in Emma's attitude.

Kit decided to wait until Friday morning at the zoo to tell Mac, so that she wouldn't have to talk on the telephone where Emma could hear her.

He was checking out a scratch on the right haunch of the big silverback gorilla when she told him. "Don't make too much of it," she said. "Emma's a smart kid, and I know my father's been talking to her about you — just casually, you know. Maybe she's becoming a little more realistic about her crush on you."

"I miss her," Mac said simply. "I never thought I'd say that about a ten-year-old child. Or any child, for that matter."

"You're an old softie."

"How about you put on a dress and I'll put on a tie and we go someplace ridiculously expensive and very romantic?"

"How about we rent a movie and order pizza?"

"Are you still worried about the boys in blue?"

"Just wary. And I don't want Emma hearing that the minute she's out of the way, you and I start having romantic dinners in expensive restaurants."

"So long as we're together, I don't mind if we do it over pizza."

Neely, who had been checking on a golden lion tamarin a couple of cages down, sauntered up to them. "Think he needs stitches, Doc?" He pointed at the gorilla.

"Doesn't look that bad. Stick some antibiotic capsules in his bananas. That ought to do it. I'd prefer not to have to anesthetize him if we don't have to."

"I agree. How about you, Kit? You ever see a gorilla up this close?"

"No, and I'm not all that certain I want to again. I had no idea he was so gigantic."

"He's very gentle. One time about five years ago one of the keepers left the door of his holding cage unlatched. Five of the keepers were in the middle of a poker game in the primate office when in comes Cedric and hunkers down behind his keeper to kibitz. His keeper says you should have seen their faces. He got up quietly, took Cedric's hand and walked him back down the hall and into his cage."

Kit laughed.

"True story." Neely held up his hand to swear. "Of course, nobody remembers who won the pot."

The day dragged for Mac. He checked the supplies in the mobile clinic, saw five clients whose dogs and cats had minor ailments, did one interesting surgery to remove a rolled-up sock from a puppy's stomach and watched the clock.

Kit wanted to drive to his apartment in her own car. He'd asked if she wanted to be able to escape. She'd simply smiled and touched his cheek.

She and Kevlar came into Mac's apartment just after six. She carried two hot packs. "When I told Dad about your romantic-dinner idea, he decided to send us one." She put the packs on the kitchen counter and unzipped them. The smell was wonderful. "Let's see. We have beef bourguignonne over homemade fettuccine." She opened the other pack. "Some roasted veggies to go with it, and a hot tarte aux pommes for dessert with crème fraîche."

"Delicious. But not as delicious as you, Kit," he said, bending over to kiss her.

No one had ever kissed Kit the way Mac did. He practically swept her off her feet. She adored him — she couldn't help it. Her feelings overwhelmed her.

Without thinking about what she was doing, she whispered, "I love you."

She felt him tense. Why had she said that? He didn't love her. He'd talked all around the word *love,* but he'd never said it about her or even about Emma.

She acted as though she'd never spoken. She kept her arms around his neck, and her face down so that she couldn't read anything he might say.

Just then, he pulled away from her. "Phone," he said. He answered it, but his face was in profile, so she couldn't tell what he was talking about. He was scowling, however.

When he put the telephone down, he took her in his arms again. "We've been placed on rescue alert. I'm not on call this weekend except for dire emergencies, but Rick has decreed that those of us who are scheduled to go with the van need to come in tonight and get things organized."

"We'd better eat fast, then."

"I'm sorry, Kit."

"It's fine, really."

"Would you let me take you out to breakfast tomorrow, to make up for being on call?"

"That depends."

"I'll take you to Perkins. Best pancakes on the planet."

"It's a deal," she said, half disappointed, half relieved that their evening had been cut short. She still couldn't believe the L-word had come out of her mouth. He hadn't given any sign that he'd heard her — maybe she'd said it too quietly.

Yeah, and maybe pigs could fly.

"How did you get Kevlar?" Mac asked over their second cup of coffee at Perkins the next morning.

"There's a national group that trains and provides helper dogs, everything from Labrador retrievers who will open refrigerator doors for people who can't use their arms, to Seeing Eye dogs, to hearing dogs. The closest group is in East Tennessee. The dogs are free to the recipients, but most people try to make a sizable donation when they get one. Dad put me down for one before I even came out of the hospital.

"At first I was dead set against using a helper dog. I didn't want anyone to know I had a problem. He convinced me that was stupid. Kev was no different and no less necessary than a wheelchair if I were paralyzed. So when they called to say they had a dog trained and ready, I flew to East Tennessee, trained for a week while my parents looked after Emma, and came home with

Kevlar. They certainly had no idea he had a deformed kidney."

"I'm sorry I yelled at you that night."

"Did I just read the word *sorry?* You aren't supposed to know the meaning of that word, according to Nancy."

"You've taught me a lot."

After breakfast they took Kevlar to the park where he chased the tennis ball Kit kept for him, until his tongue was hanging out. They browsed in the largest bookstore in the area, bought a couple of paperbacks and wound up eating thick Reuben sandwiches at a local deli for lunch.

"Do you have any idea what you want to do in the long run?" Mac asked. "You're overqualified for the clinic."

"It's gotten me back into the workforce. I'm grateful for that. Actually, I've been thinking of going back to college."

"Graduate degree?"

"I wish. I didn't need but two years of college before I went to the academy. I planned to go back, but then Emma came along. Now that she's a little older, I'd like to finish."

"What in? Criminal justice?"

"Speech pathology. I ought to be able to help people with speech and hearing problems. I'd also like to train dogs for the hearing ear dog program. They have nobody doing it between Knoxville and Oklahoma."

"When would you start?"

"Not until September at the earliest. Why, are you trying to get rid of me?"

"Absolutely not. But I don't want to see you getting antsy. You've got too much drive to scrub kennel floors, but not enough technical skills yet to do the simple stuff without supervision."

"That drive is what infuriated Jimmy."

"I like it. Whatever I can do to help, I'll do."

"Really?" She looked at him quizzically. "You mean that?"

"Yes. And on another note, I hadn't planned to say this, but maybe you could convince Emma to let me teach her to ride."

Kit started to say something, but he held up a hand to stop her. "Give it time. I know."

"She'd do almost anything to ride. It would be something the two of you could do without me. It might work."

Suddenly he grimaced. "Phone." He clicked it open and listened. Kit couldn't catch every word, but she knew what the call meant. She felt their perfect day slipping away.

When he hung up, he said, "Come on. We

just got the call to arms. We're leaving for Mississippi before dark."

She composed her face to smile. "I'll come with you to the clinic. Run me by your place so I can pick up my car."

"Good. I'm taking the Suburban to Mississippi. We have to have a big car to pull the boat trailer, and there's no place for passengers in the van. Want to stop by your place so you can call Jimmy and tell him to drop off Emma at the clinic?"

"You can call him from your car."

Mac raised his eyebrows.

"Who cares what he thinks," Kit said.

CHAPTER FIFTEEN

"Big and Kenny have the van packed," Rick said. "Big's tested both motors on the john-boat. All we have to do is hook up the boat trailer to Mac's Suburban and you're good to go."

"I've got the laptop and the portable printer," Mabel said. She hefted a computer case and an overnight bag into the back of Mac's Surburban.

"How long do you think you'll be gone?" Sarah asked Mac.

"With luck, only a couple of days. Eleanor's husband, Steve, said he'd hire a chopper to bring in more supplies if we needed them. I'll let you know."

"The phones are down all over that part of Mississippi. So's the power."

"The sheriff's office says the high school where they've set up the shelter has its own generator. It's on a knoll, so it's high and dry and should stay that way. The dormitory is in the gym. We'll set up animal rescue cages and log-in desks in a couple of classrooms. We can do any surgery required in the van. Where's Kit?"

"Helping Kenny load the portable cages into the back of the van. He'll drive down in the van with Big. His father says he can stay the entire weekend if we need him."

Mac loped down the hall toward the storeroom behind the kennel. As he reached the door, Alva Jean called from the front, "Dr. Mac, can you tell Kit she's got a call? He says to tell her it's Jimmy."

Mac ground his teeth. Kit did not need this. She had enough on her hands. He told her about the call and followed her to the reception room. If Jimmy started one of his tirades, Mac planned to take the phone from Alva Jean and rip into him.

"He wanted to speak to Emma first, but I told him she wasn't here," Alva Jean said to Kit. "That's when he asked to speak to you. I've got the speakerphone on. I'll repeat what he says for you."

"Jimmy?" Kit asked. "What's this about Emma? She's supposed to be with you."

"See, I got called back to duty this morning because of the floods."

Alva Jean repeated Jimmy's words for Kit to read.

"What time did you get called this morning?" Mac heard the rising panic in Kit's voice. "You didn't leave her alone in your apartment, did you? Jimmy, I swear . . ."

"Of course I didn't. I — uh — dropped her at Momma's."

Alva Jean repeated.

"Jimmy, you promised —"

"Kit, I left messages on your answering machine, but you didn't call me back. I couldn't get hold of your mother and father. What else was I supposed to do? Not my fault you're never home."

Alva Jean reproduced Jimmy's words precisely, but without the guilty inflection.

"Isn't she still at your mother's?"

"I told Momma not to go anywhere because of the weather. She was only supposed to drive Emma to meet you at the clinic. I told her to be there before four this afternoon."

"It's nearly five. She's not here and I haven't heard a word from her or anybody else. Did you call my house? Emma would pick up the phone if she's there. Did your mother just drop her off there? Emma has a key. She could let herself in, but Jimmy, she's too young to be left alone, and certainly not in this storm."

"Nobody's answering the phone at your

house. Vince drove by. The lights aren't on, and nobody answered the door."

"So she's still at your mother's or on the way here. Maybe she got stuck somewhere, tried to drive through some water and stalled the car. Does your mother have a cell phone?"

"She keeps losing them, so now she won't let me get her another one. Says it's a waste of money."

"Have you looked for her?"

"I put the word out. So far nobody's spotted her."

"Could she have stopped at the grocery or the bank?"

"I've checked parking lots everyplace she might have stopped."

"Where on earth could they be?"

"I don't know. I mean, she wouldn't —"

"Jimmy, what are you not telling me?" Kit was trying to keep the rising panic out of her voice.

By this time Alva Jean was even parroting the inflection in Jimmy's voice. "Kit," she repeated. "You know Momma. This morning when I dropped Emma off, Momma was all worried about the homeplace. Said she wanted to make sure everything was all right at the farm."

"What? In *Mississippi?*"

335

"She promised me she wouldn't go. Said she'd call one of her old neighbors to check, but you know my mother. She may have figured she could drive down there in a couple of hours and be back to drop Emma at the clinic with time to spare."

"Have you called the farm?" Kit asked quietly.

"Phone's been disconnected for a long time. The last renters moved out three months ago, so the house is empty. I've been trying to convince Momma to sell, but she flat-out refuses."

"Surely she'd have better sense than to drive down there with Emma. Even if she started out, I don't think she'd have been able to get through. Can't you have somebody down there go by the house?"

"I've tried. Can't get a line through."

"Probably been evacuated anyway," Mac said.

"I ought to know this, Kit, but I don't. Does Emma carry a cell phone?"

"Jimmy, the school system will not allow children to have cell phones. Don't you even know *that?*" Kit's hysteria was mounting.

Mac took the phone out of Alva Jean's hand. "Jimmy? This is Mac Thorn. Where exactly is this farm?"

"It's just the old farmhouse. The land's

been rented since Momma moved to Memphis. Pays for her condo."

"I don't care if it pays for a trip to the moon. Where is the farm?"

"Two miles outside Nettawamba." He sounded defeated.

Mac dropped his head into his hand. "Nettawamba's where we're headed right now for animal rescue. The levee's broken north of there. The whole county's flooded."

"Please, what's he saying?" Kit begged.

Mac put his hand on her arm. "Give me a second." He spoke into the phone. "Would your mother have tried that drive in this weather? And with Emma along?"

"I don't know. She's been getting strange lately. Keeps talking about showing Emma her roots."

"What kind of car is she driving?"

"Maroon Crown Victoria. I've alerted the locals, the sheriff's office and the staties down there already. They have the tag number. They should be able to find her if she's still on the road."

"No reports of cars winding up in ditches or canals?"

"Not that I've heard. If anything's happened to Momma and Emma . . ."

"Someone will find them, Lockhart, or I will. Now, give the details about the car and every telephone number you can think of to Alva Jean here. Tell her exactly how to get to the farm from any direction. Give mileage as precisely as you can. We may not have landmarks or road signs to guide us. We'll take a map with us. I'll talk to Kit."

She grabbed his arms. "Tell me. Where is she?"

He drew her to the far side of the reception room by the windows and told her as quietly and gently as he could. With every word her eyes grew more terrified. He could see the pulse jump in her throat. "That woman! If she's hurt my baby . . ."

"We'll find her, Kit. We're headed down there right now. We're setting up the rescue unit at the high school in Nettawamba." He turned toward Alva Jean. "Did you get that information from Lockhart?"

She nodded. "He said he can't take off himself until after midnight, and maybe not then."

"You get in touch with the rescue people down there any way you can and tell them they may have to rescue a couple of people they didn't know about before, then give them directions."

Kit said, "It'll take hours — maybe days — to get everyone they *know* about to high ground. There could be more than a hundred people in the outlying areas. They can't look for possibles until they've got all the people they know about to safety," Kit said. Her eyes were wild, but she was trying to sound rational.

"Ten to one they're sitting high and dry by the side of the road in Mrs. Lockhart's car, Kit," Mac said. "They probably never made it past the roadblocks. Some of the roads down there have been closed since noon."

"Noon?" Kit cried. "She might have left the minute Jimmy did, long before the roads were closed." She was quiet for a moment, then added, "I'm coming with you."

"What if Emma shows up here or calls looking for you?"

"Alva Jean will be here. She has everybody's cell phone numbers." Kit turned to Alva Jean. "How late do you plan to stay?"

"My momma's got the kids. I'll stay until somebody comes in to take over. Don't you worry about Emma. If she shows up or calls here, I'll make sure she's safe and I'll let you know. I'll hang on to that Mrs. Lockhart, too, for good measure." She patted Kit's shoulder. "Don't you worry, honey. She'll be all right."

Her glance at Mac showed she wasn't as certain as she sounded.

He nodded. "Kit, grab your stuff and let's go."

Big drove the mobile veterinary clinic. Kenny rode along with him. Mac followed in the Suburban, towing the johnboat.

Kit sat beside him, her fists clenched in her lap. From time to time he squeezed her knee. It was as close as he could come to comforting her without taking his eyes off the road. Kevlar crouched on the floor at her feet. Even he seemed worried.

The rain was unremitting. Lightning ripped the sky.

The thunder crashed so fiercely that Mac was glad Kit couldn't hear it. Even he started at some of the larger claps.

Mabel and Eleanor sat in back. While Mac concentrated on his driving, they organized the setup for the rescue.

"We won't be able to assess the problems with the large animals until daylight," Eleanor said. "Even with searchlights we couldn't do much about getting them to high ground."

"Kenny and Big can set up the cages for the animals we rescue," Mabel said. "I've got the animal rescue program in the computer. It's just a matter of filling in the blanks so we can match pets with owners. I understand why they don't allow people to take animals with them into flood shelters, but I sure wish they would. Everybody would breathe so much easier if they knew their pets were safe."

"With luck, they'll be safe until we can get to them," Eleanor said. "I worry about the covered kennels. If the runs aren't covered, the hounds can usually manage to climb out and swim away. If not . . ."

"Have you done this before?" Mabel asked.

"Twice," Eleanor answered. "Once when an old dirt dam broke and flooded a resort area in East Tennessee. Another time a whole town got torn to pieces by a tornado. Ten people died. We managed to save most of the pets but we weren't so lucky with the livestock."

Mac glanced at Kit's set jaw. She couldn't read any of the conversation from the backseat. She was locked into her own silence. In the dark with his face toward the windshield he couldn't even say anything to cheer her up.

South of Como, a highway patrol roadblock was stopping all cars and sending them back the way they had come. Mac climbed out of the Suburban and walked down to the highway patrolman manning the barricades.

"We're part of the rescue effort. Any way we can get through?"

"What's in the van?" the man asked.

"A mobile veterinary clinic. Animal rescue."

The man looked up. "Hey, I read about you folks. My wife saw a story about some flood in North Carolina a couple of years back where they managed to bring out everything from rabbits to snakes."

"That's us. Or at least the same national association that we're part of. So, can you tell us how we *can* get to Nettawamba?"

"Road's only got about a foot of water on it, but it's running swift, rising fast and the road corkscrews. We closed the road 'cause you can't tell where the pavement leaves off in the dark. If we lead you through you can make it okay, but follow close or you'll wind up roof-deep in a ditch."

"Thanks." He gave a thumbs-up sign to Big, who was waiting in the van.

They crawled along the submerged road behind the state patrol car for the better part of a mile before they pulled safely out onto clear road at the far end. Mac leaned out his window to thank the policeman. "Can we make it all the way to the schoolhouse in Nettawamba from here?"

"Last report said the road was clear into the north-side parking lot of the high school. That's where they're taking people they've evacuated. Water's all the way up to the base of the hill on the south side. Supposed to rise a couple of feet more before it crests. Better get a move on if you want to beat it."

Mac climbed into the truck and turned Kit's face toward his. "He says we can make it to the school where they're bringing the people they've rescued. From there we can launch the boat to hunt for Emma."

Her face was wet with tears, but she managed a weak smile. "Hurry."

After the pitch black of the road and the countryside, the lights that spilled out of the open doors of the school onto the wet parking lot beckoned like the Great White Way.

"Their generator's working," Eleanor said. "Good."

A dozen official cars from the Mississippi Department of Transportation were parked along the perimeter of the parking lot. Three-fourths of the remaining paved area was full of cars and pickup trucks, squad cars from the state and county, a pair of ambulances, two fire trucks and a fire chief's car. At the eastern end of the lot close to what was obviously the gymnasium, heavy electrical cables ran from a large trailer to the roof of the school. When Mac lowered his window to ask for directions, he could hear the hum of the generator in the trailer like a horde of angry wasps.

A deputy routed both the SUV and the van to the southern end of the parking lot. "Where can we launch the boat?" Mac asked.

"Right down there." The deputy pointed south past the school. "Take the same road you came in on past the school. There's a gravel road about a quarter of a mile down. At least it used to be a gravel road. Now it's a boat ramp. That's where the rescue boats are putting in. What group you folks with?"

"Animal rescue."

"You gonna start that tonight? We haven't brought in half the people from the houses yet. Better wait till morning when you can see. Rain's supposed to slack off later tonight, but we're due to get more tomorrow afternoon. You should have four or five hours of good daylight tomorrow to work before we get hit by more of this stuff."

"Thanks for your advice." No sense in telling the man that he and Big were a one-boat rescue team to find a small girl and an old lady. He had no intention of getting bogged down in red tape or having to coordinate with anybody official. He and Big would simply go and do it. If they got in trouble afterward, so be it. They'd apologize and say they hadn't understood the protocol. The animal rescue part of their assignment would have to wait until Emma was safely back in Kit's arms.

"What did they say?" Kit asked him.

"They're still bringing in people. It could be tomorrow before they get everyone who's been flooded out."

"I can't stand to wait that long."

He took her arm and made her look up into his face. "We're going to launch the boat, then Big and I are going to take the directions Alva Jean sent with the map, and we're going to the Lockhart place. Kenny can help here while we're gone. Big and I will ride the boat in as close as we can to the Lockhart farm, then if we have to walk the rest of the way through the water, we will. If they're not there, we'll use that as a starting point and keep backtracking until we find them."

"Don't be in such a hurry, Mac," Eleanor said. "They might both be safe inside already. Why risk anybody else's life in this mess until we're sure?"

"She's right," Mabel said. "Come on, Kit,

grab a duffel. No sense in making more trips than we need to."

Kit took off toward the lighted gym without even a glance at the duffels in the Suburban. She ran flat out like a sprinter.

Mac ran after her.

He caught up to her at the open door to the gym where a tall man wearing a muddy navy business suit held a clipboard.

"Have you seen a ten-year-old girl and a seventy-five-year-old woman?" Kit said.

"We have all the names, ma'am, if you'll just calm down."

"Calm down? How calm would you be if it was your little girl out there somewhere?"

"I understand, ma'am, but this is the best way to check. Names?"

Mac stepped in quickly before Kit could throttle the guy. He gave the names and waited while the man licked the end of his pencil and ran it down the list on his clipboard.

"They're not in alphabetical order yet," he said. "So I have to check the sheets one at a time."

"Can't you hurry?"

"I am hurrying, ma'am."

Behind them a fresh boatload of refugees lined up. Mac heard plaintive wails of "Can't we at least get in out of this rain?"

and "What on earth are they *doing* up there?"

At last, the man flipped all his sheets back over. "No. No Lockharts here."

"Could you have the spelling wrong?"

"This list is accurate. Now if you'll just step aside, I'm sure they'll be in the next few boatloads."

"Come on, Kit."

"But, Mac, nobody's looking for them!"

"Jimmy said he notified the sheriff they might have come down here. If the rescue parties are working their way out from here, they may simply not have gotten as far as the Lockhart place."

"I've got to find her."

"That's why we brought the boat." Mac dragged her away into the semidarkness of the parking lot. "Big's probably already got it launched. Go help Kenny and Mabel set up cages. It'll keep your mind occupied."

"Don't be silly! I'm coming with you."

"No, you're not."

"Of course I am. She's my child."

"You're going to have to trust me and Big."

"I'm a trained police officer. I have done rescue work. I know CPR and emergency medical procedures. I am coming with you." She started toward the road.

He caught her and swung her to face him. "You're going to stay here. We'll be two big men in that boat, and we'll be floating over who knows what debris and obstacles. We're going to have to communicate fast. It's dark. You couldn't read our lips even if you wanted to. We can't take the chance you won't react quickly enough."

"She's my baby. She's out there someplace crying for me."

He took a deep breath. He might never be forgiven for this. "If she is crying for you, Kit, you can't hear her. We can."

She recoiled as though he'd slapped her. It was almost as though she stopped breathing for a moment. Then she took a deep breath and said quietly, "Of course. You're right. You can hear her. I can't."

She turned and moved toward the main door of the building.

Mac found Big holding the painter of the johnboat at the edge of the launching area. The heavy Johnson outboard motor was tipped forward over the gunwale so that the rudder wouldn't bash into some hidden obstacle. The small trolling motor, made to kick up out of the water when it ran into submerged debris, chugged softly in the water beside its big brother.

In his orange life jacket, and with the

bright miner's lantern shining out from the front of his cap, Big looked like a giant cyclops. He tossed Mac a life jacket and handed him a hat. "Save the light. Don't need but one to steer by. May need the other to hunt later on."

"You know how to get us there?"

"I know we got to go slow right down the center of what used to be Main Street. Otherwise we're liable to pile up on a car or a parking meter or something. After that, you got to guide me. I'm not too good with maps. Once we turn south toward the Lockhart place, ought not to be much in the way except stobs and branches and such. We can go faster then."

"You're the boss." Big was in his element. Mac didn't even fish. He was used to ocean water and clear breezes and a boat that had a sail. This was like rowing across the Styx.

At least he couldn't ask for a more conscientious and capable Charon than Big.

As they pulled away, a larger flat-bottom johnboat with heavy motors pulled into the muddy bank they had just left. A man in a firefighter's jacket with fluorescent stripes nodded to them. Five people sat huddled in life jackets in the bottom of the boat. As that boat grounded, two men stepped forward and began to hand the passengers to shore. One child in its mother's arms cried. The others were strangely silent.

As Mac and Big turned down Main Street, the trolling motor chuckled so softly that they could talk without raising their voices. "What'd that Lockhart woman come down here for anyway?" Big asked. "Those weather-people have been screaming flood, flood, flood for a month. Don't she listen?"

"From what Jimmy Lockhart says, she's pretty hardheaded."

"Anything happens to that little girl . . . well, it just won't."

"You got that right," Mac said.

The rain stopped as though a tap had been turned off.

"That's a break," Big said. "The way that rain was coming down, thought we might have to bail this here boat out before we got to the house."

"Lockhart says his mother drives a maroon Crown Victoria. At least it's a big, heavy car. You see any cars parked on the street that might fit that description?"

"Can't see much but the top four or five inches. Don't know if I'd recognize a Crown Victoria, and in this light, maroon looks black." They puttered past the last small building in town and into relatively open country.

A three-quarter moon broke through the clouds revealing floodwaters that stretched all the way to the horizon, broken only occasionally by a barn or cluster of drowned trees.

"Don't look much like soybean fields and pastures now, does it?"

From a group of trees fifty yards to their right Mac heard the lowing of frightened cattle. He prayed they had dry footing, and if not, that they could stay afloat until they could be rescued after daylight. No way to do it now.

"Hey. See the top of that fence post?" Big pointed his cap with its light toward the sign. "Don't that say Lockhart Lane?"

"Looks that way to me. We're supposed to turn right there."

"How far you think we got to go?"

"Should see the house any minute now."

Fifty yards ahead was an old frame farmhouse perched in the middle of the moonlit lake. Water had risen above the floor of the broad front porch that fronted the house.

Big stopped the motor for a moment. "You see any lights?" he whispered.

Mac shook his head. "How deep would you guess the water is?"

"Probably three, four feet." Both men continued to whisper as though afraid to awake some malevolent spirit that lay under the floodwaters.

"Get closer. The moon's shining on something by the front door. Looks like the roof of a car."

"Oh, boy. Is it maroon?"

"Can't tell. Dark, anyway."

The motor puttered closer to the house. "Hey!" Big whispered. "I swear I saw a speck of light upstairs."

Mac looked, but saw nothing. Then he saw the faintest flutter behind the upstairs curtains. He started to shout, but Big put a hand on his arm and shook his head. "Old lady might have her a shotgun in there. Scared to death, no telling what she'll do. Don't want to come this far and get blown to smithereens. Here, let's tie up to the porch railing. If that front door's locked, I can break it in easy."

"Then she'll really let fly with the shotgun. Let me go first."

Mac climbed out of the boat and felt the icy water slosh over the tops of his gum boots.

"Should'a worn waders, Doc, like mine." In a pair of waders that came up under his armpits Big looked very much like a sperm whale walking. "Try the door."

It was unlocked, but impossible to force

open against the pressure of the water. "Try the window," Mac said.

The window beside the door slid up with a screech like an owl that has spotted a particularly succulent squirrel.

"Well, that's torn it," Mac said. He leaned in the window. "Emma? Mrs. Lockhart? We've come to get you."

Lovely choice of words. Guaranteed a couple of loads of buckshot in the brain. "I mean, this is Mac Thorn and Big Little. We've come to rescue you from the flood."

From upstairs came the sound of quick whispers, then the sound of the scrape of a shoe on wood. "I will too go out there!" Emma shouted. "Mac, Big, we're up here!"

Mac leaned against the banister to the second floor. He wasn't certain, but he thought he was crying. "Emma, Emma, honey? Come on down, we've come to take you to your momma."

Emma pulled away from someone outside Mac's line of vision and stood at the top of the stairs. She held a lit candle. Behind her, a strong but aging female voice said, "We're just fine, young man. Go away. The water will be gone before morning."

Mac forced his way up the submerged stairs to the first dry one. The moment Emma came down within reach he pulled her to him. She jumped into his arms, threw hers around his neck, buried her face against his shoulder and wrapped her legs around his waist. "I knew you'd come. I told Meemomma you wouldn't leave us here to drown. I was so scared. Is Mom all right?"

"She's fine. She's waiting for you at the rescue station. And watch that candle. I don't have much hair as it is."

"Die, candle!"

Mac heard the hiss as the candle hit the water behind him. So she hadn't lost her sense of humor.

Big pushed past them and climbed to the top of the stairs. He turned the corner and held out his hand. "Hey, Mrs. Lockhart. I'm Bigelow Little. Jimmy sent us to bring y'all back home."

"He's not supposed to know I came down here. This wasn't supposed to happen. We should have been safe at home by now and nobody the wiser."

"I know, ma'am. Now, Big's gonna pick you right up like a little kitten. You hold on to ole Big and we'll have you back with Jimmy in a little minute."

"I don't know . . ."

"He's not mad. He's worried. You dassen't let a good boy worry about his mother."

"Of course you're right. Are you certain

you can manage to carry me?"

"Oh, yes, ma'am. You just hold on tight."

"And you, missy," Mac said. "Swing around to my back. It'll be easier to get you in the boat."

"Okay." She kissed him on the cheek. "I love you."

His throat filled. "I love you, too, honey."

It was true. He did. The words he'd hesitated to say for so long came out so easily. He loved Emma. He loved Kit more than his life. Why hadn't he told her that? Why hadn't he said those words to her?

He would say them the instant he got back to the rescue station with Kit. And then he would ask her — them — to marry him.

Mrs. Lockhart kept up a running commentary as Big walked down the stairs with her in his arms. "I didn't want to take the child back to her mother," she said. "Not at work. The woman should be home where she belongs, not gallivanting around working with diseased animals . . ."

"Ma'am," Big said gently, "you'd best hush up now."

And she did.

Mac managed to crawl out the window without getting Emma too wet, and settled her in the boat with a life jacket fastened tightly around her, along with a dry blanket.

Then he went back for Mrs. Lockhart. Big passed her to him through the window, climbed after him and helped Mac settle her. They practically had to force her to put on a life jacket. She wore a pair of soggy jeans and a heavy red sweater. She was almost as tall as Kit but bony. Mac could sense the strength of will in her. He didn't think she was used to taking orders.

As Mac settled a blanket around her shoulders, he felt something wet on his hand. In the light from his hat he saw his palm was red.

"Mrs. Lockhart, you're bleeding."

"It's nothing."

"Yes, it is. Mac, Meemomma slipped on the stairs and bumped her head."

"Was she unconscious at all?"

"Of course I wasn't unconscious. I've bumped my head worse than that on the edge of the chicken coop."

"Was she?"

Emma shook her head. "No, she just said 'Ow' and rubbed the back of her head. I didn't know it was bleeding. Is she all right?"

"I'm sure she is, but they'll check her out at the rescue station."

"Rescue station." Mrs. Lockhart snorted. "I've lived through four floods in my lifetime sitting on the second floor of that house. I could just as easily have lived through this one. I did not need rescuing."

Mac realized the woman was trying to justify her actions, but he couldn't let her get away with it. He was too angry. "You have no food or water, your car is obviously ruined, and nobody knew for certain where you were. Emma needed rescuing even if you didn't. Let's get going, Big. Think we can use the large outboard?"

"Hmmph," Mrs. Lockhart said.

"Sure, Doc. I know where the stobs are sticking up now."

As Big began to crank up the Johnson outboard, Mrs. Lockhart shouted, "Wait! You left the window open!" Mac rolled his eyes at Big, but he climbed out and closed the window. It would be a miracle if the house survived this particular flood without collapsing, but that wasn't his problem.

Mac was certain they'd face official reprimand when they showed up with Emma and Mrs. Lockhart, but there were too many boats coming and going for the workers even to notice them get out of their boat.

Mac picked Emma up, life jacket, blanket and all, and started toward the school. He could hear Big behind him arguing with Mrs. Lockhart. If anybody could handle her, Big could.

He expected Kit to be standing around outside the high school waiting and worrying. Instead she had taken his suggestion to heart. He found her struggling to open one of the portable wire cages that would be used to house the rescued animals. Her back was to him.

When he touched her shoulder, she jumped a foot. When she saw Emma her eyes lit. "Oh, baby! You're all right!" Emma went to her and clung to her as she had clung to Mac.

Obviously this was a moment for mother and daughter. Not for him to intrude. He was bursting to tell Kit he loved her, but that could keep. There would be time to tell her again and again.

He nodded and turned away.

"Mac." Her voice stopped him. "Thank you."

"You're welcome."

"Oh, baby," Kit said to Emma, "you're freezing! Let me find you something dry. Have you had anything to eat? What possessed that woman anyway? Where is she? Is she okay? Does she need us to do anything for her?"

"I need to go to the bathroom really bad."

"Sure. Then we'll get you some dry clothes

and something to eat."

Mac watched Kit carry Emma off. Emma was too old and too tall for Kit to carry, but he knew why she was doing it. He'd done the same thing.

"Mac."

Mabel Halliburton grabbed his arm. "We just had one of the boats bring in half a dozen bluetick hounds that got pushed into a barbed-wire fence by the current. They're cut up pretty bad. Eleanor's already scrubbing, but we're going to need you, too."

He glanced at Kit and Emma with longing, then went with Mabel.

After the hounds were stitched and cleaned — but before he could go looking for Kit — Mac was faced with a half-drowned cat with a broken leg and a pair of bedraggled guinea pigs whose cage had broken. They'd embedded shards of glass into themselves. He had to find and carefully remove each shard, then treat the guinea pigs with antibiotics.

When he finally looked up, the clock at the end of the van read 6:45 a.m. He needed coffee.

He needed Kit. Time at last to find her and Emma, tell her he loved her. Ask her to marry him and the sooner the better. Emma had said she loved him. Surely that would help persuade Kit.

He climbed down the steps of the van. Kenny sat on the bottom stair with his head in his folded arms. Asleep. The kid could sleep anywhere.

Mac rubbed his own neck and shoulders. His hands ached from the endless stitching of the hounds. He'd felt as though he were working on a hairy jigsaw puzzle. They'd all survive, but they'd be sore for a while.

He found Mabel half-asleep over her computer.

"Morning, Mac," she said. "Have a productive night?"

"Coffee."

"Here." She poured a cup of steaming coffee into a foam cup.

"Thanks."

"In case you want relief, forget it. Eleanor's out with Big and a couple of farmers trying to move livestock to higher ground. Rick called and said he was driving down to relieve you now that the road between here and Germantown is clear, but he probably won't be here before noon. Kenny just got back after rescuing that . . ." Mabel pointed to a glass case in which a pair of six-foot boa constrictors slept. "He said the cage floated right out the front door of the house when he opened it. Straight into his arms.

Good thing, too, the way Kenny hates snakes."

"Where are Kit and Emma?"

"Left for home hours ago."

He felt his stomach twist.

"The paramedics took Mrs. Lockhart to Southhaven to the emergency room to be checked out, and Kit cadged a ride with one of the highway patrolmen who was going that way. Her mother and father were going to pick her and Emma up at the station."

"Is Emma all right?"

"Chilly, but otherwise fine. I swear, Mrs. Lockhart ought to be locked up."

"I wouldn't feel so charitable if anything had happened to Emma, but as it is, she's Jimmy Lockhart's problem and welcome he is to it. You think Kit's had time to make it home?"

Mabel looked at her watch. "Probably not if they stopped for breakfast or went directly to Kit's parents'."

"I'll try to call later."

"She wanted to say goodbye to you, but when she looked into the van, you didn't even glance up. She didn't want to disturb you. Said she'd talk to you later. And thanks again for saving Emma."

"Yeah."

He flopped down on the chair behind the teacher's desk at the front of the classroom. It was the only chair in the room from which he could stretch his legs. He felt drained, frustrated, annoyed and exhausted. He wanted to catch the first patrol car headed north. He wanted to call Eleanor's husband, Steve Chadwick, and tell him to send that helicopter so that he could get back to Kit and Emma.

At the moment what he wanted didn't much matter. He couldn't leave until Rick arrived.

Not for the first time he resented the fact that he couldn't even call Kit on the telephone unless she was in her own bedroom.

His head fell back, and he knew he was drifting into sleep.

Mac began to call Kit's home late on Sunday afternoon with no result. He left messages on her machine telling her to call Mabel so that he could talk to her. That would restrict his conversation. He didn't much want Mabel having to relay, "I love you, please marry me."

A couple of hours later, he dialed Kit's parents.

"Dr. Thorn, Mac!" Catherine sounded glad to hear his voice. "Kit and Emma told me what you did. I can't thank you enough."

"Um, Mrs. Barclay . . ."

"Catherine, please."

"Catherine, is Kit there?"

"I'm afraid not. But Emma's here. She's bouncing up and down wanting to speak to you. Here, Emma, don't run the man ragged."

"Dr. Mac? Thank you, thank you, thank you."

"You're welcome, you're welcome, you're welcome."

"Mom said she was scared to death. Me, too. Meemomma said the last flood, water moccasins got in and they had to beat them off to keep them from coming upstairs."

Great. "Didn't see one water moccasin."

"Mom's gone to the doctor."

His heart lurched. "On a Sunday? What's wrong?"

"It's just Dr. Zales, you know, the guy who does her ears. She sees him a lot."

"Will you ask her to call me when she gets home?"

"Sure. Dr. Mac?"

"Yes?"

"Can we go riding again sometime?"

"Sure. Soon as the weather improves."

Catherine came back on the line. "Well, you've certainly made *her* day. The young are incredibly resilient. I'll be a nervous wreck for years."

"She does seem to have forgiven me."

"I think that little expedition yesterday gave Miss Emma a lesson in priorities. When you rescued her you went from monster to hero very quickly." She laughed. "She's always adored you, of course. She wouldn't have been so angry at her mother otherwise. Apparently, she's decided to make the best of things."

"That's a relief." He hesitated. "Mrs. Barclay, is there something wrong with Kit? Doctors don't usually see patients on Sundays unless there's an emergency."

"Reuben's a friend as well as Kit's ear doctor. Emma says the minute Kit got to her house, she called Reuben. Emma doesn't know what they talked about, but Reuben wanted to see her this afternoon. Kit swears it's nothing bad." Catherine sighed. "She'll tell us when she comes to pick up Emma, I expect."

"I'm sure she will." He tried to sound reassuring. "Please ask her to call me."

"Of course."

"Thanks." He hung up. Now he wasn't merely frustrated, he was worried.

When Mabel finally called him to the phone, he jumped for it. "Kit?"

"No such luck, Doc."

"Jimmy."

"Thanks, man. I owe you one."

"How's your mother?"

"Mild concussion. I took her car keys away from her. She's still mad as a wet hen that she had to get rescued. Swears she and Emma would have done fine." He sighed. "Guess that's my problem."

"I'm just glad everyone's okay."

"Me, too. Thanks, Doc."

Mac said goodbye and hung up, feeling drained but too keyed up to sleep. It was going to be a long day.

Chapter Sixteen

By the time Rick finally relieved Mac at seven on Sunday evening, Mac was so tired he took the drive back to Germantown very slowly and stopped for coffee twice. The road that had been submerged on their way down was now clear. At least the roadway itself was. Water ran fast and high in the drainage ditches alongside.

He ate a couple of burgers from a fast-food drive-through and opened the door to his cold, dark apartment praying that the light on his answering machine would be flashing.

No such luck. He stood in the shower until the water ran lukewarm, put on some fresh clothes and waited to hear from Kit. Even if she'd tried to reach him in Mississippi after he'd left, Mabel would have told her he was on his way home. He knew his remark about her not being able to hear Emma cry had been devastating, but he hadn't expected this . . . silence.

When he hadn't heard from her by midnight, he climbed into his Suburban, drove to her house and rang the bell. Kevlar would alert her that there was someone downstairs.

But the house stayed quiet. Mac rang and pounded until he was certain he was waking up the neighborhood. He expected a prowl car to show up and arrest him for disturbing the peace.

Finally, he gave up. Too late to call the Barclays.

He tossed and turned all night and went out for breakfast at six-thirty in the morning. He rang Kit's doorbell again with the same result.

He called the Barclays from his car phone. Tom Barclay answered. He didn't sound as though he'd woken from a sound sleep.

"Sorry to call so early, Tom, but I'm worried about Kit and Emma," Mac said after identifying himself. "I haven't heard from Kit. Are they all right?"

"Where are you?"

"Outside Kit's house. Is she with you?"

"Come on over. I'll fix you some breakfast. We need to talk."

Mac broke every Germantown speed law before he slid to a stop in front of the Barclay house. Tom met him at the front door before he had a chance to knock.

"Come in. Coffee's on."

He followed Tom into the sunny kitchen.

"Bacon and eggs?"

"I didn't come for breakfast."

Tom handed him the coffee. "No, of course you didn't. Sit down."

"It's Kit, isn't it? Something's happened."

"Yes and no. You and I have gotten to be pretty good friends, haven't we?"

"I thought so."

"I've wanted to ask you this for a while. Don't answer if you think it's none of my business. Are you and Kit in love?"

Mac's mouth felt dry. "I'm in love with her. I hope she's in love with me."

"Does she know you love her?"

"I don't know." He stared into his coffee. "Probably not. I'm not good with words."

Tom poured milk into his coffee. "What are you going to do about it?"

"Marry her, if she'll have me."

"And Emma?"

"Jimmy would never let me adopt her, but she means a great deal to me. I've never been a stepfather, but I'm anxious to give it a try."

"Good."

"You approve?" Mac felt the edges of his mouth quirk.

"I do. Took a while to convince Catherine, but rescuing Emma seems to have turned the tide in your favor."

"Cut to the chase, Tom. What's this about? Where is Kit?"

Tom glanced at the clock over the refrigerator. "Three hours from now she should be landing at Logan Airport in Boston."

"What?" Coffee sloshed onto the back of his hand. He felt the sting but was too stunned to react.

"I don't know what happened in Mississippi exactly. Something you said to Kit really shook her up."

Mac sank back into the kitchen chair. "I was simply trying to keep her from going with us to rescue Emma. I told her that even if Emma was crying for her, Kit couldn't hear her." He ran his hand over his face. "I knew at the time I shouldn't say it, but I couldn't think of any other way to keep her out of that boat."

"I see," Tom said.

"She took it so quietly. I'm sorry."

"Don't be. That's one of the reasons she didn't call you before she left. She knew you'd think you had something to do with her decision, maybe try to stop her. It seems she and Reuben Zales, her doctor, have been working toward this special operation for nearly a month — doing X-rays, blood work, whatever you do to get a patient ready for surgery. Reuben originally told her it might be years before he'd feel comfortable recommending the operation, but when he began talking with the doctors in Boston who do this procedure, he decided he'd been wrong. Frankly, I think Kit pressured him. She didn't tell anyone — not us, and apparently not you, either."

"How experimental? What is it?"

"Some kind of new ear implant is all I know."

"Why keep it a secret?"

"She said she didn't want us to get our hopes up or to worry or to try to talk her out of it." He took a deep breath. "If I'd known earlier, I *would* have tried to talk her out of it. She says there are risks."

"*Any* surgery is risky, Tom. You can have an ingrown toenail cut out and die from a staph infection. How long has she known she was on the schedule?" He vacillated between anger that she'd left him in ignorance, and fear that whatever she was experimenting with could kill her.

"She saw Reuben on Sunday and asked him to see if he could possibly have her moved up in the schedule. I gather he wasn't real happy about it, but he managed

to get her a place for sometime this week —
maybe as early as tomorrow. Lab work's
been done. There's no reason to wait."

"What hospital is it? Who are the surgeons? How can I reach her in Boston?"

"Whoa! Slow down. Kit didn't want anyone to go with her." Tom got up and re-
trieved a plain white envelope from the top
of the refrigerator. "She said she knew you'd
be angry, so she left this letter for me to
give you. I planned to call you later this
morning."

Mac took the letter with trembling fingers.

Dearest Mac,
You were right. I couldn't hear Emma
crying, or know what your voice sounds
like, or how Kev barks. I've about
reached my limit. I'm willing to take a
chance to be able to hear.
Hopefully this operation is the right
thing to do.

I love you,
Kit

P.S. I called Rick and told him I won't
be in for at least a week. Hope he doesn't
fire me.

"What hospital will she be in?" Mac asked.

"It's a private clinic. Boynten and Stern-wood."

"You're going to sit here and wait for the results of the surgery?"

"That's what Kit wanted, but Catherine wouldn't hear of it. We're all three on a plane to Boston this afternoon. I've made arrangements for Emma to miss school. Vince Calandruccio is going to look after Kevlar while we're gone."

"How is Emma dealing with it?"

"She's scared."

"Can I see her?"

"She finally dropped off to sleep, and I'd rather not wake her."

"Tell her I'll see her in Boston." Mac set down his cup and walked out without another word.

He heard Tom call out behind him, "You won't change Kit's mind."

He turned. "I don't intend to try. But I plan to be there when she wakes up."

When Mac walked into Creature Comfort twenty minutes later, Alva Jean looked at him in surprise. "I didn't think you'd be back so soon."

"Rick came down and took over. Did Big tell you we found Emma safe and sound?"

She nodded. "I'm so glad. I guess Kit's

keeping Emma out of school today and staying home with her. I haven't heard from her."

"She called Rick in Mississippi." He hated admitting that Kit's call had been to Rick and not to him. "She won't be in for a while."

"Oh? I hope everything's okay."

"It will be. Now, here's what I need from you. You'd better write it down."

She reached for a pen and held it poised over a steno pad.

"Cancel everything I've got scheduled for the next week and book me a ticket on the next flight to Boston Logan. I'll change planes if I have to, but I'd rather not. Then get me a guaranteed reservation at the Copley Plaza. King-size bed. Rent me a full-size sedan to be picked up at the airport. Open-ended on both car and hotel. Open return on the airline return. Got that? Let me know when you're finished."

"Don't you have to go back to Mississippi?"

"Rick says they'll finish down there today and be back in the office tomorrow. He's going to handle the zoo until I get back."

"What about surgery?"

"They'll split the surgeries." He turned to Alva Jean with a sigh. "I know you mean well, Alva Jean, but I really do need those reservations."

"Well, excuse me." She turned to her computer.

Mac hadn't wanted to call Rick in Mississippi, but he couldn't wait until Rick came back to the office to tell him he was leaving for a week. The only thing that had made him feel less guilty was Rick's assertion that the whole Creature Comfort crew, flushed with success, would be leaving for Germantown by late afternoon. "We may still have to hit the road again if another levee gives way, but so far they're holding," Rick had said. "Everyone down here was very impressed with us."

He'd sounded pumped.

Then Mac had dropped his bombshell about leaving for a week.

"You can't just walk out with no warning. A whole week? What's going on? Kit's not coming in, either. If you two are planning a vacation — this is not a good time. We can't —"

"Not a vacation, although I haven't taken time off since this place opened, and I *am* a partner. This is an emergency."

"What kind? Is Kit sick? What's happening up there?"

"Later. I'll call you from Boston to explain."

"Boston?" Rick shouted after him. "What's in Boston?"

He'd hung up before Rick could quiz him further.

Now, while he waited for Alva Jean to make his travel arrangements, he slammed his office door behind him and sank into his desk chair. He did not want to pick up his telephone, but he had to. He dialed the Boston area code, and a number that he thought he'd long since forgotten.

"Thorn Surgical Associates," the voice at the other end trilled. "How may we direct your call?"

He hesitated. "Dr. Thorn, please."

"Dr. John Thorn, or Dr. Joanna Thorn?"

"Dr. Joanna Thorn."

"I'll connect you with her assistant."

A click and another female voice answered, "The office of Dr. Joanna Thorn. How may we help you?"

"I'd like to speak to Dr. Joanna Thorn, please." Again he hesitated. "Tell her it's her brother."

"Her brother? Oh, Mr. Thorn, I'm sorry, but the doctor's in surgery. She probably won't be back in the office until after five this afternoon. May I have her call you?"

"Please. On second thought, can you switch me to my . . . to Dr. John Thorn's office."

"Certainly."

Again the series of clicks and the phone was answered by another female voice.

"May I speak to John Thorn please?"

"Who may I say is calling?"

"Dr. John MacIntyre Thorn. His son."

This time there was no reaction from the other end. "I'll see if he's in, sir."

Right. What the receptionist meant was "I'll see if he'll talk to you."

He heard his father clear his voice at the other end of the line. "Good morning, MacIntyre."

"Good morning, Dad."

His father's voice sounded higher than Mac remembered. Perhaps not as strong as it had once been. "It's been a while since we heard from you."

About ten years, actually. But who was counting?

"I called Joanna first, but it seems she's in surgery. Still not married?"

"Unfortunately, no. And you?"

"Not yet, but soon if I'm lucky. How is Mom?"

"As usual."

"And you?"

"Also as usual. I'm very busy this morning, MacIntyre. How can I help you? Do you need money?"

Mac nearly hung up the telephone. But he'd crawl on broken glass for Kit. This was only marginally worse. "I'm making plenty of money, thank you."

"Glad to hear it. What *do* you want if it's not money?"

"I need you to have one of your staff check on a private clinic, Boynton and Sternwood."

"I don't have to check. I play golf with Harry Boynton. Best otolaryngologist in the world for my money. Are you having ear problems?"

"No, but a friend of mine is scheduled to have an operation at his clinic. I need information about the surgery itself, risk factors, success rate, et cetera, plus what time the surgery is scheduled and how long it's likely to take. Recovery-time prognosis, that sort of thing."

"Some of that information is confidential."

"You can find out anything you want to."

He heard his father's cavernous sigh. "Very well. I'll see what I can do. Name?"

"Kit — Catherine Barclay Lockhart."

"I'll have my secretary call the clinic. Leave her your number so she can call you back. Is this the possible marriage on the horizon?"

"I hope so."

"And her hearing problem is?"

"She's deaf. What's more, she has a ten-year-old daughter. I intend to marry her if she'll have me."

"Do you plan to come to Boston for the procedure?"

"As soon as I can get a flight out."

"Do you plan to see . . . your mother? I'm sure she would like to see you."

"What about you, Dad, would you like to see me?"

"I —" His father stopped. Mac could hear him catch his breath. "Yes, I would like to see you! So would Joanna. You haven't written or called or come home in *years*. Not a day goes by that I don't wonder what's happening to you and how I lost you." His father's voice broke.

Mac sat stunned. That was more emotion than his father had shown in twenty years. He took a deep breath. "Of course I'll see you if you want me to. I really am sorry I couldn't be the kind of son you wanted."

"Come home, MacIntyre. I'm getting old. I don't want to die estranged from my only son."

"Okay, Dad. We'll give it a try."

"You could stay at the house, you know."

"Not a good idea, but I'll call you from my hotel. Better break the news to Mom gently."

"MacIntyre. This woman . . . would you like me to witness the procedure?"

Mac closed his eyes. "Thank you . . . Dad. I'd like that very much. You're the finest surgeon *I* know."

"Then I'll ask Harry if I can attend." His father actually chuckled. "Thank you, MacIntyre. For once, you and I agree on something. I'm also the finest surgeon *I* know."

CHAPTER SEVENTEEN

Mac had hoped that the Barclays and Emma would be on his flight, but they weren't. He checked in at his hotel just before six in the evening. He wanted to drive to the Boynton and Sternwood Clinic immediately to see Kit, talk to her, tell her that she didn't have to do this, that he didn't care whether she could hear or not.

He sank back onto the king-size bed. This wasn't about *him.* The point was that *she* cared. It was her life, her choice, her chance. He had no right to interfere.

She must be scared to death alone in a strange clinic in a strange city surrounded by strange people. He fought the urge to go to her. The night before surgery was not the time to upset the patient. She might be sedated by now anyway. Who knew what the clinic's visiting hours were? Or whether they'd even let him see her, since he wasn't family. He finally admitted he was scared to see her.

In the meantime, his own family was waiting for him to call.

His mother sounded breathless when she answered the phone. When she heard his voice, she burst into tears.

He felt awful. Maybe she had tried to marry him off to some of the most high-maintenance debutantes on the East Coast. Maybe she had put up with his father's tirades and never taken her son's part, never protected him. She was his mother and he'd missed her.

That was what love was all about. To see the person you loved clearly, faults and all, and to love anyway. He'd learned that from Kit — she seemed to love him no matter what idiotic thing he did or said to her.

He declined an invitation to have dinner at the family home. Too many bad memories. He did, however, agree to meet his parents and his sister downstairs in the hotel restaurant.

He was sitting at the bar when he saw the three of them come into the lobby.

Joanna looked like a ship in full sail. He'd forgotten how tall she was. She looked well.

His parents had shrunk.

His father saw him first and whispered to

his wife.

She caught at her throat with both hands. For a moment no one moved or spoke. Then Joanna strode forward with her hand out. "Hi, Mac, long time no see."

They shared the fine French dinner and the beautiful wine like four strangers. Everyone seemed afraid to start a confrontation, so they kept to safe subjects. Mac ached for them all, himself included. Maybe the barriers were too high and too thick. Maybe the hurts ran too deep.

He saw his parents into his father's Mercedes and came back to the bar where Joanna sat with her coat thrown carelessly over the chair next to her.

"You've grown into a really beautiful woman," he said. When she didn't answer, he asked softly, "You still hate me?"

She set her glass down. She looked up at him, and the shiny sophistication seemed to slip away.

"I used to think I hated you. I lived in a state of constant anxiety trying to be the perfect daughter, while you were the world's worst screwup. You were the only one Dad could see, just because you were a boy. I was invisible."

He grinned. "I hated you because you *were* the world's perfect daughter. I couldn't understand why Dad was determined to force me to be his successor. I figured if I screwed up badly enough, he'd pay some attention to what I wanted instead of what he wanted for me. I'd rather have hot needles stuck under my fingernails than work with Dad."

"He's not so bad. I can afford to ignore him most of the time."

"You haven't married?"

"What, and give up the Thorn name?" She raised her finger to ask the bartender for another glass of wine. "Actually, I live with a very nice man in a loft down by the river. Maybe one of these days we'll get married. But it's not important to either one of us at the moment."

"I'd like to meet him sometime."

"I suspect you two would bond. He's a freelance graphic designer."

Mac laughed.

"I know. Mother nearly died. An artist! To top that, his family's only been in Boston for fifty years. Mother considers them newcomers." She grinned. "You managed to escape the marriage net."

"I'm hoping I'm about to be ensnared."

"The girl in the hospital?"

He nodded.

"I went by the clinic this afternoon and

met her."

"You *what?*"

"Don't freak out. She doesn't know who I am. I took my name tag off. She thinks I'm one of the nurses. Great lip-reader. I liked her. I think she's probably tough enough to handle you."

"She is. I'm in love with her."

"Good for you." She tipped her wineglass so that it emptied down her throat. "Come see us more often, big brother. *Les parents* aren't getting any younger. Even plastic surgery can't stop the clock forever. Good luck with your girl." She let him help her into her coat.

At the front door as they were waiting for her car to be brought around, she turned and touched his cheek. "You know, I think you turned out pretty well, all things considered. I could get to like you." She leaned over, kissed his cheek, climbed into her sports car and drove off with a wave.

Catherine and Tom Barclay were in the waiting room in the clinic the following morning, when Mac arrived. Emma was asleep on one of the couches with Tom's coat over her. Catherine looked up from her magazine, put a finger to her lips and pointed to the sleeping child.

He sank into a chair across from the pair.

"Kit's already in surgery," Catherine whispered. "Your father came by to reassure us. What a nice man!"

A nice man? His father?

"He said that if the operation is a success, Kit should gain some hearing immediately. She should be able to hear the nurses in the recovery room."

"Dr. Boynton came down to see us, too. He says if this operation is a success, they might want to do the other ear in a year or so," Tom said.

"Of course, it won't be perfect hearing," Catherine continued.

She sounded calm, but Mac noticed that she was quietly shredding the magazine in her lap.

"Like a scratchy old record, Dr. Boynton said." She smiled at Mac. There were tears in her eyes. "That's better than nothing, though."

He covered her hands with his and took the magazine away from her.

"How long will the procedure take, Tom?" Mac asked.

"Several hours, then she'll have to come out of the anesthesia. We may not get to see her until late this afternoon. Why don't you go on, Mac? I know Boston is your hometown. Don't you have people you'd like to look up?"

He shook his head. "Thanks. I'd rather be here."

The day dragged. Every hour a nurse would call to tell them that Kit was doing fine.

When Emma woke and saw that Mac was there, she smiled sleepily, then came to sit beside him. "Is my mom done yet?" she asked.

"Not yet." He checked his watch. "How about some lunch? I think they have a cafeteria somewhere downstairs." He turned to Catherine Barclay. "Catherine? Tom?"

"I'll stay, thank you," Catherine said. "Tom, you go."

"No, thanks. How about bringing Catherine and me a couple of ham and cheese sandwiches and some sodas when you come back?"

"You got it."

Emma ate most of a ham sandwich and two desserts. He realized she probably didn't need that much sugar, but he couldn't deny her. Watching her spoon up banana pudding he was struck by how little he knew about the logistics of raising children. Could he learn?

He delivered the Barclays their sandwiches, then took Emma for a walk around the clinic. A chill wind blew straight off the Charles River. He took off his own jacket to wrap around her and was half-frozen by the time they made it back to the main entrance of the hospital.

In the gift shop he bought her a couple of paperbacks about girls who rode horses. He bought himself the latest *New York Times* bestselling thriller.

Emma read her books and dozed off again on the sofa. He kept reading the same page over and over.

At three the nurse came out to say that Kit was in recovery and would be going back to her room shortly. The doctor might allow them to see her for a few minutes after she was awake.

"Was the operation successful?" Mac asked.

The nurse smiled blandly. "The doctor will be out to talk with you shortly."

Mac saw his father before he saw the man who must be Boynton. Both men were stripping off masks and chatting casually to one another.

"Hello, son," his father said. He acknowledged the Barclays and even smiled at Emma.

"Well?" Tom asked.

"Should be even better in six months, but at the moment, Mr. Barclay, your daughter is responding to sounds extremely well. Better than we'd hoped."

Catherine broke into tears and clung to Tom.

Emma broke into tears and clung to Mac.

Mac narrowly avoided tears and clung back.

"When can we see her?" Tom asked.

"Now. She's in pain and still groggy, but she's making sense, at least part of the time. I want to be there when you see her. I ought to warn you that the entire left side of her face is swollen and her ear looks as though she's been fighting a heavyweight boxer, but that will go away in time, possibly before her stitches come out."

Catherine and Tom walked down the hall with Dr. Boynton. Mac and Emma followed. Surprisingly, his father fell into step beside Emma. "We met this morning," he said. "Emma, isn't it?"

"Yes, sir."

"Ever considered going into medicine when you grow up?"

Mac gaped at his father.

"Actually," Emma said, "I plan to be a veterinary surgeon like Dr. Mac. I like animals much better than people."

Mac watched his father's bushy gray eyebrows climb most of the distance to his hairline.

Then he began to laugh. In a moment all three of them were laughing.

At the door to Kit's room, Catherine grabbed Tom's hand.

As Dr. Boynton began to open the door, Tom said softly, "Let Mac go first."

"But —"

Tom nodded at Mac. He opened the door the rest of the way and stepped in behind Dr. Boynton.

Kit looked as though she'd been smacked in the face with an anvil. The entire left side of her face and neck were swathed in bandages. She had a black eye.

Mac wanted to hold her and kiss every one of those bruises.

"Kit?" he whispered.

"Use a normal tone of voice," Boynton told him.

"Kit!"

She opened her good eye and looked up at him. "Mac? What are you doing here?"

The words came out in a rush. "I love you. Will you marry me?"

"Wha— ?"

"Read my lips."

"I heard you the first time." She smiled

sleepily. "I knew you were a baritone."

"I love you. Will you — and Emma — marry me?"

"Okay." She yawned, grimaced as her face stretched, and began to snore very softly.

"She heard me!" he said to the group assembled outside the door.

"Son, the entire hospital heard you," his father said.

"You mean it? About me, I mean?" Emma asked.

"Of course. Haven't I already told you I love you?"

"I wasn't sure you meant it."

"Of course I meant it."

"Can I see Mom now?"

"She's asleep," Dr. Boynton said. "But you can go in. Don't stay too long. Children under twelve really aren't supposed to be on this floor."

"Try and stop her," Mac said with a grin. "That's Kit's daughter. Nobody stops her."

"I think under the circumstances a dog is a perfectly acceptable ring bearer," Joanna Thorn said. "Kevlar is well trained. He knows what to do."

"It's still unusual," said her mother. "It's normal nowadays to have the bride's children as flower girls — sometimes even as matrons of honor. When did people give up marrying once and staying married?"

"When women stopped tying their husband's shoelaces."

"Joanna, I haven't tied your father's shoelaces in years. Not since the arthritis in my hands got so bad."

"I must admit," Joanna said, "I thought Scots pipers were only for police funerals."

"They do weddings, too. Blame the piper on my mother," Kit said from across the room. She was putting on a pair of peach satin pumps. "They're honoring *her* record with the department, not mine. I've always liked the pipes, though."

Catherine Barclay opened the door to the bride's room. "Kit, Emma is pitching a fit over her hair."

"That's why she's in another room with you and not with me," Kit said. "At the moment I'd probably brain her. Tell her to knock it off. Her hair looks fine." She thought a moment. "Tell her Mac says it's beautiful. That ought to fix things."

Her mother nodded and closed the door.

Joanna looked at her diamond-encrusted Piaget wristwatch. "Time to sweep down the aisle, Mother."

"I don't sweep, dear. I glide." Her mother went to Kit. "My dear, I don't know whether you have old or borrowed. Here's a sixpence for your shoe . . ." She pulled a shiny sixpence from the open wrist of her kid glove. "And just in case you don't have something old . . ." She opened the small velvet box she held. "These were my mother's. They're for pierced ears like yours. They're not terribly large, but they *are* nice diamonds."

"Oh, Mrs. Thorn, I couldn't."

"Never turn down diamonds, dear, no matter who offers them. Now, I'm off. I never expected to see MacIntyre married. I'm so glad he picked a nice girl."

"You've just got time to stick Mother's diamonds through your ears before we start," Joanna told her. "I'm really sorry Antonio couldn't come, but he's got a deadline."

"That's all right. I enjoyed meeting him in Boston. He's as good a cook as my dad."

"Only on Portuguese stuff. He learned from his mother."

For a moment both women were silent.

"Am I doing the right thing?" Kit asked.

"You're asking *me*? He's my brother. Actually, he turned out pretty well. So, yes, I think you're doing the right thing. For him, certainly. For you?" She waggled her hand. "Who knows. Do you still plan on going back to school in the fall?"

"Absolutely. I've already talked to University College. And since Vince was able to find land for his kennel within easy driving distance of the new house Mac bought, he's going to let me train hearing ear dogs from there. And there's Emma's riding lessons, of course. She's already angling for a horse of her own. And our house is a long way from finished. We've got Mac's things and my old things, but it seems nothing will fit." She laughed. "I'm doing it again. Overscheduling. Beats sitting home reading captions on my television set."

393

"Overscheduling never hurt any," Joanna said. "Besides, when my brother spends sixty hours a week at that clinic, you'll need something to keep you occupied." Joanna grinned at her.

"Oh, get out of here." As Joanna started out the door, Kit called, "And he's cut back on his hours."

"Right. See how long that lasts."

The small, intimate second wedding that both Kit and Mac had envisioned had gotten completely out of hand the minute Catherine Barclay and Elspeth Thorn formed an alliance. The two women couldn't have been more different, but they'd bonded instantly.

The church was festooned with ribbons and flowers, the altar glowed with white roses, and a white carpet covered the red carpet that normally graced the center aisle of the small Episcopal church in which Kit had been baptized.

Kit had refused to have bridesmaids, or her father give her away. "He gave me away once already. This time I'm on my own."

She'd also refused to wear an elaborate white wedding dress and a veil. "I'm not a virgin. No veil. No white. I'm wearing a simple peach silk dress and a circlet of greenery in my hair, period."

Her mother had argued that the peach would clash with Kit's hair, but Kit had stood firm.

"Are you ready?" her mother asked.

"Is Emma?"

"Your father has her under guard at the back of the church."

"Does Kevlar have the rings?"

"The box is securely fastened to his collar."

"Then let's do it."

"Now, remember, Emma, our flower girl, goes first, then wait until the piper starts piping before you start down the aisle."

"Got it."

Kit followed her mother into the vestry to wait for her cue. *Her* cue. The sound she could hear. Not CD quality, maybe, but better than she'd expected.

Every day in the three months since she'd said that bleary "okay" to Mac's marriage proposal, she'd drunk in the warm baritone of his voice, listened to his words with her eyes closed, talked to him on the telephone half a dozen times a day.

He had become her haven. She hoped she had become his. He told her that for the first time in his life he longed to come home at the end of the day. He even seemed to enjoy Emma's demands on his time. He took her riding at least once a week. Quite a change from the curmudgeon he'd seemed the first night Kit had met him.

With so much to do, Kit no longer had time to work at Creature Comfort. She did miss seeing Mac at work, but she thoroughly enjoyed working at the new house by herself. She was no longer isolated in a silent world. At Vince's kennel, she was surrounded by sound — bullfrogs and birds, the buzz of wasps. Once the first of her hearing ear dog candidates arrived in a month, there'd be barks and yips as well. Vince's newly imported German shepherd was due to give birth at almost the same time. Mac was already on call to deliver the puppies.

Kit peeked down the aisle. Her side of the church was packed with cops and their families. Many of them she didn't even know. They were friends of her mother's. Jimmy sat halfway down with a blond bombshell beside him. She was surprised he'd come.

Mac's side was full of his clients and colleagues.

She saw Mac and Rick Hazard enter to stand beside the altar. Joanna had been delegated to start Emma down the aisle with her basket of flowers after both mothers had been seated. Joanna would not put up with any histrionics on Emma's part.

In his own velvet cape, Kevlar sat quietly beside Emma. The box holding the rings that she and Mac would give and receive bobbed cheerfully from a ribbon tied to the back of his harness.

Emma gave her mother one pleading glance. Kit nodded and mouthed, "You look beautiful."

"I'm going to trip and die of embarrassment," Emma mouthed.

Kit rolled her eyes. "Go. You'll do fine. I love you."

Casey Stuart, the police piper, winked at Emma. She grinned and dropped her eyes. He leaned over to Kit. "Better than a funeral."

"I'll say."

Emma took a deep breath and stepped out down the aisle with Kevlar at her heels. She wore her first big-girl pumps and a blue silk dress that was a hard-won compromise between the ruffled and tucked dress Elspeth Thorn and Catherine Barclay wanted and the teenage sophistication Emma longed for.

Suddenly the church went quiet. No more Bach partitas or Purcell voluntaries.

In full-dress Stuart tartan, Casey pumped

his bag, then let fly with full skirl.

The sound bounced off the stone walls of the vestibule. Casey swung off down the aisle.

Everyone in the church stood up.

Kit took a deep breath and let it out through her mouth.

For a moment she stood at the head of the aisle and looked into Mac's eyes. He looked calm.

Then he began to move his lips soundlessly. "From this day forward and forevermore," she read. "My love."

ABOUT THE AUTHOR

RITA® Award nominee and Maggie winner **Carolyn McSparren** has lived in Germany, France, Italy and "too many cities in the U.S. to count." She's sailed boats, raised horses, rides dressage and drives her Shirecross mare to a carriage. She teaches writing seminars to romance and mystery writers, and writes mystery and women's fiction as well as Harlequin Superromance books. Carolyn lives in the country outside of Memphis, Tennessee, in an old house with four indoor and six outdoor cats, three horses, seven raccoons, at least two foxes and one husband.